THE IRRESISTIBLE IMPERSONATION

Anne would have curtsied to James Galt, but he gave her no opportunity for such social niceties. Instead, he took her in his arms and pulled her close. Anne's lips opened in surprise as he buried his face in her hair. Then he raised his head and drew back so he could look into her eyes.

"I have missed you every moment," he told her. "I knew it would be wrong for me to come to you, to love you, Amelia. But I cannot let you go."

Anne tried to say something, to admit she was not Amelia, but before she could do so, he bent his head and kissed her—and she forgot everything but his warm, insistent lips and caressing hands.

Anne knew full well that this was one time when turnabout was not fair play—but then again, when was all supposed to be fair in love . . . ?

The Turnabout Twins

Barbara Hazard

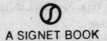

A SIGNET BOOK

NEW AMERICAN LIBRARY

NAL BOOKS ARE AVAILABLE AT QUANTITY DISCOUNTS WHEN USED TO
PROMOTE PRODUCTS OR SERVICES. FOR INFORMATION PLEASE WRITE TO
PREMIUM MARKETING DIVISION, NEW AMERICAN LIBRARY,
1633 BROADWAY, NEW YORK, NEW YORK 10019.

SIGNET TRADEMARK REG. U.S.PAT. OFF. AND FOREIGN COUNTRIES
REGISTERED TRADEMARK—MARCA REGISTRADA
HECHO EN CHICAGO, U.S.A.

SIGNET, SIGNET CLASSIC, MENTOR, PLUME, MERIDAN AND NAL BOOKS
are published by New American Library,
1633 Broadway, New York, New York 10019

First Printing, May, 1986

1 2 3 4 5 6 7 8 9

PRINTED IN THE UNITED STATES OF AMERICA

I

William Fairhaven, the Duke of Severn, arrived back at his principal seat in Devon two days earlier than expected. He had dispatched the business that had taken him to London quickly, and, anxious to rejoin the duchess, had spent only two nights on the road.

As his coach passed through the gates of Severn and bowled up the broad, well-raked avenue, he smiled to himself. Even after five years of marriage, he was still unhappy when he was separated from Juliet. It was as if an important part of his body was inexplicably missing.

He glanced out the window as the well-sprung vehicle rumbled over the bridge that spanned one end of the lake, remembering as he always did the day he had first seen her. She had been swimming with his daughters then, and he recalled how furious he had been at her, a complete stranger, caught almost naked on his estate. Thinking her the new governess, he had given her an icy setdown and called her a wanton jade, only to discover later that she was Lady Juliet Manchester, his vicar's sister.

Now he was distracted from his memories by the sight of a figure on horseback who had pulled his mount to the side of the drive to allow the coach free passage. As they drew abreast and passed, the rider swept his hat from a head covered with chestnut curls

and bowed low over his horse's mane. The duke had
no idea who this young man might be, but he waved a
careless hand. And then he shrugged. One of Will's
friends, no doubt. They seemed to be constantly
underfoot these days.

As the coach swept around the circular drive and
pulled up before the main front, the duke inspected his
mansion. Before him, Severn rose five stories, solid
and massive. Its extensive wings and the impressive
portico topped by marble statuary were as familiar to
him as his own hand. One of the liveried grooms
hurried to open the door of the coach.

The duke descended and nodded in dismissal to his
coachman before he took the long flight of stone stairs
more quickly then usual. Behind him, his valet
remained to supervise the unloading of the baggage.

The butler had already swung the twelve-foot-high
double doors open, and the duke walked into the huge
main hall without a check. On the wall facing the
entrance hung a large, full-length portrait of himself
that faithfully portrayed his tall, well-formed figure,
his dark eyes and aristocratic face.

The duke handed his hat and gloves to his butler and
looked around. One mobile dark brow rose as she
saw another young man being helped into a caped
driving coat by one of the footmen. As soon as he was
able, this gentleman made a deep bow, his color
slightly heightened.

"Your Grace," he said.

The duke nodded. "You have the advantage of me,
sir," he said in his deep drawl. "You are . . . ?"

"Viscount Rawling, er, Frederick Mason, I mean, at
your service, your Grace," the unexpected guest stam-
mered.

The duke's black eyebrows rose higher. "Viscount
Rawling?" he asked. "From Great Torrington? No
doubt you were just—mm—passing by?"

The red on the viscount's cheekbones deepened.

Great Torrington was a good twenty miles away, even riding cross country.

"Er, not exactly, sir," he managed to get out. "I came because I heard Will had returned from abroad. Beg you to excuse me, long ride home, must be on my way."

"Of course," the duke drawled, and his sarcastic tone of voice caused the discomfited young viscount to bow again and hurriedly take his leave.

The duke forgot him before the door closed behind him. "Where is the duchess, Devett?" he asked his butler.

"I believe she is in her rooms, your Grace," Devett said, and then a burst of laughter came from one of the salons that opened off the hall. The duke's eyes questioned his butler.

"The Lady Anne, sir," the old retainer explained. "And a Mr. Stephen Young and Sir Whitney Blake."

The duke's expression did not change. "And who might they be, Devett?" he inquired.

"Friends of Lord Will," the butler replied, using the diminutive all the servants employed to differentiate between the duke and his twenty-two-year-old heir. He coughed a little, and then, looking over the duke's broad shoulder, he added, "They arrived the day after you left for town, your Grace. They were passing through Devon on their way to London from Wales, and stopped to break their journey overnight."

"And that was nine days ago," the duke remarked. "Have they decided to take up residence here, Devett?"

A ghost of a smile passed over the elderly butler's lined face. "Not to my knowledge, sir," he said.

The duke frowned, impatient with the delay. "I suppose I shall have to go and meet them," he said, almost to himself, and then he added, "Oh, Devett, who was that young man I saw on the drive?"

"Squire Reading's eldest son, your Grace. He has just

recently returned from five years in the West Indies."

"No wonder I didn't recognize him," the duke murmured.

His butler coughed again. "The curate is also visiting, sir," he said.

The duke paused. "How gratifying it is that Will is such a popular young man. But although we must all applaud this sudden affinity for the church, I must admit it surprises me. I never thought curates much in my son's line."

His voice was dry, and the butler vouchsafed no answer, merely bowing as the duke turned away and walked to the salon as another burst of laughter sounded.

As he entered the room, his daughter Anne rose quickly to her feet. "Father, you are home! Why, we did not expect you until tomorrow at the earliest. What a delightful surprise!"

As she ran into his arms and hugged him, the duke looked over her dark head at the three gentlemen who had risen to make their bows. From their suddenly sober expressions, he could see that none of them thought his return delightful at all. He did not know the two sprigs of fashion who were visiting Will, but he was well acquainted with his curate, Mr. Barnaby. At his glance, this gentlemen bowed again. He was a man in his late twenties, a few years older than the others, and he was dressed in his customary black, relieved only by the white of his clerical collar. William Fairhaven had always thought him a prig; he wondered what he could find to do here in such frivolous company.

"Your Grace," the curate said now, in his slow, pedantic way. "I trust you had a pleasant journey?"

"Tolerable," the duke replied. His dark glance went to the others, and Anne said, trying to hide the laughter in her voice, "Allow me to present Sir Whitney Blake and Mr. Stephen Young to you, father. They have come to visit Will."

The duke eyed them as they bowed low in unison, not a muscle moving in his face. "Indeed?" he drawled. "Then where *is* Will? It is most remiss of him to leave his—er—*guests* to their own pursuits."

"He rode out with the agent, father," his daughter explained as she drew him to a sofa and sat down close beside him, her slim hand still entwined with his. "There was some problem with one of the tenant farmers, I believe."

The duke nodded and waved the young men back to their seats. Then he said, his voice cold and a little bored, "I understand you are on your way to London, sirs?"

"Yes, that is so, your Grace," the taller, blond gentleman in the wasp-waisted maroon coat said with a nervous smile. "We just popped in on the off chance that Will was still here. Haven't seen him this age, y'know, and well, too good an opportunity to miss."

The duke felt his daughter press his hand as the other young man said eagerly, "Very good of you to put us up, sir! Severn is impressive, most impressive, indeed."

The duke was about to remark how enraptured he was that they found it worthy of their continued attention when the door to the salon was thrown open and a gay young voice cried, "But what a terrible welcome I have been given! It is too bad, especially since I have been away such a long time!"

The duke did not have to turn to know that the newcomer was his other daughter, Amelia. The faces of the two strangers were stiff with shock, and both their mouths dropped open in a way they would have deplored if they had been aware of it. They stood as Anne gave a shriek and jumped up in a whirl of skirts to run to her sister.

"Melia! We expected you the end of last week. Oh, my dear, how I have missed you!"

As the two embraced, the duke rose and went toward them, smiling at their happy reunion. His daughters were hugging each other still, and whispering together, and he was not surprised at his unwelcome guests' stunned reactions. It was obvious that even if someone had mentioned that Anne had a sister, they had neglected to add that the Fairhaven girls were identical twins. They were as alike as two peas from the same pod, even now when they were not dressed the same, for Anne's afternoon gown was of pale primrose, and Amelia wore a scarlet traveling outfit with a saucy, matching bonnet.

As he reached them, Amelia threw her arms around him. "How glad I am to see you, Father," she said after she had kissed him. "I could hardly wait to get back to Severn. Indeed, I told Henry to spring the team over the last stage."

"And did he, minx?" her father asked, one arm around each twin.

"Not the way he would have sprung them for you, sir," Amelia admitted as she removed her bonnet from her dark curls.

The duke waited impatiently as Anne introduced her twin to the dazed young men. He was anxious to go up to Juliet, but he did not like to leave his daughters here alone. He took out his timepiece and inspected it, and Mr. Barnaby was quick to make his bow.

"I am sure you will want to be alone with the Ladies Anne and Amelia now, your Grace," he said, looking meaningfully at the other two men. As one, they bowed and excused themselves.

"Yes, run along, all of you. I cannot attend to you right now," Anne told them, her voice casual in her dismissal.

The duke was amused by her cavalier behavior, but in a moment, the salon was emptied of everyone but the three Fairhavens.

"Now this is much better," Anne said happily. "They are such pests sometimes!"

"You were not very polite, Anne," the duke remarked, trying to keep his expression neutral at her tactless description of them.

"Oh, they don't heed it, father, I assure you," she told him. "Sometimes I think they are impervious to even the broadest hint or most stunning setdown. But never mind them! Melia, I am dying to hear all the news of Blagdon and what you have been doing there all month. Come, sit down beside me and tell us everything."

The duke had the fleeting thought that Amelia looked a little self-conscious, and he wondered at it, but before she could begin to speak, he said, "You must forgive me, my dears. I have only just arrived myself, and I have yet to see Juliet. Although of course I want to hear about your stay with the Tysons', Melia; perhaps you will not mind repeating your news later?"

Amelia smiled at him and agreed, and he kissed both girls before he left them alone in the salon.

Behind him, he could hear Anne's breathless questions, and Amelia's soft replies, and he told himself it would be much better to let the first spate of girlish chatter diminish before he tried questioning his younger-by-five-minutes daughter himself.

He went up the broad marble flight of stairs impatiently, and strode down the upper hall to his duchess's rooms. Waiting for only a moment after his knock, he entered and closed the door behind him. To his surprise, Juliet was not sitting in her favorite chair in the spacious salon, although evidences of her were everywhere—an unfinished letter on the graceful writing desk, her needlepoint spread over a table, an open book face down on a chair. There was no sound of voices from her bedroom, and he wondered where she could be as he moved in that direction.

The impressive bedchamber of the Duchess of Severn was decorated in soft shades of gold and green. William Fairhaven had had it refurbished right after their marriage, to compliment her hazel eyes and ash-blond hair. Now the room was dim, sheer curtains pulled across the tall, broad windows to diffuse the late afternoon sunlight. The duke's eyes grew intent as he saw his wife lying in the wide, canopied bed, covered by a satin throw.

He walked up to the bed, the haughty planes of his face softening as he stared down at her. She was fast asleep, lying on her side with one hand cushioning her cheek. For a moment he was content to drink in her dear, lovely face. Those luminous eyes were hidden now, but her mouth curved in a little smile and she sighed in her sleep.

Unable to help himself then, the duke sat down on the bed and took up her other hand to kiss. At once, her eyes flew open and she stared at him, a little bemused.

"William!" she exclaimed, sitting up to reach out with her free hand and pull him close. "Oh, my dearest!"

He put his arms around her and bent his head to kiss her. For a long moment, they were lost in their embrace, and for the first time, the Duke of Severn truly felt he had come home.

That evening, the sounds of the dinner bell had died away long before the twins made their appearance in the drawing room. Waiting for them, the duke eyed his guests' fashionable attire with a twisting little smile that made his duchess frown at him in warning. She hurried to speak to the young men before William gave vent to the sarcastic comments she was sure he intended to make about their high shirt points and the excessive amount of fobs, rings, and quizzing glasses with which they had adorned their persons. His own son, Will, was much more quietly dressed, and that young man soon drew his father aside to discuss the problem the agent had brought to his attention that afternoon.

William Fairhaven, Earl of Maitson, was only

twenty-two, but he had cool good sense that was
unusual at that early age, and a genuine interest in the
estates. Although physically he was a younger version
of his father, and just as darkly handsome, the duke
was sure he had inherited such qualities from his
mother. Anne had been a calm, lovely young woman
who had died giving birth to the twins eighteen years
before. Although the duke had not loved her, and had
chosen her only for her family background and agreeable disposition, he had reason to thank her for the
traits she had somehow passed on to her sons. Besides
Will, there was Gregory, aged twenty-one, who was
presently traveling abroad, and Charles, just turned
nineteen, who was distinguishing himself at Cam-
bridge.

And then the duke heard his guests' sharp intake of
breath as once again they rose speechless to their feet,
and he knew the twins had come in at last. He turned
to greet them.

This evening they were dressed exactly alike in slim
gowns of aqua silk trimmed with matching braid
sashes confined under the bosom. He watched them
with a connoisseur's eye as they came down the
massive drawing room, hand in hand, to join the
group around the fireplace. It was true they were
beautiful girls, the duke thought as his heart swelled
with pride. And then he shook himself mentally. No,
they were more than beautiful, they were breathtaking. Their clouds of black hair had been brushed
high on their heads before falling in soft curls to their
white shoulders. They had his eyebrows, soaring and
arrogant over large dark blue eyes, but their aristocratic features, so like his own, were softened by skin
so clear and pale it was almost translucent. They were
taller than average, but they held themselves with
grace and dignity, and their supple figures, while as
slender as anyone could wish, had lovely high breasts
and curving hips above long, shapely legs. He was not
at all surprised they drew such swarms of admirers.

The duke's dark eyes went to Juliet's face for a moment, and he shook his head in sudden foreboding. If he were not mistaken, they were both about to enter a period full of stress and turmoil, for the twins were to make their debuts this Season. Heaven help us all, he told himself, and then he spared a sympathetic thought for all the unattached young men in London who were as yet unaware of the beauty and charm that was about to be unleashed in such generous abundance.

Will shifted his feet impatiently as the twins greeted his awestruck friends, and then he mumbled, "What cakes they are making of themselves, Father! I would never have believed either Stephen or Whitney could be so muttonheaded."

"I am sure they were better company before they met the stunning, vivacious Fairhaven girls, Will," the duke reminded him. "However, I think we will dispense with their continued residency here. That is, we will unless there is some burning reason you wish them to remain?" he asked, his courteous words at odds with the impatient disdain in his voice.

"None at all, I assure you, sir," Will told him. "To tell the truth, I'll be glad to see the back of them. I know my sisters are well enough looking girls, but all this sighing adoration, this tongue-tied stammering, is a dead bore!"

The duke's dark eyes shone with suppressed amusement. "I advise you to take care not to call them "well enough looking" after we reach town, or you will find yourself involved in countless duels with their smitten admirers for so maligning them. I realize it is hard for you to accept, as their brother, but they are so beautiful they are sure to be hailed as the Twin Stars, or some equally ridiculous title."

As Will snorted, the butler announced dinner, and the duke murmured, "Someday you will understand your friends better, son. I am glad, however, that you yourself have not been caught in any young lady's web. In my opinion, and from my own experience, twenty-two is much too young to be considering matrimony."

Will was quick to agree with him, and the duke went to take Juliet on his arm and lead his guests to the dining salon. Behind him, he could hear the young men making admiring compliments to his daughters, and he was delighted with Anne's and Amelia's light, disbelieving replies. If twenty-two was too young for a man to settle down, so too was eighteen, no matter how lovely the girl. He hoped his daughters would not fix their interests too quickly, but wait until they had been about the world a bit, and knew their minds and hearts better.

During the soup course, he asked Amelia about his friends, the Tysons, the Marquess and Marchioness of Blagdon. Amelia had stayed with them for a month. She had considerable talent with her pencil and brush, and Claire Tyson, an outstanding professional herself, had been delighted to give her some instruction in her own studio.

"They are all well, and send their love, father," Amelia told him now, smiling down the vast expanse of the dining table.

Beside her, Mr. Young grinned foolishly, having transferred his devotion in a moment. Both he and Sir Whitney had been delighted that Lady Anne had an identical twin. Their close friendship had become strained during their visit to Severn, with each one trying to cut the other out. This way, as Sir Whitney had been quick to point out, there was a beauty for each of them.

"I had a wonderful time, and Lady Tyson was so kind to me," Amelia was saying now, all unaware that her future had been settled. "I am sure I learned more from her in a month than I ever did from any of my drawing masters. If I had not missed you all so much, I would have been happy to remain there longer."

Her fair skin flushed a little, and then she added,

"The marquess sends his remembrances. He said they will call on you both in London next month."

The duke nodded to his butler to refill his glass. "You mean Andrew has finally convinced Claire to try another London Season after all these years? I can hardly believe it."

Amelia smiled at him. "She is anxious to see Turner's new etchings, sir, and since the children are busy with their lessons and well cared for by their nanny and governess, she feels she can indulge herself in what I have heard her call worthless frivolity."

She paused, as if she felt the conversation must be boring their guests, and then she turned and asked the fatuous Mr. Young a question about his home. Silently, the duke applauded her tact. Of the two girls, Amelia had always been the kinder, more gentle twin, and as she had grown to young womanhood, these traits had increased. Although Amelia had all the charm and intelligence of her sister, she was much more introspective and even-tempered by nature. Anne was like a whirlwind beside her, full of laughter and high spirits, and with a definite flair for the dramatic. And yet they could exchange places easily, acting the other's role, and still did on occasion. They could not fool their father and Juliet anymore, not after a few moments, but the duke had often deplored their behavior when he saw them trading names to tease some hapless beau who was not even aware he was being tricked.

As the others began a discussion of the coming Season, the duke turned to his wife and said softly, "I am afraid, my dearest Juliet, that you are about to be treated to a most unusual spring."

The duchess nodded, not at all perturbed by his prediction. "Yes, it is more than time to present them, William. Otherwise, you will continue to have these armies camped at your door, and Severn will remain in a state of siege. So much better to take them to London where their beaux will have to return to their own lodgings every evening." She laughed a little then, and added, "I cannot wait for them to stun the *ton*, and for all the fun that is to come!"

Her hazel eyes twinkled, and the duke smiled in return. "Pray you will still think so, love, when the Season is over. You, of all people, know that where the twins are there are sure to be extravagances, escapades, and excitement. You may have turned them into seemingly demure young ladies of quality, for which I am eternally grateful, by the way, but I cannot think them completely domesticated even now."

"They will be domesticated someday, my dear," his duchess told him, her eyes relaying a secret message.

The duke's dark eyes lit up, and he lifted his glass to her in a silent toast.

By some method neither young man understood, the duke made it clear to his son's guests that their continued residency at Severn would be most unwelcome. He was not openly sarcastic or blatant, but almost as soon as the ladies had left the dining room, they found themselves announcing their plan for an early morning departure. The duke assured them that both he and the duchess, as well as his daughters, would be delighted to renew their acquaintance when they themselves came up to town.

At Mr. Young's eager question, William Fairhaven said he had no idea precisely when that would be, but certainly in the not too distant future. With this, the two beaux had to be content.

Meanwhile, in the drawing room, the duchess was listening to Amelia's account of her stay at Blagdon. When the twins had turned sixteen, she had suggested to the duke that they be separated part of every year, although neither girl was aware that the subsequent traveling was part of a preconceived plan. Last spring, Anne had spent a few months in Vienna, visiting some distant relatives, and this year Amelia had been invited to Blagdon. Juliet had told her husband it would be easier for the twins when they married if they grew accustomed to an occasional separation now. Someday they would be forced to live apart. How could they contemplate such drastic surgery with any degree of ease unless time spent apart had already become commonplace? The duke was quick to agree her plan had merit.

In much the same way, the duchess had tried to encourage the twins to dress differently, but in this she had been less successful. They invariably appeared in the same outfits, even though when questioned, each said she had not known what her sister had planned to wear when she chose her gown. Their closeness continued to worry their stepmother. She could not help feel a little foreboding whenever she thought of the time when one of them fell in love, and someone else became more important to her than her twin.

As she listened to Amelia's soft voice telling of her visit, Juliet shook off her apprehensions. Blagdon, which was only a few miles east of Bath, had been delightful, Amelia told them. The young Tyson children had been such fun, she declared she was sorry she was the youngest rather than the eldest Fairhaven. And how she had loved being able to work hard for so many hours in Lady Tyson's studio, aided and instructed by her. She was so talented, so good!

"I have begun to paint in oils, too," she announced, her voice proud. "Claire—Lady Tyson, I mean, although she did ask me to call her Claire—told me I had a genuine aptitude."

"How wonderful, Melia, although I am not at all surprised," the duchess said with her warm smile. "I have always thought your talent extraordinary."

Anne chuckled as she hugged her stepmother. "You are besotted with us, ma'am, although we are very grateful. You not only think Melia's artistic talent wonderful, you admire my singing till there is almost no bearing it!"

Her Grace studied the glowing young lady beside her. "I do not think everything you do is wonderful, Anne," she remarked.

At her wry tones, Lady Anne shrugged. "You are thinking of the way I spoke to the curate the other day, are you not, ma'am? But Mr. Barnaby has become impossible! He seems to call here all the time, and he is not an easy man to entertain, nor is he easy to dismiss." She turned to her twin then and said, mischief gleaming in her dark blue eyes, "How glad I am that you are home, Melia! Now we can take turns being bored."

Amelia laughed and shook her head. "I wouldn't think of it, Anne! Why, Mr. Barnaby is *your* beau. I would not steal him from you."

Anne groaned a little. "You may steal him from me with my blessing, twin. In fact, I ask it of you as a favor. Besides, you are much more his type; soft and quiet and kind. I have often wondered why he decided to make *me* the object of his devotion, for surely we are most unlike."

The duchess watched them both, a little smile curling her lips. They were so very young in her eyes, so heady with their success. For months now, every man they had met had fallen under their spell. Sometimes she worried that they would become arrogant, as arrogant as their father could be on occasion. And of the two of them, she was much more concerned about Anne than Amelia. It was so obvious that she had inherited more than her share of the Fairhaven pride. She accepted the admiration and attention that was heaped on her as her right, for was she not the Lady Anne Fairhaven of Severn, the daughter of the duke of the realm? Juliet hoped with all her heart that life would not treat Anne too harshly, even as she realized there were bound to be disappointments and heartbreaks ahead. No one, not even the glorious young beauties beside her, so sure of their power, and with the overwhelming optimism of youth, ever got through life without paying the same dues demanded of lesser mortals.

"You are very quiet, dear Juliet," Amelia remarked, taking up her hand and pressing it. "Are we tiring you with our chatter?"

Juliet hugged her. "Not a bit of it, Melia. I was thinking of something else for a moment, and my mind wandered."

Before Anne could demand to know what that might be, the gentlemen entered the room, and their private conversation came to an end. Almost immediately, Sir Whitney begged Anne to sing for them. She would have demurred, until she learned that he and Stephen Young were leaving for London very early, and then she smiled and went to the piano.

The duke settled down in his usual chair to listen critically to her performance. Her soprano was true and pure, and she looked so beautiful as she sang and played that he did not wonder at his guests' rapt attention. Even Mr. Young forgot Lady Amelia for a moment in his admiration of her twin.

Anne would not allow the others to remain only her audience, and a short time later, all the young people were clustered around the piano singing glees and rounds with a great deal of hilarity.

Amelia excused herself soon after the tea tray had been brought in, claiming she was still tired from her journey. She knew why Anne was looking perplexed, and she sent her a silent message of reassurance as she curtsied to her father and their guests, and gave Juliet her customary kiss.

"Yes, do go and sleep, my dear," the duchess told her, patting her cheek a little. "You will feel more the thing in the morning."

Amelia went gracefully to the door. She did not even notice the disappointed expression of her newest beau, for she was deep in thought. As she went up the broad stairway, she sighed. Of course it was wonderful to be home, but she could not help feeling regret that her stay at Blagdon had come to an end. She was abstracted as the maid she summoned helped her to undress, and when at last the girl left her, she blew out her candle and went to the window to draw the curtain aside. There was some faint moonlight, but she did not look down into the familiar grounds of Severn. Instead, her eyes sought the far horizon to the north.

He was there, so many miles away. She put her hand to her mouth as she wondered if he were thinking of her too, perhaps even now? Saying she had been tired had been only an excuse. She had wanted to remember him, and to do that she had to be by herself. She had realized on her journey back to Severn that she must take care when she was reunited with Anne. Since they could read each other's minds, she would be forced to put her memories aside except when she was alone.

She did not know if she had been entirely successful, for she had seen more than one questioning look in Anne's eyes today, and she knew her twin was bewildered by the change in her. As the moon disappeared behind a cloud, she wondered why it was so important that Anne should not learn what had happened to her while she had been away. They had always been so free, so open before this, telling each other all their dreams and plans and feelings. What was there about Mr. James Stuart Galt of Edinburgh, Scotland, that made her feel she could not bear to share even his memory with her beloved sister?

Amelia sighed again, and her eyes grew sad. In all probability, she would never see him again. It hurt to think of that, so she turned her thoughts to the start of her visit.

Was it only a month ago that she had gone into Wiltshire? Somehow, it seemed a lifetime, for she knew how much she had changed. She was not at all the little innocent, her heart intact, that she had been when the duke's carriage deposited her and her maid at Blagdon's doors.

She leaned her forehead against the cool pane, and then she whispered to herself, "I will remember. I know I will remember him always. . . ."

II

The first few days at Blagdon had passed quickly, as she made the reacquaintance of the marquess and his wife and their four children. Amelia had always enjoyed her visits there, the noise and activity and the high spirits of the Tyson family, and now she was quickly involved in all their current pursuits. Claire Tyson—talented, outspoken, and independent—was her idol as well as her teacher, and Andrew Tyson was so pleasant he made her feel immediately at home. The children, too, had always made her welcome, treating her like a beloved aunt.

She had met James Galt a week after her arrival. He was visiting on a neighboring estate, and his host had brought him to Blagdon to be introduced to the marquess and his wife.

Amelia had not left the studio with Lady Tyson that afternoon, for she was intent on a drawing she was making. It was not until a housemaid came to summon her that she realized the Tysons were entertaining guests. A little flustered, she had done no more than shake out her crushed skirts and smooth her hair before she ran down the stairs to the drawing room.

As she came in, the gentleman standing next to the marquess turned and their eyes met. Amelia could not restrain a tiny gasp. Surely she knew this man! She had no idea why she felt this so strongly, but it was true, as if they had met at another time, another place, a long

time ago. And then she reminded herself he was a
stranger. As she studied him, she saw he was not handsome for his expression was stern, almost forbidding. A
little above average height, he had dark brown wavy
hair that she was soon to discover gleamed with
chestnut highlights in sun or candlelight. His hazel
eyes were deep-set and penetrating in a face composed
of rugged planes, and he had a firm jaw and a
determined mouth. As she made her curtsy, Amelia
saw how intent his eyes became as they inspected her,
and she wished she had changed her gown and
brushed her curls before she hurried down.

When he spoke to her and bowed, she heard the
accent in his baritone voice that told her of his Highland background. It intrigued her, it was so different
from the drawled English she was accustomed to, and
she smiled.

From the glances she stole at him as often as she
dared, she saw he was not a young man. She was not a
judge in such matters, but she was sure he must be in
his late twenties. With all her heart she wished she
were older. Why would he be interested in a gauche
eighteen-year-old, she asked herself miserably. Oh, if
only she could chat as easily and as knowledgeably as
Lady Tyson, and thus draw his attention to her!

The marchioness had many questions to ask her
visitor. She had never been to Scotland, and her
intense interest in the country was obvious. Amelia
had to be content passing the tea cups and listening to
Mr. Galt's terse replies. She noticed he rarely smiled,
and she wondered at it.

When the callers rose to leave, she was somewhat
mollified to see him smile at her. It was only a little
smile, but it lightened his cool, contained expression
and made him look years younger. His eyes lingered on
her face as if he wished to memorize it. She wondered
if anyone else had noticed, and then, when everyone
appeared quite normal, scolded herself for imagining
things.

She did not see James Galt for several days after that. Claire Tyson told her he had been invited to dinner at the end of the week, and with this to look forward to, she tried to be content. She told herself his absence was all for the best, for she needed time to think about this strange thing that had happened to her, these unusual feelings she was having. What did she know of the man after all? She had met him only briefly; could she trust her first reactions to a complete stranger? How Anne would stare and laugh at her if she knew! To even think that the Lady Amelia Fairhaven, the Duke of Severn's daughter, was remembering a little polite smile again and again and building impossible dreams around it, was ludicrous.

One afternoon that was unseasonably warm for late March, Amelia went out for a walk alone. She had spent the morning in the studio, having her first lesson in oils, and when Lady Tyson had excused her at last and suggested some fresh air might do her good, she had been quick to agree. She paused only long enough to put on a dark blue hooded cloak and a sturdier pair of shoes. As she strolled along, the sketchbook that was never far from her hand under her arm, she came to a clearing in the home woods. It was spangled with snowdrops, their brave petals white against the dark, still dormant ground, and running through it was a small stream. She sat down on a flat rock to listen to the cheerful sound of the water as it gurgled over its rocky bed.

In only a few moments, she had opened her sketchbook and begun a drawing of the scene. Completely absorbed, she did not hear the horse that approached, nor see the way the rider checked and then dismounted to stride toward her. He stood behind her silently for a moment, studying her drawing, and then he said in an admiring voice, "You are very accomplished, m'lady. My congratulations."

Amelia dropped her pencil and gave a startled little cry as her hand went to her heart. At the fright and confusion in her eyes, Mr. Galt was quick to kneel beside her.

"I beg your pardon, m'lady," he said, taking her hand and pressing it. "I did not mean to startle you."

Amelia gulped and tried to calm her breathing. She had been thinking of the Scotsman, and his appearing just now made it seem as if her thoughts had willed him into being. Now, with his face so close to hers as he bent over her with concern, she was sure he could see not only her confusion, but her helpless attraction for him as well.

"Are you all right?" he asked gruffly.

She nodded, and then, afraid he might think her nothing but a tongue-tied child, she said, "Quite all right, thank you. It was just that I thought myself alone."

He looked relieved, and a little smile quivered on her lips. And then he picked up her pencil and ruefully studied the broken point. "I have caused you to break your pencil, too. It is too bad, for how will you be able to finish your excellent drawing now?" he asked.

Amelia dug into the pocket of her cloak and withdrew a small knife. "I am well prepared for emergencies, you see," she told him, hoping he would not excuse himself and leave her. She had lost all desire for drawing now that he was close to her.

"Were you riding to Blagdon, sir?" she asked politely, trying to think of something she could say or do to keep him here beside her. "I am sure the marquess will be delighted to welcome you."

"I was riding to Blagdon," he agreed, "but not to see the marquess. I hoped to see you, m'lady."

As Amelia stared into his stern face, he added, almost as if the words were torn from his throat against his will, "I had to see if you were really as beautiful as you seemed the other day."

For a moment, all the joy she felt shone in her eyes, and then she lowered her lashes in confusion. James Galt settled down beside her and calmly took the knife from her unresisting hand. As he began to whittle a new point on the broken pencil, he said, "I find my memory was at fault, however. You are even more beautiful than I remembered. Surely such loveliness is unique."

Amelia searched her mind for a light reply. "Why, thank you, sir," she managed to get out at last. "I fear you are mistaken, however. I have an identical twin sister."

She stole a glance at him, feeling safer in doing so now that his head was bent over his whittling. She wondered why she had mentioned Anne so quickly, especially since for one brief moment she had wished she did not have a twin, that she was truly as unique as he seemed to think her. Now she felt a wave of guilt for her traitorous thoughts.

He looked up, his expression more than a little incredulous as he presented her pencil. "I find that hard to believe, m'lady. Surely two of you would be an overabundance of beauty."

As Amelia put the pencil in her pocket, she made herself say, "Perhaps you have only recently arrived in England, Mr. Galt? I am sure you will discover many women more comely than I."

James Galt stared at the brook bubbling away at their feet, and one hand came up to rub his chin. "I have not been here for long, that is true, nor do I plan a long stay. To be honest with you, I hated the very thought of the trip to England, but it was necessary for my work."

"What do you do?" Amelia asked, glad the conversation had turned from her looks.

"I am a writer," he said. "Oh, not a bard like our great Rab Burns, or even the novelist Walter Scott who is being embraced with such fervor these days. No, I am a historian, a bit of a scientist, and a part-time inventor."

"So many talents," Amelia marveled. "Most people would be content with only one. Why, I can do nothing but draw! How I envy you your many interests." As she spoke, she wondered why he had not wanted to come to England, why his voice grew so cold and gruff when he spoke of their country.

"I am only here to exchange information and ideas with my host, Lord Barton," he was saying now, and she listened intently. "He is writing a modern history of England, and he asked me for information on the Jacobite Rebellions. Since I myself am engaged in a book about that period, we thought to meet and compare notes." He paused for a moment, and then he said bitterly, "Perhaps in doing so I can correct the many misapprehensions so many English have about those rebellions, and about my country and my people as well." He turned those brooding hazel eyes to hers, and added a little stiffly, "As soon as my work here is done, I return to Edinburgh."

Amelia swallowed a quick comment that she hoped his work would take a very long time. "Tell me about Scotland, if you please, sir," she said instead.

James Galt's eyes grew distant. "It is a beautiful, wild country, very unlike this cultivated Eden," he said, waving a dismissive hand. "I know there are those in England who consider us savages still, and it is true that there was bloodshed and war for many years between the clans. But Scotland has much more than her past, she has a glorious future. New Edinburgh is a city London might strive to emulate, and within her gracious buildings live many learned scholars, and doctors and inventors as well. I myself have a house in Charlotte Square in the New Town."

"Have you always lived there?" Amelia asked.

"No, I was born near Fort Williams at Inverlochy. My family have always been lairds there. But when my brother came into the title, I moved to Edinburgh." He laughed harshly, and Amelia had to twist her hands together in her lap to keep from touching him, comforting him, he sounded so bitter. "Inverlochy can only support the laird and his family now. We have seen harsh times since our bonnie prince died, and if I am not mistaken, we are about to see more."

He paused, and then he shook his head. "But why am I telling *you* all this?" he murmured to himself, as if he were confused. He stood up quickly, and held out his hand to her. As he drew Amelia to her feet, she protested, "But what you have told me is very interesting. I admit to an abysmal ignorance about Scotland, for I have never traveled. How I envy Lady Tyson! Why, she went to Brazil and Greece when she was only a child!"

James Galt smiled a little at the naive awe in her voice. "Scotland is not like those places, m'lady," he told her. "There are no jungles, nor any Parthenons either, although our castle at Edinburgh is an imposing sight. At least we think it is," he added, almost defiantly.

Amelia wondered why he was so much on the defensive, even as she resolved to search the marquess's library for a book about the north this very afternoon.

"May I walk with you a little way?" he was asking now, and Amelia heard the little pleading note in his voice, and felt a surge of elation. She had heard the same tone in other masculine voices, but never before had she welcomed it as she did now.

She nodded, and Mr. Galt untied his horse from a branch and began to lead it behind them.

"You must tell me about yourself, m'lady," he said after a few moments. "I fear I have monopolized the conversation. Unfortunately, the one thing no Scotsman is stingy with, is words."

Amelia considered his request, very conscious of the broad-shouldered, masculine body so close beside her. "There is very little to tell. I am the youngest daughter of William Fairhaven, the Duke of Severn, and I have lived most of my life in the country. This spring I am to go to London with my sister so we can make our come-outs."

"London must be holding its breath, or at least it should be," he said, the little frown back between his dark brows. Amelia wondered what she had said that was so upsetting, but then he went on, "But there must be more than that. Have you other sisters, brothers perhaps? Where did you learn to draw so well? Have you been studying long?"

He seemed genuinely interested, and Amelia told him all there was to know about her past, wishing it had been more exciting.

They reached the edge of the home wood then, and he halted. "I must return to Lord Barton's now," he said, and then he turned and faced her squarely. His deep-set hazel gaze seemed to burn as it lingered on her face.

Amelia held out her hand. "I am glad we met, Mr. Galt," she told him. As he took her hand, almost reluctantly now, she noted, she added, "I shall look forward to seeing you at dinner in a few days' time. I hope your work goes well."

He nodded, but he did not speak, and Amelia felt her breathing grow shallow as she looked up into his dark, frowning face. He raised her hand, and for a moment she was sure he was about to kiss it, and she waited, holding her breath. But then he merely pressed it briefly, and nodded to her before he turned away to mount his horse. He nodded again before he wheeled it and cantered away. Amelia watched him ride out of sight around the first bend, and then she made her way slowly up to the house. Mr. James Galt was a difficult man to understand. In the beginning, she had been sure he was going to flirt with her, but then his manner had changed. And by the time they had parted, his face was as black as a thundercloud. She did not understand him. What had she said, or done, to make him look so forbidding?

Although she looked for him often in the days that followed, he was nowhere to be seen. She often walked in the home wood, hoping to find him there, but she was always disappointed. In the evenings, she read everything she could find about Scotland, its history, and its people. She was a little confused when she discovered that his country had been a part of England for over a century, and yet surely he had spoken of it as if it were separate still, and owed no allegiance to the English throne. She hoped she would have the chance to ask him about it, when next they met.

That was not to be until the evening the Bartons and their guest had been bidden to dinner. Amelia dressed very carefully, choosing a gown of deep rose silk Claire Tyson had admired. She wished she could wear her hair up, and had some sophisticated jewelry to add to her toilette. Unfortunately, both Juliet and the duke had very stringent ideas about what was suitable for a young lady not yet out, and she was forced to go downstairs completely unadorned.

She saw Mr. Galt the moment she entered the drawing room, and even though she conversed easily with Lord Barton and his wife, and replied to some questions from the marquess, she was always conscious of him, standing beside his hostess engaged in easy conversation. He was dressed in the same evening clothes the other men were wearing, but Amelia did not think he looked comfortable in them, though perhaps that was due to the stiff, controlled expression he wore on his face.

They barely exchanged more than a few words before dinner was announced, and then Amelia was disappointed to find Lord Tyson bowing to her to take her to the dining room. The marchioness led the way on Lord Barton's arm, and his wife and Mr. Galt brought up the rear.

At table, things were no better, for James Galt had been placed across from her. Amelia resigned herself to an evening of chitchat with Lord Barton and her host.

She did manage to steal a glance every now and then at the Scotsman she found so intriguing, but more often than not, she was treated only to a view of his rugged profile. During the second course, however, she was able to stare at him as much as she liked when he held the company enthralled as he told them an old Scottish folktale. He had all the flair of a born story-teller, and he was roundly applauded at the end.

Amelia wondered if Mr. Galt would come and speak to her after dinner in the drawing room. When he did not do so, and did not even look in her direction, Amelia decided she had had quite enough. She rose and went to his side, marveling at her temerity. He was not like anyone she had ever known, and his refusal to pay her the kind of homage she was used to, made her bold.

"I trust your work with Lord Barton is going well, sir?" she asked him, smiling as she did so.

James Galt did not return her smile. "Thank you, m'lady. Tolerably well, although it is taking much longer than I had hoped. But Lord Barton has been very kind, and there is a great deal more we must explore together before I can return home."

Amelia heard Lady Barton's plummy voice behind her, and hidden in her skirts, her hands made two fists in her frustration. "I do assure you, Lady Amelia, they work throughout the day, and if I did not insist on their stopping for dinner, would no doubt continue through the night. Was there anyone like a scholar for forgetting the time?"

Mr. Galt bowed to her, a little twinkle in those deep-set eyes. "You have been most patient, ma'am," he said.

"I shall forgive you, James," his elderly hostess said. "But only because you have brought such pleasure to my husband. There is nothing he likes more than a deep historical conversation, and the stories you regale us with at table are fascinating!"

She turned aside then, in response to a question from the marquess, and Amelia said quickly, "May I ask you something, sir?"

She waited until he nodded, looking a little puzzled, and then she said, "Why did you speak the other day as if Scotland was a different country? I have discovered the Scots have been English subjects since 1707. Are you not, therefore, as English as I am?"

She saw him stiffen, and she wondered at it, and at the way he frowned down at her. At last he shook his head. "We may be subjects of your king, that is true, but we are not English. We will never be English!" His voice had quickened and grown harsher, and Amelia raised her hand as if to implore him to speak more softly. He saw the distress on her face and lowered his voice.

"But where had you this information, m'lady?" he asked. "Can it be that someone as lovely as you has been studying some dusty history books?"

He sounded so sarcastic that Amelia felt a blush starting at her toes and rushing up to her face, and she was sure her complexion exactly matched her rose gown. Before she could try to answer, he took her hand in both of his. "I beg your pardon, m'lady! I did not mean to embarrass you. Indeed, I am honored you took the trouble. So many of your countrymen cannot be bothered with anything but their own glorious past, and think of the Scots merely as a conquered nation to be raided and ravaged to enrich their coffers."

He paused, and then with a visible effort he said more calmly, "Let us speak of something else. You are very beautiful this evening. The color of your gown reminds me of the rose and pink heather that blooms all over Scotland."

Amelia was not appeased. Why did he always seem to take offense when none was offered? And then she remembered something from her reading, and she said, "I thank you, sir, but I cannot return the compliment. No, for to me you seem more like a Scots thistle, prickly and difficult."

She put up her chin, her dark blue eyes flashing fire, and James Galt's dark brows rose in astonishment. Amelia curtsied a little and turned to leave him.

"But the English rose has thorns, too, and now I see she does not hesitate to use them," she heard him murmur behind her. Amelia pretended not to hear him as she walked to Claire Tyson's side.

The rest of the evening passed in a blur of misery for Amelia. She was careful not to look at James Galt unless she had to, and when she bade him good-bye, her eyes were cool. Only for a brief moment did she search his face, and then her hand trembled where it lay in his at the light she saw deep in his eyes.

She saw him again the very next afternoon. She was taking the older Tyson children for a walk, and when she saw him cantering up the drive toward her, she was sorry she had volunteered to do so. Introducing the little girls allowed her to regain her self-possession, but a moment later they ran ahead to the swings in the garden, and she was left alone with this irritating, infuriating, impossible, *fascinating* man.

"I have come to apologize, Lady Amelia," he said in his abrupt way. "I am sorry I offended you last evening."

Amelia inclined her head, but she did not speak.

"No doubt you think me a savage boor. You must not feel you are alone in your assessment. Most English think of my countrymen that way."

Amelia stared up into his rugged face. It was carefully expressionless. "Why do you speak and act the way you do?" she asked him, as abruptly as he had spoken. "Why are you so quick to assume people are sneering at you, maligning you?"

Mr. Galt stared back at her, and then he swung from his horse's back and came to stand before her. "I cannot explain . . . you would not understand," he said.

"Try me," Amelia invited, her dark blue eyes steady on his face.

"There is a sea between us that can never be bridged," he told her, his deep voice harsh. "I am a

Scotsman, and you the lovely daughter of an English duke."

"But we give obeisance to the same king," Amelia pointed out.

"But only one of us does so from choice," he said. "We are a conquered people, we did not join England of our own free will."

"I cannot believe this!" Amelia exclaimed. "The union between our countries is over a hundred years old. How can you still feel your defeat so strongly?"

"My family was out for both Rebellions, m'lady. My grandfather fell at Culloden, and my father remained loyal to Prince Charlie. The English have made us pay for that. Most of our lands were stripped from us, and it was only after many years that my brother was allowed to call himself Laird of Inverlochy again." He gave a bitter laugh. "Little did those condescending conquerors know that he would always be laird, no matter how they ruled. The lowliest sheepherder of our clan still bends his knee to a Galt, not to any English king."

Amelia was horrified. The hatred and disdain in his voice, his dark expression, made him seem truly savage. Without thinking, she put her hand on his arm. Under his riding coat, she felt his muscles contract, but she did not release him.

"Can you never forget? Must you hate us—all of us —always?" she whispered.

James Galt stared down at her slender white hand, and his mouth twisted, almost as if he were in pain. "Perhaps someday there will be Scots who hold no grudge. But we are a long-headed, proud people. It is hard for us to forget," he said, more quietly now.

Amelia dropped her hand and stepped away from him. "You are telling me I am your enemy, are you not?"

Suddenly, he moved forward and swept her into his arms. Amelia put her hands on his broad chest, feeling weak and confused. "You are not my enemy, Lady

Amelia. I could never hate you," he said. "But between a member of the English nobility and a loyal Scotsman, there can be nothing."

As his voice died away, Amelia grasped his lapels. "Nothing?" she whispered. "But there is already . . . something."

His hands tightened at her waist, and she felt a wild exaltation as she lifted her face expectantly. And then he groaned a little and bent his head until his lips covered hers. Amelia's arms flew up around his neck, and she pressed closer to him. That they were standing on the drive, in full sight of dozens of windows faded from her mind, as did the laughter of the two little girls swinging some distance away.

All too soon, James Galt raised his head, but only to put his hard cheek against hers. His warm breath stirred her hair as he whispered, "Yes, there is something indeed, m'lady."

And then he put her away from him, his hands firm on her arms. "And that must be the end of it," he told her sternly.

Amelia looked at him as if she could not believe her ears. He had kissed her as if he were starving for her, a kiss full of a passion she had never even known existed. How could he say that kiss was the end? She knew he loved her, wanted her. Surely he could not walk away from her now, and for such a reason as he had given.

"No, I don't believe it!" she cried. "I won't have it end!"

For a moment they stared at each other. The dark, inflexible look was back on his face now, and even the tears sparkling in Amelia's eyes had no power to move him. "Your pardon, m'lady," he said harshly. "I should not have kissed you, but I could not resist. You are much too lovely, too sweet. Someday you will understand. In a short while you will be in London being courted and admired. And someday you will be the bride of some English noble. That is how it should be—will be—and if you don't know your destiny, I do!"

He strode away from her then, and just before he mounted his horse, he bowed. "The likes of a James Galt is not for you, m'lady. You deserve better. I am so sure you will have it that I wish you happy now. There is, after all, little likelihood that we will ever meet again."

He did not wait for a reply, but swung into the saddle and wheeled his horse. Amelia watched him ride away through tears that blurred her vision and streamed down her cheeks. How could he do this? How could he leave her? She did not understand.

By the time the little girls ran back to her, she had composed herself. She knew what she knew, and she would not give James Galt up without a fight. She did not want some nameless duke or earl, she wanted him, prickly and difficult, and oh, so dear!

Now, home at Severn, Amelia sighed with her memories. She had not even had a chance to try, for she learned the very next day that James Galt had left Wiltshire. The marquess told them how disappointed Lord Barton had been that he had had to curtail his visit, but he had had some news of his brother that had him taking coach for Scotland within an hour of receiving it.

Amelia continued to try and eat her dinner, letting the others speculate about this sudden departure and Mr. Galt's unusual personality. She knew why he had gone. It was the only way he could make sure that he did not weaken in his resolve. What she was to do about it, she did not know.

And then she heard Anne coming into the adjoining room, and she wiped the tears from her eyes as she ran to her bed. In the days that had followed James Galt's departure, she was sure no one at Blagdon had even suspected the momentous thing that had happened to her, or the loss she had suffered. She worked hard in the studio, she played with the children, and she was always agreeable and smiling. Only at night did she give way to her grief. And it would be that way at Severn, too, she promised herself. She could not share this even with Anne, not now, and probably not ever, she told herself as she pulled up the covers. But she wondered if the pain she felt would ever leave her, or if she was destined to spend her life in bitter regret for a lost love she could never have.

When Anne opened the door, she pretended to be fast asleep.

III

"How restful it is at Severn now that Will's friends have gone," Anne remarked the next morning at the breakfast table. Amelia looked up from her porridge and smiled in agreement.

"I do not think we can count on it remaining this way, Anne," the duke said, nodding to his butler to refill his coffee cup. The duchess had not put in an appearance yet this morning, and since Will had gone out very early, only three Fairhavens were together in the sunny morning room that overlooked the gardens.

"Whatever do you mean, sir?" Anne asked, her eyes dancing.

"You know very well what I mean, minx," her father replied in his cool drawl. "Any moment now, Devett will announce that the young lord of this or that is in the hall, hat in hand. Indeed, I was surprised not to find several smitten puppies underfoot when I came downstairs."

"I hope you do not think we encourage them, father," Amelia said, her voice demure.

"Of course you do not, Melia," he said as he cut a piece of ham. "But as you have been aware for some time, encouragement is not required. They continue to storm the barricades all unbidden. Do not, I pray you, make your smiles for them any warmer, for that will really put the cat among the pigeons."

As a knock sounded on the door, the duke added,

"What did I tell you? But not, if you please, before breakfast, Devett!"

The old butler bowed. "Certainly not, your Grace," he agreed. And then he took the note that was handed in and brought it to Lady Anne.

As she opened it, William Fairhaven murmured, "Do not feel it is at all necessary to read that aloud, Anne. I do have my digestion to consider."

"It is from Mr. Barnaby, Melia," Anne explained to her twin. "I told you how it would be. He wants me to come to the church this morning so I might assist him with the selection of Sunday's hymns. What a bouncer! He must think I have more hair than wit to believe that."

The duke looked a reprimand, but he did not speak until his daughters' laughter had faded away. "I was not aware that you were so involved in spiritual things, Anne," he said. "It is a side of your nature that, alas, we have seldom seen."

Lady Anne tossed her head. She was wearing a morning gown of sprigged muslin, and she had tied her curls back with a pink band. Lady Amelia was similarly attired.

The door opened and the duchess came in. At once, William Fairhaven was on his feet to go and hold her chair for her, and to drop a light kiss on her ash-blond hair. Amelia saw the fleeting glance that passed between them, and she could not help a little pang for the obvious love they shared.

"Just some tea and toast, Devett, if you please," the duchess said, and then she turned and smiled at her stepdaughters. "You are very merry this early in the morning, my dears. I heard you laughing all the way from the hall."

"And how many eager bodies were you required to step over, ma'am?" the duke asked, his voice courteous.

"Father!" both his daughters said in unison.

"Indeed, it is too bad of you, sir," Amelia told him.

"He has been teasing us unmercifully, Juliet. Do tell him it is not our fault that Will's friends keep calling."

"He already knows it, my dear," the duchess said, shaking her head as Anne offered her the marmalade. "But I hope you will both be pleased to learn we have decided to beat a hasty retreat. We plan to go up to town as soon as it is possible."

"Oh, good!" Lady Anne exclaimed. As she buttered a muffin, her lips curved in a little smile, and the duke raised his brows at his wife.

"Anne is anticipating a somewhat larger audience, William," she told him, chuckling a little. "As well she should. Severn has nowhere near the scope she requires."

"I am not the only one at fault, Juliet," Anne protested. "You know yourself Tom Reading has been here almost every day this week to ask for news of Amelia."

The duke snorted as he wiped his mouth. "He is airdreaming, as is Mr. Barnaby. Do either of them really think a daughter of Severn would consider a country squire or a lowly curate?"

Juliet noticed how quickly Amelia's head came up, and the careful way she searched her father's haughty face.

"Do you mean we must choose our husbands only from the nobility, sir?" she asked in a quiet voice.

"I would prefer it, for it is definitely more suitable," her father told her. "But I do hope you will not marry anyone for a long time. You are only eighteen. Enjoy your girlhood while you can. Marriage lasts a very long time."

"Is marriage so inferior to the single state, then, ma'am?" Anne asked the duchess. Again a little look passed between the duke and his wife, and Amelia lowered her eyes to her cup.

"It is much to be preferred," Juliet told her stepdaughters. "However, there is one problem, and a serious problem it is." She waited, and then she said solemnly, "You must be sure you are marrying the right man."

The duke rose and put his napkin beside his plate. "I shall take my leave of you now, my dears. It is obvious that you are to have a treatise on matrimony that perhaps it would better for me not to hear."

He paused at the door, and then he said, "I shall instruct my agent that we intend to leave Severn within the week, Juliet, if that will give you enough time."

The duchess smiled and nodded, and he went away.

The three ladies did not mention marriage again after he left; instead they talked of the clothes they would take with them, and those they planned to purchase.

"Our first order of business in town will be to set London's finest modiste to making your ball gowns," the duchess said. "Have you any preference as to color?"

"Why, white I suppose would be best," Anne said, and then she added quickly, "I hope you mean to let us dress alike, dear Juliet."

"On this occasion, I think it entirely appropriate," her stepmother agreed. "Your gowns must be not only simple and modest as befits debutantes, but stunning as well. I have been picturing ice blue satin in my mind—a very pale ice blue, almost a silvery white."

"That sounds beautiful, Juliet, but you do have such excellent taste," Amelia told her.

Anne had a score of questions about their presentation ball, and although Amelia joined in on occasion, the duchess was thoughtful when she dismissed the girls to their own pursuits. She sat alone at the table for several minutes, staring out at the blustery April day with unseeing eyes. At last she nodded, and rang the bell. After her customary interview with the housekeeper and chef, she intended to write a letter to Lady Tyson. She was sure something had happened to Amelia while she had been at Blagdon, but she could see the girl had no intention of mentioning it. Perhaps Claire would know, she told herself. Juliet Fairhaven loved all her stepchildren very much, but the twins were her special favorites, for they had been friends even before her marriage. Being a perceptive person, she could see beyond Melia's pleasant smiles and gay chatter, and there had been a look in her eyes once or twice that had alerted the duchess to some secret unhappiness.

In the gold salon the twins had appropriated for their own use now they had outgrown the schoolroom, Anne was busy promoting a scheme to her sister. "How can you be so stuffy, Melia?" she scolded. "It is not as if we have not changed roles often. And I did so want to ride this morning with father. Why can't you pretend to be me, and take my place in church? I am sure you can choose the hymns as well as I can, and Mr. Barnaby will never know."

Amelia knew there was no way she could tell her twin she did not have the heart for such girlish pranks anymore. "Why don't you just write to him and say you cannot come?" she asked instead.

Anne jumped up to run to the mirror to adjust her hairband. "If I did that, he would come hotfoot to Severn to inquire if I felt quite the thing, and it would be ages before I got rid of him." She sighed, and came to sit beside her sister. "I shall be glad when we leave Severn, Melia. Mr. Barnaby has been hard to bear, for Juliet forebade me to give him a crushing setdown. She said it would be unkind, for people in love are easily bruised."

Silently, Amelia agreed with the duchess, as Anne went on, "But he is such a bore! All he does is prose on and on about church matters, and his illustrious family tree. Ugh."

Amelia laughed. "Very well, but this must be the last time, Anne. We are really too old for such tricks."

Her sister gave her a considering look, and seemed about to question her, and Amelia was quick to squeeze her hand before she went to order the carriage for eleven. For a long while, Anne sat in a brown study and pondered her sister's behavior, much as the duchess had done. She was only recalled to the time when a footman came to tell her the duke had sent a message to the stables, and then she flew upstairs, calling for her maid as she went.

Later that morning, Amelia had not spent many minutes in Mr. Barnaby's company before she was in complete agreement with her sister. The curate was so solemn, so deliberate in his choice of words, that it was all she could do not to finish his sentences for him. And he had nothing of interest to say, although he spoke at great length. He sat beside her at the organ, turning the pages of the hymnal, and begging her to play the music and sing for him.

Amelia made herself laugh, much as Anne would, to distract him, for her voice was nothing like her sister's and her playing inferior. At once he frowned, and placed a finger to his lips.

"My dear Lady Anne," he said in reprimand, "You must remember where you are. Such a display of mirth is not seemly in God's house."

"Do you think God does not want us to enjoy ourselves, sir?" Amelia asked pertly, and then she raised her chin as Anne was so apt to do. "I cannot believe it. I should think He would be glad to see some of His children happy, when there is so much misery in the world."

Mr. Barnaby made a steeple of his fingers, and looked even more serious. "You raise an interesting theological point, my dear lady. Allow me to instruct you. I do not believe God wishes us to go about in a constant gloomy piety, but on the other hand, we must ever . . ."

Amelia easily put Mr. Barnaby and his sermon from her mind. She began to wonder if James Galt would admire her in ice blue satin, and she was not recalled to her surroundings until she heard the curate say, in a slightly warmer voice, "But you are very young, my dear Lady Anne. I consider it my duty as well as my pleasure to instruct you, for I am your spiritual guide." He coughed a little then, and added, "And someday I look forward to instructing you in other matters very dear to my heart. I shall say no more at this time, but I am sure you understand my meaning. We have spoken of it before."

Amelia looked at him amazed. Did he really think Anne would marry him some day? It was ludicrous! She wondered if Anne had ever encouraged him, in a fit of devilment, and was sure somehow she had. She wished she had never agreed to take her twin's place.

As she rose from the bench, she drew herself up and said, "If I ever feel the need for spiritual guidance, you may be sure I will go to my dear Uncle Romeo, Mr. Barnaby. As for your other remarks, I am afraid you have mistaken my intent."

Her voice was cold, and the curate coughed again, and said in a placating way, "Of course you would prefer an older man for your girlish confidences, would you not? I quite understand. The vicar is your dear stepmama's brother, too. And you must not think I mind that you want to—dear me, what is the cant expression?—*cut a dash* in town. But when you have done so, my *dear* Lady Anne, I am sure you will return to Severn, and if I am not too bold to say so, to one who has all your interests close to his heart."

Amelia gasped as he bowed and smirked at her, and then she about-faced and marched down the aisle, beckoning to Anne's maid who had been waiting for her in one of the pews, as she did so. She knew she must speak to her twin as soon as she could manage it, for Mr. Barnaby's statements, in spite of being just so much pompous fustian, had been too confident, too assured.

She had intended calling on Vicar Manchester, since she had not seen him for such a long time, but now she took her seat in the carriage to be driven home immediately.

Devett told her the Lady Anne had returned from her ride and was entertaining Mr. Thomas Reading in the red salon, and Amelia shook her head in despair. She did not go and join them, for she knew very well Anne was pretending to be her. The squire's eldest son was as single-minded as Mr. Barnaby. Ever since he had returned from the West Indies, where he had stayed at the wealthy uncle's plantation he was in such great expectation of inheriting some day, he had pursued her. He had decided that the Lady Amelia would make a beautiful, gracious wife, and before she had gone to Blagdon, had spent many afternoons telling her all about the islands. He was, in his own way, as pompous as the curate, and if ever he felt any doubt at his temerity in courting the daughter of a duke, he was able to quell it by thinking of his future position as a wealthy landowner in a fascinating part of the world far removed from stiff English conventions.

Amelia went upstairs to the north-lit room the duke had had fitted out as a studio for her. She decided she would work on some of her unfinished drawings of Blagdon until Anne managed to send the eager Mr. Reading on his way.

Half an hour later, Anne knocked and entered the room. She was still wearing her habit, and Amelia could see her eyes were dancing with mischief. After she had closed the door behind her, she leaned against it and began to laugh. A sympathetic answering smile curled her twin's lips as she straightened her working materials and put her sketchbook away.

"The fragrance of the bougainvillea—ah, the bright red bougainvillea, my dear Lady Amelia!" Anne exclaimed at last. Putting one hand on her hip, and pushing out her lower lip in imitation of the hapless suitor, she began to stride about the studio, waving her other hand for emphasis. "How you would stare to see the turquoise sea, the waving fields of cane! And I daresay the villa would astound you, so richly appointed as it is. Only the finest, the *finest* furnishings, my dear lady, have been used. Nothing the least bit shoddy or second rate, 'pon my honor. It lacks but one beautiful thing to make it complete." Here Anne paused and leered at her sister, who could not help giggling. Anne was such an accomplished mimic, it was almost as if Mr. Reading was standing before her in person.

Suddenly Anne dropped her pose and said in her own voice, "I was obliged to invent an errand for Juliet in order to escape him before he threw propriety to the winds and clutched me in his arms. He was aching to do so, I can tell you."

She stopped, and then she asked, her voice guileless, "You did not *want* me to fall into his arms, did you, Melia? Oh, I do so hope my dismisssal was not untimely!"

"Behave yourself, twin," Amelia told her. "Of course I don't want to be clutched in Mr. Reading's arms, and you know it. But I am glad you escaped him, for there is something we must discuss. Something serious."

Anne sank onto a tall stool, clasping her hands before her. "So something did happen at Blagdon! I knew it!" she crowed.

Amelia's heart beat a little irregularly for a minute. "I do not know what you mean, Anne. It has nothing to do with Blagdon. No, indeed. I must tell you that Mr. Barnaby seems very sure you are going to marry him. I was never more shocked! How could you have let it go so far, encouraged him that way? It would have been better to—"

"Give him that icy setdown," Anne finished for her. Then she frowned and began to arrange the paints on the table beside her in neat rows. "I never meant to let him make such assumptions, but one day when he called here, he kept prosing on and on, and I—well, I stopped listening. I was wondering if my mare really had a sprained hock, for I had detected a limp that morning when I was riding her. And so, I just kept nodding every once in a while when I thought to do so, so Mr. Barnaby would think I was attending. Imagine my surprise when he kissed my hand in parting, and actually patted my cheek!"

"And he went away thinking he had secured your promise just from that?" Amelia asked, somewhat awed. "I wonder what he said?"

"I tried to get him to repeat it many times, so I could refute it, but he never did. He just kept hinting, and— and I didn't know what to do," Anne admitted. "But what did you say to him, Melia? Dare I hope you gave him a setdown?"

Her twin grimaced. "Of a sort. It was more luke-warm than icy, though. But I did tell him he had mistaken your intent. Even that did not discourage him, so I came home at once to discover what game you were up to, before I said any more."

Anne shrugged. "When we are safely in London, perhaps I will write a letter to him. A cold, formal dismissal would be easier that way."

"But nowhere near as kind," her twin pointed out.

Anne rose and went to the window, her skirts swinging with her impatience. "Kind?" she repeated, her voice rich with scorn. "I consider I have been quite kind enough not to take him to task long ago for his ridiculous presumptions." As her sister looked at her in distressed surprise, she went on. "How dare he think I would even consider him? Or Tom Reading imagine you would accept his hand either? Men, I am discovering, Melia, are the most arrogant creatures alive. Our birth, our nobility and wealth, they dismiss with an airy wave of their hands, for they are so conceited and think themselves so *devastating*, they are sure we are nothing but helpless pawns, easily manipulated to their will. Well, they shall see."

She nodded then, her chin coming up in that

familiar gesture. Amelia wondered that she had never realized how like her father Anne was. And then she remembered one man who was not so arrogant, the man who had told her harshly that between the daughter of an English duke and a plain Scotsman, there could be nothing. She forced herself to forget James Galt when she saw Anne looking hard at her, her dark blue eyes intent with her determination to see into her twin's mind.

Suddenly, Anne was aware of the dark wall her sister had erected between them, and she wondered at it, feeling very hurt that Melia would not confide in her. I shall find out what it is, she told herself. It is not at all like Melia to shut me out.

"I think both of us should speak to the gentlemen before we leave," Amelia was saying now, coming to put her arm around her sister, for she knew the hurt Anne was feeling. "And I will promise to do so, if you will too, Anne."

Lady Anne's flair for the dramatic was aroused, and she smiled. "Perhaps we could do it together, Melia?" she asked. "We could line them up across from us and deliver a speech in unison. What fun it would be to watch their horrified expressions!"

She did not notice Amelia's frown as she rose to elaborate her plan. " 'My dear sirs, you have misread our intent and attributed to us an interest in your august persons we do not feel. We take this opportunity to tell you both now that between the Ladies Anne and Amelia Fairhaven and yourselves, there can be nothing but friendship. Good day.' And then we can bow a little, a haughty expression on our faces, and leave them to commiserate with each other."

Before Amelia could scold her sister for her flippancy, a maid knocked to deliver a message from the duchess. She wished to see the Lady Amelia in her rooms as soon as it was convenient.

Amelia nodded and left the studio. Her twin remained by the window, deep in thought. Anne was more than hurt; she had felt real pain when she realized that Melia intended to keep her own counsel. Something had happened while she was away, something so momentous, so private, she could not even tell her other self what it was. But what could it be, Anne pondered as she walked to the table where Melia's sketchbook lay. She herself had always been the stronger twin, it was she who had led the way ever since they were children. And always she had felt protective of her twin. She knew Amelia was not as brave, not so much of a daredevil as she was, and she had tried to shelter her and reassure her all their lives.

Now she put her hand on the sketchbook and thought hard. Surely Melia would not object to her looking at it, for she had always been quick to share her work. Still Anne hesitated, wishing she did not feel as if she were spying somehow.

And then she squared her shoulders and opened the large book. In this instance she must do as she thought right. She could not bear to see her sister unhappy, and if she were going to help, she would have to overcome her foolish scruples about privacy. Melia might think she could handle whatever was bedeviling her by herself, but Anne knew better. And two heads are better than one, she told herself as she flipped over the drawings and watercolors. She did not find anything that gave her a clue to the trouble, and so she turned back to the first drawings to study them more closely.

For page after page, there was nothing unusual. And then, near the end, she found what she was looking for. The page contained several thumbnail sketches; a small drawing of a child's hand, the detail of a piece of molding, a tree branch and a bunch of snowdrops, and over to one side, a careful, detailed sketch of a man's eyes. Anne frowned and bent closer. They were not the eyes of any man she had ever seen. These were too deep-set, too penetrating, and they were frowning. Anne studied the sketch for several minutes. Surely she would remember if she had ever seen those eyes before, for there was that about them that made them impossible to forget. She wondered what the rest of the man's face looked like as she closed the book and put it back where she had found it.

As she went down to luncheon, she wondered why Amelia had drawn him frowning, and what there was about him that was making her so unhappy.

That afternoon, Amelia wrote a letter to Claire Tyson to thank her for her stay at Blagdon, and for the time and instruction she had been given in the artist's studio. Writing to the marchioness brought back all her memories, and after she had sealed her letter and written the direction, she sat still for a moment, tapping it against her cheek.

When she looked down, she saw a blank piece of hot pressed paper on her writing desk, and without thinking, she took up her pen again to dip it in the inkwell to begin a letter to James Galt.

She felt a little breathless as she did so. It was unheard of for a gently bred young lady to write to a man who was not a relative, a man, moreover, who had put any liaison between them firmly aside. But Amelia knew she had to write. It was the only thing she could think of to do. She had to let him know what was in her mind and heart, for only then could she gain any respite from the memories that were causing her so much pain.

In spite of her resolution, her letter was a shy, restrained effort, and she shook her head as she read it over. She had addressed him as Mr. Galt, before she told him how sorry she had been that he had had to leave Wiltshire so suddenly. She said she hoped his research was going well, and how much she was looking forward to reading his book when it was published at last. And then she picked up her pen, and her guard slipped a little. She wrote that she missed him, that she was sorry he felt as he did about any future relationship between them. For herself, she told him, she did not think she would ever forget what had passed between them.

And then she crossed that paragraph out, and took a clean sheet to begin again. It was a long time before she was satisfied. There was nothing in her final effort that the entire world could not have read, but she hoped with all her heart that he would read between the lines and sense her longing and her pain.

She signed her letter "Amelia Fairhaven," and then she added a postscript, telling him she would be delighted to hear from him. She gave him the address of the duke's townhouse in Berkeley Square, London, where she said she expected to be situated for the next few months.

As she wrote his name on the outside, she remembered he had said he had a house in Charlotte Square. Even if she did not know the number, surely her letter would reach its destination safely.

She was careful to burn all her earlier attempts in the fireplace before she took her correspondence down to her father's secretary to be mailed. She did so at once before she had a chance to regret her impetuous, unconventional behavior.

IV

By the time the Fairhavens arrived in London ten days later, most of the masculine faction that made up the *ton* was all agog. Sir Whitney Blake and Stephen Young had wasted no time extolling the Fairhaven twins to the skies. Every one of their acquaintance was treated to a detailed account of the young ladies' beauty, talent, and grace, and if some of the more skeptical of their friends decided it would be prudent to wait and see for themselves, there were many more who eagerly accepted their account of these paragons, and who had every intention of forming one of their admiring court as soon as they reached the capitol.

They were to be disappointed. Anne and Amelia were very busy addressing the cards of invitation to their ball, assisting the duchess in her plans for decorations and refreshments, and having fittings on all their new gowns.

Mr. Percival Collingwood had caught a glimpse of them stepping into their carriage in Bond Street one day, and he was quick to inform his cronies at Brooks's Club that for once, Stephen and Whitney had not exaggerated.

"Such gorgeous black hair, such well-proportioned figgers and slender ankles," he enthused to an avid audience. "And perfectly matched, too!"

"One would think them a team of horses that you

saw this morning at Tattersall's from your description, Percy," a deep voice drawled. The owner of the voice lowered his journal to stare at the red-faced, freckled young man. "Do try and contain your ecstasy, dear boy. Some of us came here to read in peace and quiet," he continued. As he disappeared behind the paper again, he murmured, "When you have seen as many Seasons as I have, and witnessed the never-ending parade of pulchritude that inevitably appears each year, you will learn to control your enthusiasm."

"No, no, m'lord," Mr. Collingwood protested, his Adam's apple bobbing with his fervor. "There can never have been anyone to compare to the Ladies Anne and Amelia Fairhaven, I do assure you, on my honor."

"Indeed?" m'lord asked in a bored voice. "Remind me to give you my—er—expert appraisal after I have seen 'em."

"But when *are* we going to see them?" Lord Anders asked quickly, ignoring the Earl of Burnham's cool, casual indifference. It was obvious to him that when a man reached thirty he became blasé. He was not looking forward to it, himself.

"Yes, when?" another young lord chimed in. "I have looked for them at every party I've attended, but they are never there."

"Stephen told me they are busy preparing for their ball, and that their father, the Duke of Severn, does not care to have them jauntering about until they have been properly presented to the *ton*," Mr. Collingwood explained.

"How perfectly gothic of him!" Lord Anders exclaimed in a horrified voice.

At the threatening cough that came from behind the journal that was being rattled in two elegant, although impatient hands, the young men removed themselves from the reading room, to continue their discussion in more convivial surroundings.

The Duke of Severn was well aware of the speculations and whispers, for more than one gentleman of his acquaintance had demanded news of his daughters, claiming their sons' eager questioning was driving them to distraction. To one and all, he returned a light answer, saying that although he himself considered his daughters extraordinary, he had no doubt a father's pride had made him partial. He said he would leave it to the *ton* to decide.

The duke was enjoying himself very much. Outside of Sir Whitney and Mr. Young, no crowd of beaux were underfoot as yet. Since they had not been introduced to the young ladies, they could not call on them, and since Will was remaining in Severn until the ball, they could not gain entrance to the mansion in Berkeley Square on the pretext of coming to see him.

The duke and his wife exchanged many a chuckle when he related the growing interest in the twins. Juliet told him that just as many ladies with sons were flocking to the doorstep, to ensure that they received an invitation to the ball, and how Lady Jersey had come to inspect them for herself. This patroness of Almack's had declared she was delighted by the twins' beauty and manners, and vouchers to that hallowed club had arrived barely a day later.

None of these anecdotes were repeated in Anne's and Amelia's hearing.

"They would grow puffed up with conceit, William," his duchess had warned him. "They will discover their power soon enough; in the meantime, let us enjoy this peace that reigns now for as long as we can."

The duke agreed, and although Juliet wished he would take Anne to task for some of her more outrageous statements concerning her infallibility, she had to be content. She knew her husband did not see Anne's arrogance. How could he, she asked herself, when he is so arrogant himself? Of course the Ladies Anne and Amelia were superior to other mortals. Were they not Fairhavens of Severn? she could hear him asking in a cold voice, those black brows soaring in surprise that anyone could doubt it. The duchess shook her head, and tried to temper any unseemly display of conceit by pointing out on as many occasions as she could manage it, that a modest demeanor was much more attractive in a young woman making her come-out, and that nothing got people's backs up so much as vain boasting and inordinate pride.

She noticed Amelia's little smile of agreement as her twin tossed her head and looked mutinous, as if she would like to disagree but did not dare. The duchess had not had a return letter from Blagdon, although the duke had told her that Tysons had promised they would attend the ball, and so she was still in the dark about Amelia's unhappiness. The girl had such lovely manners, however, that no one else suspected anything was wrong, and if she was very quiet on occasion, it was put down to the fact that she had never been the whirlwind her sister was.

The evening of the ball arrived at last. The large ballroom of the duke's townhouse had been decorated in a rich shade of blue accented by silver. Masses of hothouse flowers stood in tall vases, the crystal chandeliers and wall sconces sparkled, and even as the twins put the final touches to their toilettes, they could hear the orchestra tuning up two flights below them.

When Juliet came to see if they were ready to receive the thirty guests who had been invited to dinner before the ball, Amelia clapped her hands. "How fine you look, Juliet!" she exclaimed, her eyes admiring. As Anne agreed, Juliet smiled. She was wearing a gown of navy brocade, embroidered all over with silver thread, and the Fairhaven diamonds. The matching tiara on her ash-blond hair made her seem very regal.

"Thank you, my dears," she told them, coming to give them a kiss. "I chose my gown to complement yours, for this is your night, and you are perfect! I knew that blue satin would be a success!"

The twins inspected themselves in the pier glass, arms entwined. "Remember how we used to worry that we would never have a shape, Melia?" Anne asked her sister.

"It seems a long time ago," Amelia agreed.

The duchess admired their graceful, curved figures. Their gowns were cut with low necklines that showed off their slender necks and white bosoms before falling in a fluid sweep of satin to the floor. The only adornment was the faggotting around the neckline and down the outside of the tight sleeves, and their long white kid gloves. Juliet knew that modest as they were, the gowns were daring in their very simplicity. Where were the pearl rosettes, the braid and flounces and tucks and knots of ribbons with which most ball gowns were adorned? But she had not wanted anything to detract from the twins themselves, and now that she saw what a success their gowns were, she was pleased.

As the girls turned slowly so she might inspect them and their maids fussed around them, a knock sounded at the door. The duke came in and bowed to them, and then he held out two blue velvet cases.

"For you, my dears, to mark this most momentous occasion," he said, not even trying keep the pride he was feeling from showing in his deep voice.

Anne opened her gift first, and her gasp as she reverently took out the delicate sapphire and diamond necklace and matching tiara made the duke smile.

As their maids put the jewels on, both twins were effusive in their thanks.

"I have never seen anything so lovely," Amelia whispered. "How can we ever thank you, father?"

"You can thank me by comporting yourselves as I would wish, not only tonight but in the weeks to come," he told them. His voice was serious, and then he made a sign, dismissing the maids. When the four of them were alone, he went on. "You will remember who you are at all times, and in every situation you might find yourselves in this Season. There are to be no madcap pranks, no episodes that will cause gossip and conjecture. You are Fairhavens of Severn. You bear a great name and a greater responsibility."

"Dear father," Anne assured him, her voice teasing, "we are well aware of it. Do we *look* like two little scullery maids?"

He stared at them, unsmiling. They were so young, so beautiful, he wished they never had to change; never grow old, feel any pain, suffer sadness and bereavement. Tonight they wore their hair in shining waves brushed high and then descending in a cascade of ebony curls that reached their shoulders. Their dark blue eyes sparkled with anticipation under those distinctive black brows, and the excitement had brought a most becoming color to their delicate complexions. At last the duke said, "No, you look noble, titled, and altogether breathtaking." He paused, and then he added in a softer voice, "I am proud of you."

Anne flew into his arms. "Oh, father," she said, beginning to weep.

The duke shook her a little. "I believe satin stains, m'lady?" he asked, his voice gruff with emotion. "Do control yourself!"

As Anne wiped her eyes, Amelia came and kissed him. "I hope you will always be proud of us, sir," she said. "We shall do our best to see you have no reason not to be."

The duke nodded, and then he held out his arm to Juliet, and the pair preceded the excited, whispering twins, who picked up their bouquets of white roses to go to the drawing room and await their guests.

Juliet had invited their closest friends to dinner. She knew the ball was going to be a perfect crush, for she had had very few refusals to her gilt-edged cards of invitation, and so she wanted the twins to have a little time first with those people they knew best.

When the Marquess and Marchioness of Blagdon were announced, Lord Tyson pretended to be dumbstruck, and his bow to the twins was deep and reverent, although his eyes crinkled shut in his amusement. "You are to be congratulated, William," he told the duke. "I do not think I have ever seen such loveliness."

"And multiplied by two as it is, makes it even more awesome," his wife agreed with a chuckle. "But I am well aware that the way they look is all due to Juliet's discerning eye. How are you, my dear? I have not had a moment to reply to your letter, but now that I am in town at last, we can have a long talk soon."

She kissed her hostess's cheek and pressed her hand, and the duchess smiled.

Both girls had turned away for a moment, to answer a cousin's question, and the duke said softly, "Do you care to accept another commission, Claire? I want my daughters to sit for their portraits this Season, and there is no one who can do them justice save yourself."

Lady Tyson inspected the girls with a new eye, her head tilted slightly to one side as she considered them. "Yes, they must be painted now," she agreed, and then she added absently, "Dressed in their ball gowns, too. I shall pose Amelia in a high-backed chair with Anne leaning one hand on the back of it. Perhaps a crimson drape behind? Or would a deep blue be more effective . . . ?"

The marquess took her hand to lead her away. "Now see what you have done, your Grace," he scolded. "She is lost in her plans, and we will be lucky to get a sensible word from her on any other topic for the rest of the evening."

By the time dinner was over and the additional guests had been announced and gone through the receiving line, it was after ten o'clock. Expectantly, the guests waited as the duke signaled the orchestra, and then he bowed to his daughters before he led Anne onto the gleaming floor. He had made a light comment about the elder being first to Amelia, and she smiled as she nodded. After a few minutes, he gave

Anne's hand to her brother Will, and now it was Amelia's turn to be partnered by her father. She smiled up at him and said, "But no one has thought to tell you how handsome *you* are this evening, sir! It is too bad."

The duke smiled down at her, his dark, haughty face softening. "Now why are you thinking to turn me up sweet, Melia?" he teased.

"But I mean it!" she exclaimed. "You are the best looking man in the room!"

The duke laughed at her. It was true that even in his late forties, William Fairhaven was still an intriguing man. He was as lean and handsome as he had been in his youth, and the dusting of silver in his sideburns added to rather than detracted from his good looks. He gave his daughter up at the end of the dance to the myriad of eager young men who wished to sign her dance card, and sought out his duchess, well pleased with the success of the evening.

It was true the Fairhaven ball was destined to be talked about for many weeks. All the *ton* was there, and they were in general agreement that never in living memory had two such lovely young ladies joined their ranks. The other debutantes tried very hard to conceal their envy. The more astute among them resolved to become friends with the Fairhaven twins, in hopes of joining the coterie they were sure to attract. Many a young lady told herself that being included in their inner circle of friends could only bring her to the attention of all the most intriguing men, and after all, the twins could only marry one of them each. When they finally dropped the handkerchief, there would be lots of beaux left over, hopefully looking for consolation.

The Earl of Burnham inspected the twins through his quizzing glass for a long time, and then he made his way leisurely to Mr. Percival Collingwood's side. This young man had just finished dancing with Anne, and he wore a vacant look of complete happiness.

"My sincere apologies, my boy," the earl murmured, swinging his glass gently to and fro.

"Hmmmm?" Mr. Collingwood asked absently, his eyes never leaving the vision who was now dancing with one of his friends.

"You were perfectly correct in your description of the young ladies we have come to honor this evening," the earl explained. "And I, much as it pains me to admit it, was wrong. I shall even humble myself further and say I have never seen anything like them in over a decade of Seasons."

"Hmmmm?" Mr. Collingwood murmured again, and seeing he was incoherent and probably would be for some time in the future, the earl shrugged and left him.

In spite of his admiration, the earl did not attempt a dance with either twin. It was not his style to become part of the clamoring throng that surrounded them whenever they stopped dancing, for at the age of thirty, Hugh Thomson Moreley was too sophisticated, too self-possessed to be so obvious.

Accordingly, he went to give his congratulations to the duke and duchess, and he remained beside them for some time, chatting of the ball and exchanging news of society.

He was still there when a breathless Anne, her dark blue eyes glowing and a delicate wild rose flush to her cheeks, came over to sit beside her stepmother.

"Whew!" she said, closing her eyes for a moment. "I am worn to a thread, ma'am!"

"You do remember the Earl of Burnham, Anne?" her father asked, reminding her of her manners.

Anne would have risen to curtsy, but the earl raised a deterring hand. "Please do not, m'lady. It would be cruel to ask it of you when you are in such *dire* need of a rest."

He seemed to be laughing at her, and Anne studied him just as carefully as he had studied her earlier. She

had met so many new people this evening, and she
could remember so few. Somehow, she was sure she
would not forget the elegant nobleman who stood
before her now, smiling down at her with a crooked
little smile. He had hair as black as hers, and unusual
gray eyes, and although he was shorter and slighter in
build than her father, he was just as arresting. She
sensed by his demeanor and the way he held himself,
that he was as arrogant as the duke. As she continued
to look at him, a mocking light came into his eyes, and
then he nodded to her. Anne's own eyes widened. She
had the strangest feeling that somehow a gauntlet had
been thrown down, and she was being dared to pick it
up. One of her dark brows soared, and then, hesitating
only a moment, she lifted her chin. The earl nodded
again before he turned to answer a question of the
duke's.

Suddenly, Stephen Young was before her, bowing
and looking very earnest. "My dear Lady Amelia," he
began, his voice a little strained. Mr. Young had seen
the way his friends had clustered around the lady he
had chosen for his future wife, and he did not like it
one little bit. Why, any one of them would try his best
to cut him out, he told himself, and then he called
himself every kind of fool for not asking the lady to
marry him before the ball.

"But I am not Amelia," Anne interrupted, shaking
her head. "I am Anne."

Mr. Young blushed crimson, and he began a flound-
ering apology until the duchess kindly took a hand.
"Amelia is over by the door, Mr. Young," she said with
her warm smile. "Do not be upset; everyone mixes the
twins up. Why, I often do so myself, and I have known
them for years."

Anne managed to contain her laughter until the
hapless beau had bowed himself away, but then she
began to chuckle. Juliet shook her head, and the duke
frowned.

"I beg your pardon," Anne said when she could

speak again. "But he is so ridiculous! And Juliet, you told a terrible lie. You know Melia and I can never fool you anymore."

"I did it to be kind," the duchess told her. "Poor young man! Contretemps of that sort are very hard to handle with any degree of sophistication at his age."

As Anne looked disdainful, the earl remarked, in an admiring voice, "You are very gracious, ma'am. I must tell you, there are many men who envy the duke his kind and lovely wife."

His voice seemed to imply that he himself was in the forefront of the duchess's admirers, and yet Anne felt there was a special message for her there as well. A little frown formed between her brows until her next partner appeared and she went with him to join the set that was forming.

It seemed strange to Anne that even as crowded as the ball was, she should know exactly when the earl left it, shortly after supper. He had not attempted any further conversation with her, nor looked her way again, and she was confused to find that this annoyed her. And when she came down the next morning and inspected the many bouquets that had been delivered, she was surprised again at her feeling of pique that he had not honored her with even so much as a small nosegay. When she discovered that he had sent Juliet a large bouquet of roses, she was furious.

She decided then and there, as she ate her late breakfast, that she would bring the earl around if it was the last thing she ever did. She had never been rejected before; she did not intend to be rejected now. Sir Whitney and the other young men were all very well in their way, but not a one of them could compare to this older, dashing challenge of a man. It would be quite a feather in her cap to have him dancing attendance on her, and a little smile curled her lips as she began to make plans for the gentleman's speedy capitulation.

Anne was to be disappointed more often than not in

the days that followed. It seemed that the Earl of
Burnham did not choose to attend the parties to which
she was invited. She had become accustomed to looking around the room as soon as she entered a party,
and the few occasions that he was present could not
make up for all the evenings when he was not there.
Anne told herself she did not care if he came or not,
that it was only because she was determined to have
him as an admirer, nothing more, but she began to
wonder why she felt so strongly. One afternoon as they
were dressing for a ride in the park, she asked her twin
what she thought of the earl, and she was surprised
that Amelia had trouble placing him.

"But surely you remember, Melia!" she exclaimed.
"He was at the Wilton party last evening. The dark-
haired man in gray who stayed beside Lady Preston
most of the time."

As she spoke, she lifted her chin. Lady Preston was a
beautiful, voluptuous widow who was much admired.
Admired, that is, by everyone but Anne Fairhaven.
The lady always made her feel gauche and young, and
she did not care for it.

"But I have never met the earl," Amelia explained,
watching her sister carefully. "Do you like him,
Anne?"

Anne picked up a bottle of scent and dabbed the
stopper behind her ears before she replied. "I don't
know," she said slowly. "I was introduced to him at
our ball, and I had the strangest feeling that somehow
he was laughing at me, as if he found me no more than
an amusing child. I don't know how I feel about him."

Amelia smiled to herself. Was it possible that Anne
was fretting because there was one man who would
not surrender to her charms? She had so many
admirers, what did the Earl of Burnham matter when
all was said and done? She picked up her crop and her
gloves and put her arm around her twin to lead her to
the door. "I shall make it a point to observe this
unusual earl more closely next time," she assured

Anne. "How very strange he must be, not to succumb to Anne Fairhaven. Why, he must be *mad*!"

Anne laughed at her incredulous tone as she tossed her head. "Do you think to tell me I am too haughty, Melia?" she asked as they started down the stairs.

"I have no need to tell you, twin," her sister said. "You know you are!"

Both girls were laughing as they went out to their horses. Four mounted gentlemen were there as well, all arguing about who was to have the privilege of helping the twins to their saddles. Amelia solved the problem by beckoning to the groom the duke insisted attend them at all times.

That same afternoon they were out riding, the Marchioness of Blagdon came to call on the Duchess of Severn. The two old friends caught up on all the family news before Juliet introduced the one subject she was most interested in discussing.

At her query, Claire Tyson put her tea cup down. "Ever since your letter, I have been thinking back to Amelia's visit with us, my dear, but try as I might, I can remember no reason for this shadow you say you see in her eyes. We had very few guests and there were almost no festivities. Andrew was busy with the estate, and knowing I was going to be away for such a long time, I was much occupied with the children. I remember hoping Amelia would not be bored, we were so quiet. But Amelia is such a dear! She seemed content just to spend time with the family when she was not working in the studio. Toward the end of her stay, she did seem to grow quieter, but I thought she was merely homesick. I certainly did not notice anything else that could have caused it."

As Juliet passed her guest the plate of cakes, she wished Claire was a more observant person. She had noticed this lack of hers before, and had put it down to the singleminded intensity with which she approached her work. It seemed to the duchess that if the matter at hand did not concern her husband, her children, or her painting, Claire was blind. There was no one who could look more searchingly at the skin and bone and muscle of any human being, but she was incapable of searching deeper into someone's heart and soul. Juliet wondered if all dedicated artists, musicians, and writers were like her. She knew the duke had loved Claire Tyson once a long time ago, and she was glad nothing had come of it for both their sakes. They would have driven each other mad, the *prima donnas* that they were.

She put her thoughts aside and tried to jog Claire's memory. "Were there any young men about?"

"Not a one," the marchioness said quickly, but then she raised her hand. "No, there was one. He was not precisely young, and he was such an unusual man, I am sure he could not be the cause of Amelia's melancholia."

"Tell me about him," the duchess invited, settling back in her chair and feeling she was getting somewhere at last.

"His name was James Galt, a younger brother of the Laird of Inverlochy. He himself lives in Edinburgh, for he is a historian, a writer. He was visiting our neighbors, the Bartons, and doing some research with Lord Barton, I believe. I would say he is in his late twenties, and he has never married. But Amelia only met him twice. He came to tea one afternoon, and then, on another occasion, to dinner. Now that I think of it, he seemed content that evening to talk to the rest of us, instead of seeking Amelia's company. Surely he could not have attached her by ignoring her, the only pretty girl in the room." Claire shrugged. "For myself, I found him fascinating once he began to talk about his work and his country, but he was not an easy man to entertain. He had little social conversation, although he could be charming when he chose. He was intelligent and knowledgeable as well. But even so, he appeared forbidding."

She smiled at the duchess. "I am sure you have met

the type. Men who seem to smolder with some hidden, burning resentment."

The duchess nodded. "He does not sound at all attractive," she said, trying to keep her disappointment from showing.

"Physically, he was handsome in spite of his frowning eyes and distant manner," Claire told her. "I remember thinking he would make an excellent model. His eyes were so deep-set, his facial structure so powerful. And his hair would be a challenge to any artist. It seemed a deep brown, but there were some intriguing gleams of chestnut there . . ."

Her voice died away, and Juliet tried to hide a smile. Claire was back in her studio, and she would hear no more of the strange Mr. Galt's character today.

After the marchioness left her, the duchess sat on in the drawing room, deep in thought. She had hoped that once Amelia was in town, being feted and admired, she would forget whatever was bedeviling her. But the duchess was well aware she had not. She could see it in her eyes, in the little bewilderment there when she thought she was unobserved, and it was there in her silence and her abstraction as well. And whatever it was, it was serious. Otherwise, she would have spoken of it, if not to her stepmother, most certainly to her twin. The duchess had questioned Anne carefully, for she did not want the girl to badger Amelia, but she could tell from her answers that Anne was as confused as she was herself. She was also a good deal more hurt by the change in her twin. Before Claire Tyson's call, Juliet had been sure Amelia's problem had something to do with a man. Now, after Claire's description of the Scotsman and her account of the amount of time Amelia had spent in his company, she knew he could not be the reason after all.

Amelia would have been astounded if she had known how much consternation she was causing. She thought she hid her sorrow and her disappointment very well, and that surely only Devett suspected anything. The butler had looked at her strangely once or twice, for she was always the first to come down and inspect the post every day.

Her early rising was to no avail, for Mr. Galt did not reply to her letter. She told herself there were probably a score of reasons why he had not; family problems, his work, why, perhaps he was still traveling and had not even received it! But late at night, lying sleepless in bed, she could not deceive herself that way. She knew he had read her letter, and this silence she was enduring was his way of telling her that he had meant what he had said at Blagdon, and he would never come near her again.

She was trying very hard to enjoy the Season in spite of the ache under her heart. James Galt did not want her, very well, then, it obviously behooved her to look about her world with new eyes. But when she tried to tell herself what a good husband Mr. Young would make, for he adored her so, or how exciting it would be to be the bride of the dashing Lord Williams or the Marquess of Hanover, that frowning, rugged face and those piercing eyes got in the way. In her despair, she knew that there would never, ever, be anyone else for her. And then she cried herself to sleep.

V

Anne did see the Earl of Burnham one afternoon when she was out shopping with her maid, but the meeting could not be called a success. She was alone, for Amelia had declined the expedition, saying she must work on her drawings before she lost whatever skill she had gained through misuse. When Anne saw the earl strolling toward her as she was about to step into her carriage outside the Burlington Arcade, she could only be glad that Melia was so devoted to her work. Quickly, she pushed her astonished maid into the carriage, and when the girl tried to protest, she told her to be quiet, and at once!

And then she turned and gave the earl her most entrancing smile. Of necessity, he was forced to stop and remove his tall beaver to bow to her. Anne noticed his little crooked smile was back, and the mocking light in his eyes as well.

"Lady Anne," he said, taking her hand and pressing it briefly. "But where are all your crowds of devoted admirers, my dear young lady? Never did I think to see *you* so alone."

He looked around then, and added, laughter in his voice, "Why, there does not even appear to be a maid with you. How singular!"

Anne felt herself growing warm under her pale green walking dress as he stooped to look into the carriage and spotted the cowering maid, clutching her mistress's parcels.

"I have not seen you much of late, m'lord," she said, deciding to ignore his provoking remarks, although she was sure now he had seen her push the maid into the carriage and knew very well why she had done so. "I thought you must have gone out of town."

"Why, it almost sounds as if you missed me, m'lady," he said. Before she could reply, he went on, "But I am well aware you have not. How could you miss one man when there are at least ninety-nine others about you? And such—er—eager young men as they are, too."

Anne stared at him, her dark blue eyes growing cold with her anger for the way she was being teased.

He chuckled then and flicked her chin with a careless finger. "I have just had the most intriguing thought," he said. "Can it be that your interest in me and my whereabouts is because I, unlike other men, refuse to dance to your piping?"

Anne drew in a startled breath. "Not at all, m'lord," she said. "I asked merely as a politeness. You are, after all, a friend of my father's."

Her voice was full of respect for her elders, and he put back his dark head and laughed. "*Touché*, ma'am," he said, not at all discomposed.

"And now you must excuse me," Anne continued, her head high. "I have several more errands to do this afternoon."

The earl bowed again as she moved toward the carriage. "Allow me to assist you, m'lady," he said as he cupped her elbow to help her up the step. And then he murmured softly, "No, much as it pains me to have to deny you the conquest, I shall not dance to your piping, Lady Anne, but someday I have great hopes that you will dance to mine."

Anne was sure now that she had been challenged, and she was very preoccupied during the drive back to Berkeley Square. The Earl of Burnham was cunning quarry, but she was not discouraged. Beside his mocking words, and the laughter in his eyes, she had seen something else there—admiration and attraction. She made up her mind she would not give up. Someday, she vowed to herself, Lord Burnham would dance, and to her piping, too.

After that afternoon, he seemed to become more attentive, and it was a rare occasion that he did not stroll up and exchange a few words with her. He never stayed beside her long, and he never asked her to dance. She wondered why, for she had seen him dance with many others. The earl was a confusing man, as incomprehensible as he was elusive.

One evening at a small dinner party they both attended, her hostess asked her to sing for the other guests. Anne agreed, and Amelia went with her to the piano in the drawing room to help her adjust the bench and the candles. "Are you nervous, Anne?" she whispered, her eyes full of concern. "I know this is really the first time you will sing in public."

Anne smiled as she arranged her skirts. "Not a bit of it, Melia. You know how I love to perform, and there is a special reason I want to sing tonight."

Her twin nodded in relief and went back to Juliet's side. She herself would have been shaking in her little satin slippers, but Anne was so brave, so sure of herself!

When the impromptu concert was over, the applause was generous and prolonged. Anne had carried it through with her usual aplomb. Her playing was faultless, and her clear soprano true and melodic. More than one lady had wiped her eyes at a sad ballad, and grouchy old Lord Pemberton was seen to tap his foot during a gay Italian aria.

Anne was disappointed that the earl did not join the others who came up to congratulate her, but remained in conversation with her stepmother. It was some time later before he made his way to her side.

"My congratulations, m'lady," he said in his careless

drawl. "You are indeed a talented musician. I have rarely heard such expertise even on the stage."

"Thank you, m'lord," Anne said, stifling the impulse to tell him it was good of him to finally bother to tell her so.

"My dear Lady Anne," a breathless voice interrupted, and they turned to see Lord Anders clasping his hands and exclaiming, "I had to tell you again what a beautiful voice you have, dear lady! Why, as you were singing, I was reminded forcibly of a heavenly choir, so—so angelic as you sounded!"

The earl bowed. "Yes, her voice is terribly misleading, is it not, m'lord?" His glance to Anne spoke volumes, and once again she felt her temper rising. Before she could speak, he had left them, and she was forced to listen to Lord Anders tell her that she must not heed such blasphemy, for she was truly an angel in every way.

Anne was not in very good temper for the next few days. Beside the unsatisfactory Earl of Burnham, she was still upset by her sister's refusal to confide in her.

The sittings for their portrait had commenced, and at least three mornings a week the twins went to Claire's studio to pose. They left their ball gowns there, and changed when they arrived, with the help of their maid. The marchioness did not hesitate to tell Anne to stop chattering after the pose had been decided and she set to work, and with nothing to do but stand behind Amelia's chair and stare into space, Anne grew bored. Besides, even as close as she was to her twin, she could pick up no clues from the thoughts that ranged in Amelia's mind as to what was bothering her.

One morning, she grew so upset that when the sitting was over and Amelia asked if they might remain a while so she could question Lady Tyson about one of her drawings, Anne flatly refused.

"I shall go on ahead and send the carriage back, Melia," she said as the maid buttoned up the back of her walking dress. "I want to see Juliet about something."

Amelia nodded, already going through her sketchbook to find the drawing in question, her twin forgotten.

Anne rode home in a hurt silence, staring with unseeing eyes at the streets they were passing through. When they reached the duke's townhouse, she ordered the carriage and the maid to return for Lady Amelia, and then she ran up the steps and sounded the knocker.

As Devett admitted her, he said, "There is a caller, Lady Amelia, a Mr. James Galt to see you. I did not like to have him wait, but he insisted. And her Grace is not home, dear, dear."

He looked very worried at this lapse of propriety, but Anne only smiled at him, slipping into Amelia's role with ease. Something told her that the man waiting to see her twin was the reason Melia had been so strange of late, and she could not let this opportunity to find out more about him, go by.

"I shall see Mr. Galt, Devett. I know him from Blagdon and it is quite all right," she said in Melia's soft, gentle voice.

Waving an airy hand, she went to the blue salon where she knew Devett always escorted any morning callers, and shut the door in his worried old face.

As she entered the room, a man stood up and stared at her. Anne recognized him immediately from his deep-set eyes. Of course, she thought triumphantly. The man in Melia's sketchbook!

For a moment, they simply stood and stared at each other, and then the man said in a husky voice, "Forgive me, Lady Amelia. You see, I could not stay away from you after all, in spite of my fine words and good intentions."

Suddenly, Anne had no idea what she was going to do or say, and as he came toward her, she held out her hand. She would have curtsied, but he gave her no opportunity for such social niceties. Instead, he took her into his arms and pulled her close. Anne's lips opened in surprise as he buried his face in her hair, and then he raised his head and drew back a little so he could look into her eyes. It seemed to be an eternity that they stood there. Faintly, Anne could hear Devett giving one of the footmen some instructions, and outside in the square, a carriage rumbling over the cobblestones, but she could not look away from those intense hazel eyes. She wondered why he looked so distraught, and why he was frowning.

"I have missed you every moment," he told her, sounding as if he hated himself for the confession he was making. "And when your letter came, I tried to forget it, for I knew it would be wrong for me to come to you, to love you. But, Amelia, I could not! No matter how ill-judged my love is, I cannot let you go."

Anne knew she should say something, admit she was not Amelia, but before she could do so, he bent his head and kissed her, and she forgot everything but his warm, insistent lips and caressing hands. Her own lips clung to his, and her arms went up around his neck in total surrender. She almost cried out when he stopped kissing her and put her away from him firmly.

"But you are not Amelia after all, are you?" he asked, his voice strained. "You must be Lady—Anne, is it not?"

Anne nodded, never taking her eyes from his face. How handsome he is even when he frowns, she thought. She longed to put her hands on his face so she might feel the rugged planes under her palms, and trace the contours of those firm set lips with her fingers, to memorize them. And then she wondered what on earth was happening to her, to feel this way about a stranger. A stranger, moreover, who was in love with her sister.

"Why didn't you tell me who you were at once, m'lady?" he asked, his voice cold now, and stern.

Anne made a valiant effort to pull herself together.

"Won't you be seated, Mr. Galt?" she asked, moving to the chair near the fireplace as she did so. He hesitated for a moment, and then he sat down across from her, never taking his eyes from her face. Anne looked down at her tightly clasped hands and took a deep breath.

"I must beg your pardon, Mr. Galt. Yes, I came in here pretending to be my twin. Melia and I often change roles, you see. I should not have done so, of course, but I have been very worried about Melia."

"She is ill?" he asked, leaning forward in his distress.

"No, she is not ill, but she has been so unhappy since she returned from Blagdon, and she would not tell me anything about it." Something compelled Anne to glance up. She caught her breath at the blaze of joy in his eyes, and it was a moment before she could continue. "My sister and I are very close. It is almost as if we were one person who somehow has been divided into two. We can even read each other's mind. At least, we could. But ever since she came home, Melia has put a wall between us. Try as I might, I could not break that wall down, and I was so hurt at the way she was excluding me, I could not even ask her what the matter was. So when Devett assumed I was Melia, and told me she had a caller, I decided to see you and talk to you myself. I had a feeling you might be the reason for Melia's unhappiness."

Mr. Galt settled back in his chair, running a big hand through his hair in angry confusion. "Aye, I can see you're fey, m'lady," he muttered, and Anne trembled a little at his soft Scottish burr. "Fey, and more than a little willful to boot," he went on. "What you have done was wrong, no matter how close you are to your sister. You need a good whipping!"

Anne felt tears clogging her throat at this harsh reprimand and then he rose abruptly. "You must excuse me, m'lady," he said. "I shall return another time to see Amelia."

"Oh, do not go!" Anne begged, getting up to run to

him and catch hold of his arm. At his bitter glance, she dropped her hands and blushed. "Melia will be here soon, and . . ."

"No, I will not trespass on your hospitality any longer," he said. As he turned to the door, Anne cried, "Say you forgive me, please! I—I am very sorry that I misled you, truly I am."

She waited breathlessly, but he only nodded before he strode to the door. Anne trailed after him, wringing her hands. She wished there was some way she could get him to remain, but she knew he would not heed any of her pleas. She was not his Amelia.

She stood where she was in the center of the salon until she heard Devett close the front door behind him, and then she went slowly up to her room. Now that he had gone, she hoped Melia would stay with the marchioness a very long time, for she had to think. As she trailed her fingers up the polished bannister, she realized wryly that now she too had a wall she must erect between them. She could not let Melia see into her heart anymore either.

It was three long days before Mr. Galt called again. Anne had been in an agony wondering if he had been so bitter at being tricked that he had returned to Scotland without seeing Melia at all. It was all she could do during those days not to confess everything to her sister, but she could not bear to add to her sorrow. Besides, she came to see that in doing so, she would only be gaining relief for herself, for Melia would be even more unhappy when she learned what she had done. And perhaps she would even begin to hate me, Anne thought. I would hate her if she did such a thing to me.

When Devett brought in Mr. Galt's card, the twins were sitting with Juliet in the blue salon, busy with their needlework. The duchess took the card from the silver salver and frowned a little at the strange name.

Anne held her breath and prayed, her forgotten needle still poised above her canvas.

"The Honorable James Galt, Devett?" Juliet asked. "I do not believe we know a James Galt. Please deny him."

Anne's eyes went to Melia's face. It had turned quite pale, but her eyes were shining. As she watched, her twin dropped her work to run to Juliet's chair.

"I know him, dear ma'am," she cried. "I met him at Blagdon. Oh, please let him come in, please!"

Juliet studied her white face and glowing eyes. "Ah, yes," she said at last. "*That* Mr. Galt. Very well, we will receive the gentleman, Devett."

The old butler nodded and made his slow way from the room. Amelia continued to stand very still, staring after him, until her stepmother said softly, "Do go and sit down, Melia. This breathless anticipation will not do at all. Kindly remember your manners."

Amelia started, and then she nodded and went to take her seat again, but Anne noticed her eyes never left the door.

Mr. Galt was dressed carefully, albeit in an old-fashioned style for his morning call, and his bow to the ladies was performed with grace. Anne saw him looking searchingly at both of them, but it only took him a minute to know which twin was the lady he had come to see. She tried not to feel sick when his glance left her so quickly and he began to study Melia's expectant face.

No one moved for a long moment, and then the duchess rose and came toward him, holding out her hand. "Mr. Galt? I am the Duchess of Severn. Amelia has been telling us of your acquaintance in Wiltshire. Won't you be seated and allow me to order you a glass of wine, sir?"

Thus recalled to the others in the room, James Galt raised her hand and kissed it. "Thank you, your Grace. You are very kind," he said.

Juliet smiled and indicated a chair and then she rang the bell to summon Devett.

"I trust I find you well, Lady Amelia?" their guest asked as he took his seat.

"I am very well, thank you," she whispered. Anne heard the additional word "now" even though it remained unspoken. She was sure James Galt heard it too, for his hazel eyes burned into dark blue ones until the duchess said, "I do not believe you are acquainted with Amelia's sister Anne, Mr. Galt."

With a visible effort the Scotsman looked briefly at Anne. "M'lady," he said.

Anne tried to smile. He acted as if he had never set eyes on her before, and didn't care if he ever did so again.

Juliet chatted of inconsequential things, knowing full well that in spite of Mr. Galt's polite, if terse replies, he was hardly attending to her at all. She asked some leading questions, included both Anne and Amelia in the conversation, and was delighted when Devett brought their guest a glass of the duke's excellent Canary.

"You will be in London for some time, sir?" she asked next as he sipped his wine.

"I don't know. My plans are not definite right now," he told her.

"Mr. Galt is a writer and a historian, Juliet," Amelia contributed. "No doubt he has some research he wishes to do while he is in town."

"Indeed?" the duchess asked with another charming smile. "I hope we will see you at some of the festivities as well, Mr. Galt. All work and no play, you know. London is very gay during the Season, and now you are here you must take the time to enjoy it."

Their guest opened his mouth, and then firmly closed it, and she wondered what he had been about to say before he thought better of it.

Fortunately for her grace's supply of small talk, James Galt only remained for the customary half hour.

As he rose to take his leave, Amelia rose as well, her hand going out to him as if she could not bear to be parted from him. Anne jumped up too, to distract the duchess.

"I shall hope to see you soon again, sir," Amelia said in a whisper as he bowed to her. He took her hand in his, and when Anne saw the way Melia grasped it, she swallowed hard.

But then her grace was there, and he was forced to release Amelia and bow to them all. Once again, there was silence in the salon until the outside door closed behind him.

"Sit down, Melia," Juliet said, her normally kind voice a little stern. "I think we must have a talk, and there is no time like the present."

Obediently, Amelia sank down in a chair, and as she looked from her stepmother to her sister, tears ran down her cheeks. "He came," she whispered. "He came!"

Anne ached to go and put her arms around her sister, but Juliet motioned her away. "Wipe your eyes, Melia," she said. "And then you will tell me, if you please, all about this man—who he is, where he is from, and most importantly, why he is able to reduce you to this state."

Amelia did as she was bade. Her words, released at last, ran over each other as she told of their meeting and their love. "He left me at Blagdon, and I thought I would never see him again," she told them. "He said a plain Scottish gentleman was no match for the daughter of an English duke. But in coming here, he admits he cannot accept that after all. I cannot tell you how happy I am! Oh, Juliet, Anne, I love him so much!"

Juliet wished with all her heart that Amelia had never gone to Blagdon, never met this most unsuitable man. She could see nothing but trouble ahead, and when she thought of how the duke was going to take the news, she shuddered. What, his beautiful, noble daughter to be marrying a nobody? A nobody, moreover, who was neither witty nor amusing, and whose serious, stern face did not even indicate a pleasant disposition. The duke would never hear of it, and his refusal to let Amelia accept Mr. Galt's suit would bring the girl nothing but pain. Knowing the disappointment in store for her stepdaughter made her voice softer when she spoke again.

"Hush, Melia! You must not be so unrestrained. And even if what you have told me is true, I find it very hard to believe. How can you be sure you love him, after so few meetings? You do not even know him, not really, for you know nothing of his home, his family, his fortune—"

"I know I love him," Amelia interrupted. Her little chin was stubborn and her eyes flashed. "The rest is not important."

"Melia, Melia," the duchess said, coming to take her in her arms. "It *is* important. You are only eighteen, and you have a long life ahead. You must be very sure when you give your promise, lest you spend that life in bitter regret. Perhaps what you feel for James Galt is only infatuation, something that will go away . . ."

Amelia kissed her stepmother. "It will not go away, dear Juliet, any more than the love you have for my father will ever go away."

And then she stopped and frowned. "Father will not be pleased, will he, ma'am?" she asked.

"No, he will not be," the duchess said. "He will feel that Mr. Galt is not suitable for his daughter, not at all worthy of her. He will think as I do, that what you feel for him is only a young girl's first fancy, and he will seriously doubt such a man can make you happy. The whole affair will upset him terribly."

Amelia's eyes were calm and steady. "I love my father very much, Juliet, and I hate to think that any action of mine would give him pain," she said. Then she added in a softer voice, "But I love James more."

Her voice was so determined, it sounded to the duchess just like Anne's. For the first time in several minutes, she remembered Amelia's twin. When she turned to her, she gave a little cry of distress. Anne stood holding the back of a chair with such a tight grip, her knuckles were white. Her eyes looked huge in her pale face, and Juliet could see they were glittering with unshed tears.

Remembering her premonition of trouble when one of the girls fell in love and discovered someone else was more important to her than her twin, she moved across the salon to put her arm around Anne.

"Are you well, Anne?" she asked, giving her a little squeeze. "You look so pale."

For a moment Anne closed her eyes, and then she took a deep breath. "I think I was just a little surprised, ma'am," she said, and Juliet was glad to hear the careful control she kept over her voice.

Amelia ran to them, her arms outstretched. "Dear Anne! I am so sorry I could not tell you about James, but thinking as I did that it was all over—that I would never see him again—I could not bear to burden you with my unhappiness. Do say you forgive me, twin!"

Anne loosened her fingers and tried to smile. "Of course I forgive you, Melia! But you would stare if you knew what I have been thinking was the matter. I imagined the most dire things, fit only to grace the pages of the more lurid novels. How happy I am to know that you are just in love."

She laughed a little then and moved away from them to go and stare out into the square. "Melia will not forget James Galt, Juliet," she said in the same quiet voice. "I know her, and I believe her heart has been truly given."

"Oh, Anne," Melia cried. "You do understand!"

Her twin turned to face her, her back ramrod straight, and the same little smile she had pinned on moments ago still firmly in place. "Of course, for are we not one person?" she asked, and then she said, "But I have been most remiss. I must wish you happy, must I not, Melia?"

Amelia dropped a mock curtsey. "Thank you, my dear, I shall be," she said, her face aglow with her joy once more.

The duchess returned to her chair and picked up her needlepoint. "May I remind you the gentleman has not asked you as yet? You are both very premature," she said.

"A mere formality, and you know it, ma'am," Anne told her, coming back to sit across from her. Her twin sat beside her on the sofa and picked up her hand. "You saw his face when he looked at Melia. If ever there was a man in love it is James Galt," she concluded.

Juliet folded her needlepoint, keeping her head bent. Anne was right, of course. Putting aside the fire that blazed in his eyes, by coming here from Scotland to see her stepdaughter, Mr. Galt had proclaimed both his love and his intentions. The actual proposal would be almost an anticlimax.

"Be that as it may, I must ask you to say nothing of this to anyone just yet," she told Amelia, raising her eyes to stare into the girl's face. "Let us see how you both feel after a few weeks. I, myself, will not mention anything about it to the duke until he has had a chance to meet the man and take his measure." She saw Amelia was looking a little troubled, and she added, "Surely you can do this little thing for me, and your beloved father, can't you?"

"Yes, I suppose so," Amelia replied. "But—but you will not forbid me to see James, will you, ma'am?"

Juliet wished it were within her power to do so, either that or whisk Amelia to the other side of the earth. "No, of course not," she said instead. "Naturally you must meet, at parties and other festive evenings, and of course, he may call. But there must be no announced engagement for some time yet."

She waited until Amelia nodded reluctantly, and then she excused herself. She wanted to be alone so she could think about the best way to handle this potentially dangerous situation. As she went up the stairs to her room, leaving the twins whispering together in the salon, she realized with a shock that it was not of Amelia and her unsuitable Scot that she was thinking first. No, it was Anne's pale face and tear-filled eyes, and the brave act she had put on these past few minutes.

The Lady Anne Fairhaven was more valiant than the duchess had ever realized before.

VI

Even with no one saying a word, it did not take the duke very long to discover that his younger daughter was in love. James Galt, now determined on his course, moved swiftly. By enlisting Lady Barton's aid, he managed to get himself asked to most of the parties Amelia had been invited to attend, and although she only danced with him twice every evening, as was proper, it was soon evident not only to the Fairhavens but to her crowds of admirers as well, that the Lady Amelia had a decided partiality for the stern Scotsman who seemed always to be somewhere near her.

Besides, she was wearing such a glowing air of happiness these days, it would be difficult even for someone with less than perfect vision to ignore it.

Juliet was finally forced to admit Amelia's secret. As was his custom, the duke was in her room late one afternoon so they might discuss the day's happenings. Suddenly he remarked, "Melia seems to be blooming these days, does she not? I hope Claire is managing to capture it on canvas."

The duchess only nodded, and he studied her. For once, his proud face did not soften as he looked at her. "Perhaps you had better tell me what is troubling you, my dear," he said. "Has it anything to do with Melia?" He waited, and then he added, "And that man I

84

always seem to see dancing attendance on her these days?"

As Juliet smoothed her gown, she drew a deep breath. "Yes, William, I think I had better tell you. You have been kept in the dark quite long enough, although I did have hopes that when Melia saw more of him, the whole affair would die down as quickly as it flared up. It has not; if anything, her feelings are more firmly engaged than ever. His name is James Stuart Galt, a Scotsman. She met him at Blagdon while she was visiting there and they fell in love with each other at first meeting, or very near it."

She looked a little nervously at her arrogant husband, but when she could read nothing but polite interest on his face, she went on, "Of course, in the eyes of the world, he is not a suitable match, being only the younger son of the late Laird of Inverlochy, but he seems an educated, intelligent man. He is a writer, a historian."

"Is he indeed?" the duke asked, as if he were not much interested in either Mr. Galt's ancestors, occupation, or intelligence. "I am sure I wish him every success in his endeavors, but they shall not include marrying my daughter."

His voice was implacable, and Juliet's heart sank. "Melia loves him, William," she reminded him.

"Love? What does she know of love?" he asked, crossing one booted leg over the other and folding his arms across his chest. His voice was scornful. "She has had her head turned by an older admirer, and is in the throes of her first puppy love. Come, come, Juliet! She is just eighteen and barely out. I have only to forbid her to marry him, and after a little while to sulk and brood, she will forget him."

He got up then to come and lean his hands on the arms of her chair. As he bent over her, he said, "Of course I am sorry to trouble you with her moods, my dear, but you'll see. This will soon pass."

His duchess stared up at him, and then she put one hand on his cheek. "I hope so William, for your sake. But I must warn you that I do not think it will be that easy. I believe Melia has formed a lasting attachment for James Galt, and you know she is nowhere near as mercurial as Anne. She is a steadfast girl."

He turned his head so he could kiss her palm. "You must not look on the dark side, Juliet. Melia will obey me when she learns I shall not countenance any alliance between her and this man. What, the Lady Amelia Fairhaven of Severn, with all her nobility, wealth, and beauty, to marry some Scottish nonentity? I will not hear of it."

He stood up then, brushing a piece of lint from his sleeve. "I must go and change now. I believe I told you I am promised to the Duke of Cumberland this evening, my dear? Perhaps you will be so good as to tell Melia I wish to see her tomorrow? I shall expect her in the library at ten."

He waved a kiss and left her. Juliet shook her head. She was very much afraid that the days when the duke could order his twins to obey him were gone. She felt a pang of regret for both William and Amelia. For her husband, because it would hurt him to find out that Melia cared for another man more than she did for him, and for Amelia, because even if she won her James, it would have to be at such great cost. It would not surprise her at all if her arrogant duke disinherited his daughter if she persisted, and refused to see her ever again.

At that moment, Amelia was walking in Hyde Park with Mr. Galt, and she had no idea of the storm that was brewing. Her maid trailed them at a respectful distance, keeping a sharp eye on her charge. In spite of the crowds assembled on this lovely spring day, the pair was managing a private conversation.

"This waiting is intolerable, Amelia," Mr. Galt was saying in a gruff undertone. "How much longer will it be before you allow me to speak to your father?"

Amelia pressed the arm she was holding, and she felt the muscles tighten under his dark green coat of superfine. "I know, James, I know. It is intolerable for me, too. I want to tell the whole world of our love, begin planning our wedding, and most of all, I want to be able to kiss you as often as I like."

His harsh face brightened. "I hope you will *like* to very often, love," he murmured. "And when we are engaged, surely you will be allowed to dispense with that dragon of a maid."

"But I do not think we would do very much walking in that case, sir," she teased him, smiling up at him. Stephen Young, driving by in his new perch phaeton, groaned with his disappointment, and did not even attempt to catch the young lady's eye.

"As little as possible," Mr. Galt agreed quickly and with great cordiality. "But when is that happy time to come? I want you, Amelia, and I have wasted far too much time in London."

His voice was full of distaste. Amelia knew how much he despised this city, and the *haut ton* and all their frivolous amusements. He was longing to be home again, hard at work on his book and with his own friends around him, and his hobbies and inventions. She felt a stab of triumph when she realized that even all that could not take him from her, not until he had won the right to have her beside him always.

"I don't know," she admitted. "I tried to speak to Juliet about it yesterday, but she said it was too soon. Perhaps I should go to my father myself . . ."

"Nay, you'll not do that, my girl," he commanded. "It is my place to speak to him, ask permission to address you . . ."

Amelia laughed, clinging to his arm. "To address me, James? Oh, my dear love, how silly you are when you know very well I want nothing more in the world than to marry you!"

She laughed again, and then she said, "And shall you go down on one knee, your hand to your heart,

when you propose, my dearest? I cannot wait to see
you in the position!"

He grinned down at her, all his love in his eyes. For
once, his stern face was bright with happiness. Amelia
felt her heart turn over. "You are a bold lassie," he
scolded her. "Of course I shall kneel. After all, I never
did propose to you, now did I?"

Amelia appeared to be thinking back. "No, now
that you mention it, you did not. Somehow, we forgot
that part."

Her eyes softened with her memories, and he said,
"You shall have the grandest, most eloquent proposal
ever made, my beautiful Amelia. My promise on it."

As he bent nearer, his eyes adoring her, Amelia felt
a little breathless and she looked around to see her twin
coming toward them in a smart landau. Anne was
out driving with three of her beaux. Amelia waved.

"There is Anne! Doesn't she look smart in that new
blue driving dress? Do you like it, James? I have one
just like it."

Thus adjured, Mr. Galt gave the occupants of the
carriage a brief glance. He bowed slightly as Lady
Anne waved to them, but his smile was gone. "You
will look lovely in it, Amelia," he said. "Blue becomes
you so well."

Amelia bit her lip, and then she asked, "Why don't
you like Anne, my dear? I have noticed that you never
smile at her, or even come near her if you can help it. I
know she is hurt by your attitude."

"The Lady Anne has too many other admirers to
worry that I am not one of them," he told her. When
he saw she was still looking a little troubled, he added,
"Perhaps I am jealous because she looks like you. I
want you to be unique, and I don't want to share you.
I want you to be mine alone."

Amelia looked up at him. I shall be, my dear, her
eyes promised.

That evening, the duchess and the twins joined the

Marquess of Hanover and his party for a festive evening at Ranelagh Gardens. To Juliet's relief, an invitation had not been sent to James Galt.

The marquess had reserved a prominent box in the lower tier, a thoughtful gesture he was to regret when he saw the attention the twins attracted. For some strange reason, several of their beaux had also decided to attend Ranelagh that evening, and to a man, they came and made their bows, clustering around the front of the box like so many avid bees around two pots of honey.

Anne was feeling unsettled, and a little reckless. She had seen how quickly James Galt's smile and loving expression had changed when he bowed to her in the park that afternoon, and she could not forget other occasions recently when he had been just as cold and distant. It was plain Mr. Galt had not forgiven her her deception, and she found this somehow bothered her a great deal.

Now, strolling back to the box with the others after the fireworks display, she saw Stephen Young standing by one of the dark side paths. Bent on mischief, she gave him a little smile. His expression brightened, and he came to her side at once.

"Please, Lady Amelia, I beg a moment of your time," he whispered, taking her hand in both of his.

The others had moved ahead a little, and Anne nodded demurely. To her surprise, Mr. Young did not follow them. Instead, he took her down the path he had just quitted, almost at a run.

This was so unexpected, Anne tried to break away from him. "Why, Mr. Young," she said in Melia's soft voice, "What are you thinking of? You must be mad!"

Stephen Young stopped and wiped his brow, and in the dim moonlight, Anne saw the glitter in his eyes with a little feeling of unease. "Mad? Aye, I'm mad all right," he muttered. "Mad with love for you, Amelia! But you never have any time for me anymore, not since that Scotsman came to town. Amelia, my love, you must know how I adore you! Give me some hope that someday you will be mine!"

The impassioned young man, who had had too much arrack punch, pulled her roughly into his arms and began trying to kiss her. Startled, Anne tried to pull away, tossing her head to avoid his eager mouth. He did not release his grasp.

"Let me go!" she cried, loudly, forgetting to play Melia's part.

"No, no, darling," Mr. Young said thickly. "One kiss, I beg!"

Suddenly, Anne heard hasty footsteps behind them. She felt a great sense of relief when she heard the Earl of Burnham's voice. "You forget yourself, sir," he said coldly. Mr. Young let Anne go in some confusion as the earl continued, "The Lady Amelia does not appear interested in dalliance. I suggest you beg her pardon."

He had not raised his voice, but Stephen Young fell back, paling at the cold authority in that implacable voice. "I . . . the fever of the moment . . . your pardon, m'lady, m'lord, I . . ."

Neither Anne nor the earl replied, and he turned even paler as he bowed and fled the scene.

Anne took a deep breath. "I cannot thank you enough, m'lord," she began, still imitating Amelia. The earl waved an impatient hand.

"Do not bother to playact with me, Lady Anne," he said sharply.

Anne stared at him. How could he possibly know she was not Melia? The earl began to smile at the incredulity written on her face, and then he bowed and held out his arm.

"Allow me to escort you back to your party, m'lady," he said.

Obediently, Anne took his arm. They had not walked more than a few steps before she asked in a wondering voice, "How did you know I was not Melia, m'lord?"

She glanced sideways to see him looking down at

her, and when she saw the amused expression he wore, it made her angry. "No one has ever been able to tell, why, only my family can guess, and then not at once!" she declared.

The earl chuckled. "Much as I would like to maintain an aura of omnipotence where you are concerned, Lady Anne, in this case I shall relent. Yes, you play your sister very well indeed, but I knew who you were immediately."

He began to walk again, and she had to skip a little to keep up. "I know how you love to perform, you see," he explained kindly. "Besides, it would be completely out of character for Lady Amelia to be so rash as to go down a dark, deserted path with a young hothead in his cups. She has too much sense."

Anne gasped. "And you are implying that I do not, sir?" she asked in her haughtiest voice.

The earl inclined his head. "As you say, my dear." As she gasped again, he added, "You are impetuous, rash, and somewhat short-sighted, although it is very like you to take chances."

They had reached the main path now, and he paused before joining the throngs promenading there under the bright lamps.

"Allow me to warn you, Lady Anne," he said. There was no amusement in his voice now, and Anne found herself unable to look away from his stern, handsome face. "Men do not always remember they are gentlemen, especially when they have had too much to drink, and the lady is as beautiful as you are. Remember that. Your arrogant refusal would have little effect on someone so impassioned."

As Anne stared at him, speechless, he reached out and took her chin in his hand. Under his half-closed lids, his gray eyes glittered with the same light she had seen in Stephen Young's, and she shivered. "Someday," he said softly, leaning closer, "you will discover what a man's passion is all about, and you will be glad you have had this warning. It would be such a shame if you were introduced to it before you were—er—ready."

He released her, and then he said courteously, "Shall we go on, m'lady?"

Anne nodded, but she did not speak until they reached the Marquess of Hanover's box. She was busy remembering that once, while boasting to Juliet about how easy it was to fool a beau, the duchess had interrupted her to say, "It will not always be so, my dear. Someday, you will meet a man who will not be misled, no matter how perfect your performance."

"What man?" Anne remembered she had asked.

Her stepmother had smiled at her. "The man who loves you will know you apart instantly," she had replied.

Anne had laughed at her and said she did not believe it could possibly be so, but now she was not at all sure. James Galt had known she was not Amelia the moment he kissed her, and now, here was the undeceived earl as well. It was all so confusing!

As she curtsied and thanked him in her most proper voice for his escort and assistance, Anne wondered if Hugh Moreley had fallen in love with her. If what the duchess had said was true, he must have. And yet, he had always been so casual, more apt to laugh at her than try and make love to her. She had felt he considered her an amusing child, whose antics were to be watched with indulgence. At least he had been that way until tonight. She knew she had not mistaken the light in his eyes, nor his very real concern for her welfare. And then she wondered why his capitulation, that she had been trying so hard to attain, did so little to raise her spirits.

She was abstracted for the remainder of the evening, and not at all sorry when they left the gardens at last.

The duchess told Amelia that the duke wished to see her in the morning just before they all retired. As

Amelia looked surprised, Anne kissed her stepmother good night. "I am off to bed, if you will excuse me, ma'am," she said. "For some reason, I am very tired tonight."

Juliet nodded, her attention all on Amelia. "Your father knows," she said. "He asked me about Mr. Galt this afternoon."

Amelia smiled. "I am glad. James is getting impatient, he is so anxious to speak to father. He did tell me I was not to do so, but now that will be impossible."

She saw the doubt on her stepmother's face, and she kissed her. "Do not worry, dear ma'am! I am sure I will be able to convince father of my love for James, and his for me. You'll see."

When Amelia came into the duke's library the following morning as the clock was striking ten, she wore a mischievous smile. The duke looked up from the papers he was perusing, his soaring brows asking a question.

"How this does bring back old memories, sir," she said, coming around the desk to kiss him. "Don't you remember how often you used to summon Anne and me when we had been naughty children, and make us stand in front of your desk while you delivered a scathing lecture? How I used to quake in my sandals, waiting for the beating that never came! We were wrong to call you The Dreadful Duke. Now that I come to think of it, *we* were dreadful, weren't we?"

She took a seat nearby and folded her hands in her lap. "You were indeed," the duke agreed in a colorless voice, and her smile broadened. "I often despaired of ever turning you into young ladies of quality, such madcaps as you were. I realize I have the duchess to thank for your present good manners and impeccable behavior."

As Amelia nodded in agreement, he added, "I

expect those manners to continue, and your obedience to me as well."

As Amelia stared into his dark, haughty face, she saw that the interview was going to be even more difficult than she had expected. She had known her father would not be best pleased with her choice of husband, and she was sorry for it, but she was sure that only a little resolution on her part would make him see that without James Galt, her life would be nothing but empty loneliness. She was secure in the duke's love; she could not imagine a situation where he would deliberately allow her to be unhappy, when by just giving his permission, he could ensure it forever.

She took a deep breath before she said in a calm voice, "I hope that is possible too, sir."

The duke straightened his papers and put them away before he said, "Juliet tells me you think you have fallen victim of Cupid's dart, my dear. And that you imagine yourself in love with a most unsuitable man. Before we go any further, let me tell you at once that I shall never countenance any marriage between you and Mr.—er—Galt, is it not?"

Amelia did not even try to hide her surprise. "But you do not even know him, sir, why, how can you—"

"I have no intention of knowing him," her father interrupted. "I know quite enough about him to make any desire for a further acquaintance distasteful to me. I know he is a Scots, a younger son with no title or wealth to commend him. Why he ever had the audacity to think his suit would be welcome in this house, is a mystery to me. I can only assume he is a fortune hunter, for you are a very wealthy young lady. There are men like that, Amelia, as you would know if you were not so young and innocent. In your case, however, you are fortunate to have a father to protect you from the brigands of the world."

Amelia leaned forward in her chair. "He is not like that!" she exclaimed, and her father frowned at her impassioned words. "You do not understand! He tried to stay away from me, because he knew it would be such an unequal marriage, but he could not. He . . . he loves me too much."

"I am sure he does," her father agreed, his voice so cordial she looked at him with suspicion. "It would be a strange man who would not. You are so sweet, so lovely. But even if you were ugly, with a screeching voice and the worst temper in the world, he would still try and gain you for his wife. Gold is a powerful goad, my dear."

He saw she was looking mutinous, and he continued, "I shall not see Mr. Galt, and neither shall you from now on. Trust me, Melia. You will see I am right, before long. I am sorry you must suffer a little now, but in only a few weeks you will have forgotten this unsuitable Scotsman."

He paused, a little surprised she had not interrupted him. Her face, above the primrose morning gown with its gay knots of ribbons, was very pale, and in spite of the unshed tears in her eyes, she stared her defiance. The duke stiffened. And then she said, very deliberately, "I shall never forget him, for I love him more than I ever thought it possible to love. You are condemning me to misery for the rest of my life, and I never thought you could be so cruel. I was sure you would understand, and because you loved me too, you would put aside your pride."

"Yes, I am a proud man, and you should be proud too, daughter," her father told her. "You are the Lady Amelia Fairhaven—"

"Of Severn," she finished, and then she nodded. "But when I marry, I will cease to be that young lady. I will be a wife and take my husband's name."

The duke nodded in turn. "But you will always be my daughter," he reminded her. "Come, my dear. Enough. Know that I forbid you to see Mr. Galt again. You may, however, write to him and apprise him of the situation. I am sure he will understand it immediately, and he will be leaving the capitol within

the week. The James Galts of this world can find easier
prey with unprotected girls. He will not waste any
more time here, not when he understands how
adamant I am. You may wager on it."

Amelia stood up, her face sad but not at all resigned.
"You know nothing of James at all, father. He will not
go away, he will never leave me."

"It would be wiser for him if he did," the duke said,
his voice cold. "I am not without power in this world,
my dear, and I can make it very uncomfortable for
him if I choose to do so."

They stared at each other for a long moment before
the duke said, "You are excused, Melia. Go to your
room and think about what I have told you. Know I
shall never change my mind, so you had best accept
this ultimatum with a good grace."

Amelia curtsied, but she did not speak again, and in
a moment she had closed the library door softly behind
her. The duke frowned at the wooden panels of that
door, and then he shrugged. He was surprised at the
resistance he had met, for surely the behavior he had
just been treated to was more typical of Anne than his
gentle, kind Amelia! He decided to speak to Juliet as
soon as he could. She would know best how to handle
the girl's defiance and implacability. And if this Mr.
Galt did not leave London, if he continued his pursuit,
William Fairhaven had several ways he could use to
discourage him. He realized he would even submit to
buying the man off if there were no other way.

Amelia went up to her room as ordered. Strangely,
she did not feel discouraged, even now. She would
write to James when she was a little calmer, and over
her initial disappointment, and she would tell him
what the duke had said. And then she would wait, for
however long it took. She was sure he would find a
way for them, sure he would never rest until he
married her, for she knew he was none of the things
her father had called him. As she went to the window
to stare out into the busy square, she realized that he

was a better man than her father, much as it pained
her to admit it. He was proud too, and stiff-necked
about his country, but he was not arrogant. And in
spite of his terseness and his stern face, he was not a
cold man. She wished she had thought to tell her
father of James's initial reluctance to align himself
with an Englishwoman. How the duke would have
stared to learn that there were those in the world who
did not consider the Fairhavens suitable *partis*!

Amelia saw a carriage draw up to the front door,
and her twin and stepmother being helped down by
the grooms, and she dropped the curtain. She hoped
they would not come near her for a while, until she
was more herself. She did not think she could bear to
discuss the morning's meeting with either of them.

The letter was duly written and delivered to Mr.
Galt's rooms, and within the hour, she had his reply.
His letter was short, but in it he repeated his love and
his pledge, and told her she must not despair. Somehow, he would find a way for he could not bear to
contemplate a future without her. For the first time
since that morning, Amelia smiled, and she was able to
go down to dinner with her head held high.

The Fairhavens were dining *en famille* that
evening, and the duke was pleasantly surprised when
he discovered that Melia did not intend to engage in
pouts or stiff silences, nor were her eyes red as if she
had been in bouts of tears since his ultimatum. She
bore her part in the conversation with ease, although
he noticed she did little more than toy with her food,
and the glowing happiness he had come to associate
with her was completely gone from her serene face. He
tried to still the little inquietude he felt by reminding
himself of her disappointment. Surely, all this would
pass in a short time, and his dear Melia would be back
to tease and laugh with him. He had spoken to Juliet
shortly after her return from her shopping trip with
Anne, and although she had been upset, and more
than a little apprehensive, she had not tried to get him

to change his mind. She had not mentioned to him yet that when she went up to Amelia's room, the girl had refused to discuss it with her, and that Anne had had no better luck. The duke might take heart at his daughter's calm behavior and seeming acceptance, but his duchess was not so sanguine.

Amelia did not change in the days that followed. She was polite and agreeable except for one thing. She refused to attend any more parties, or see any of the young men who were so often on the doorstep, bouquets clutched in eager hands. Nor did she reply to any of the notes or invitations she received. The only time she went out at all was for an early ride in the park with her twin, and to Claire Tyson's studio, for she had to continue to pose for her portrait.

When Juliet told the duke of this behavior, he only shrugged. "Let her stay home then, my dear," he said in an easy voice. "She will soon grow tired of her self-imposed cloister, you'll see."

The duke had had a letter from Mr. Galt, a letter that he did not show to anyone, not even his duchess. He had been impressed in spite of himself with the man's intelligent reasoning and calm determination. He did not sound like a fortune hunter, or a rogue. In the letter he had assured the duke of his undying love for Amelia, and hers for him, and although he freely admitted he was an unlikely husband for the Duke of Severn's daughter, he wrote that they were both adamant that the wedding would take place. He then asked for an interview so he might lay his credentials and fortune open for the duke's perusal. The duke wrote a cold denial in the third person.

The next day, Mr. Galt wrote to the duchess. She was in tears after she finished it, for Mr. Galt, after telling her of his love for her stepdaughter, had begged for her intervention with the duke, his fervent words eloquent. She could not go against her husband's wishes, but her letter of refusal was couched in kinder words.

More than two weeks went by, and still things continued at an impasse. Amelia had finally spoken to her twin, but when Anne would have put her arms around her in commiseration, she only shook her head. Without her saying a word, Anne understand that Melia was not discouraged, and did not want any sympathy.

Anne herself had become more quiet, and more distant. Both the duke and duchess noticed it, even in all their concern for Amelia, but they put it down to Anne's empathy for her twin.

In reality, it was because Anne had come to see she was more than just attracted to her sister's beau, and she was troubled. Even knowing now that the Earl of Burnham was not indifferent, could not lessen James Galt's magnetic appeal. She was grateful the earl had returned to his former cool, amused manner when in her company, for she did not want him playing the lover anymore. She told herself she was being ridiculous, loving the man her sister intended to marry, that it was only pique and envy that made her think she cared for him. But most nights, even after the latest balls, she had trouble sleeping. She would lie there in bed remembering the feel of his mouth on hers, his strong encompassing arms and warm, eager hands, and the passionate words he had spoken to her when he thought she was Amelia. She made herself become even gayer at every party she attended, flirting and laughing with her admirers. She was not aware that the earl, more astute than the others, saw the lost look in her eyes when she thought no one was watching her, and wondered at it.

But if Anne forced herself to become more animated and flirtatious, Amelia's quiet, polite demeanor did not change. Even Claire Tyson, as unperceptive as she was, noticed it. One morning when they had come to sit for their portrait, she dismissed the twins early, telling them to go home and rest. "It is obvious, Melia, that you have been indulging in too many late nights and festive parties, you are so pale and quiet," she said as she began to clean her brushes.

The marchioness was surprised when Melia agreed without a word of explanation, but a few minutes later, a breathless Lady Anne ran back into the studio to tell her of the situation. Lady Tyson thought for a long time, and then she wrote a note to the duke requesting an interview.

William Fairhaven came that very afternoon, and the marchioness wasted no time coming to the point. "I was very sorry to hear from Anne of Melia's predicament, William," she said as soon as the butler had served the duke a glass of wine and left the room. "I have noticed how pale and distracted she is, why, there is only a ghost left of the beautiful, vibrant girl I was painting a short time ago. Even though the portrait is almost completed, it is suffering as a result."

The duke nodded, and as he set his wine down on a table near his chair, she noticed his stiff haughty expression, and she sighed to herself as he said, "It is true Melia is feeling a little pulled, but she will soon recover from this unsuitable infatuation."

His hostess got up to stride the drawing room, her face frowning in thought. "Will she, William?" she asked at last. "Did I get over my infatuation for Andrew, even after what happened to separate us? And I had you, so attentive and persuasive, trying to get me to do so. But I never faltered, and I do not think Amelia will either."

The duke's arrested look made her bold to continue, "I think you have gone mad! When I remember how you helped Andrew and me, I cannot believe you are being so cruel now, and to your own dear daughter, too. How can you say you love her when you continue to treat her this way?"

She ignored the duke's angry glare. "Do you remember Andrew's mother, William? The Dowager Marchioness? Do you remember how she tried to get Andrew to give me up, how she refused to even acknowledge she had a son any more after he refused to do her bidding? She was a cold, proud woman who made everyone around her unhappy, and you, sir, are growing more like her every day."

The duke stood up and came toward her swiftly, to take hold of her arms and shake her. "That will be quite enough, madam," he said through gritted teeth. "Our friendship does not give you the right to speak to me that way. Take care!"

Claire Tyson tossed her dark head. "If I do not, who will, sir?" she asked him in a calm voice. The duke released her, and she rubbed her arms where his tight grasp had reddened the fair skin. "Juliet loves you so, she will never go against your expressed wishes, no matter how wrong she thinks them. I love you too, but I am not besotted with you now any more than I was as a girl."

The duke stepped closer and tilted her chin. Her serious gray eyes regarded him steadily. "So, you love me, do you, my dear Claire?" he asked, his voice softer now.

The marchioness ignored its regretful overtones. "Of course I do, I always shall. But as your loving *friend*, I cannot stand by and let you do this to Melia, and to yourself. You must see Mr. Galt and you must hear him out. Please, William, at least you can unbend that far!"

The duke would promise only to consider it, and she shook her head as she walked with him to the door. "You once told me I was an impossible woman. If I remember correctly, you said I was willful, stubborn, overly sure of my own omnipotence, and short-sighted as well." She paused, her hand on the drawing room door, and then she curtsied. "Allow me to return the compliment, sir!" she said.

When the duke called her an unprincipled baggage, she only nodded in complete agreement, and he was forced to smile a little as he bowed and took his leave.

Although the duke was still adamant that Amelia

should never marry this Scot nobody, even after Lady Tyson's pleading, he made it a point to discuss it with the duchess again. He told himself he only wished to see if she felt the same way Claire did, and it was not very long before he discovered she did.

"I know you are not pleased, my dear, but you cannot ignore the facts," Juliet told him. "It has been almost a month since you refused to see the man, and she has not faltered in her resolve. Neither has he. I saw him this afternoon near Westminster Abbey. He has not gone home, nor do I think he will do so until he has Melia beside him."

"You cannot possibly be suggesting that *my* daughter would contemplate a flight to Gretna Green, can you? Even though it *is* on the way?" the duke asked, at his most haughty and sarcastic.

To his surprise, Juliet did not deny it at once. Instead, she looked down at her clasped hands, a little frown between her fair brows. "A month ago I would have said it was impossible," she replied at last. "Now I am not so sure. It would cause her a great deal of pain to do such an *outré* thing that would surely hurt her family, but her love for him is so strong, it must be considered."

The duke's face grew cold. "Perhaps I will send her home to Severn," he said. "I could have her guarded more carefully there, and if this Galt so much as stepped on my land, I could have him thrown in jail."

Juliet got up to come and kneel at his feet, taking both his hands in hers. "You would not be so cruel! To take her away from London when she knows Mr. Galt is here, waiting—no, no!"

"But he waits in vain, Juliet. I told you that before, and I have not changed my mind. I shall never permit Melia to marry him."

The duchess stood up and turned around. Over her shoulder, she said, "Then whatever desperate thing she decides to do must be on your head, William. I very much fear that Melia's obedience, even her great love and respect for you, has been stretched as far as it can go. Women are capable of desperate acts, when they are driven to them. Remember I told you so."

The duke was so displeased with her assessment of the situation that it was all he could do to take her in his arms and reassure her before he went away to change for dinner.

Will was with them that evening, and it was to his eldest son that the duke announced his plans. "I hope you can tear yourself away from your friends and all the delights of London, my boy," he remarked during the fish course. "I want you to escort your sister Amelia back to Severn in a few days."

Will, who had been away visiting friends for the past month, knew nothing of his sister's predicament, and he nodded. Although the duke was not looking her way, he heard Melia's sharp intake of breath.

"I am to go back to Severn, sir?" she asked at last in a quiet little voice.

The duke nodded, as his dark eyes inspected her face. "I think it wise, my dear," he said. "It is obvious you are not enjoying the Season, so perhaps a change of scenery might be of benefit. I shall write to Miss Banks and ask her to accompany you, since naturally Juliet remains with me."

Amelia's eyes were steady on his face, but Anne paled at the name of their former governess. Looking at her father, she could see he meant her to guard Melia so she could not escape Severn until such time as he relented and released her. She sent a silent message of sympathy to her twin, but Melia was not able to return even a tiny smile.

The duke put his plans in motion the very next day, and when Anne overheard him telling the butler that the traveling coach would be required by week's end, she did not hesitate. Melia might not be permitted to see or write to James Galt, but she herself had been put under no such restriction. As she sat down to pen him an urgent note, asking him to meet her in the park early the following morning, she told herself that even if he did dislike her, he would come if only to get news of his Amelia.

James Galt was prompt to their appointment. Anne had slipped out of the house without anyone seeing her, and she had not brought her maid. When he remarked on it, his face as cold as her father's could be, she waved an impatient hand.

"I did not care to have anyone know I was seeing you, Mr. Galt," she explained. "It would cause all kinds of trouble! But I had to come to tell you that my father is sending Melia back to Devon."

"When?" he asked, his eyes keen.

"In a few days," Anne told him. "He has asked our old governess to go with her, to guard her. I think that he fears you and Melia might attempt an elopement."

"He need have no such apprehension," Mr. Galt told her. "I would never ask it of Amelia, never. She deserves better than some hole-in-the-corner ceremony. It would be good of you to tell your father that I am not the kind of man he thinks."

"And how do you suppose I am to do that?" Anne asked, with a trace of her old pertness. "Since you have avoided me at every party we both attended, I can hardly pretend we are suddenly the best of friends!"

Mr. Galt did not smile. "When I received your note asking for this meeting, I wrote Amelia a letter," he said. " I have not done so before, for I knew she was not permitted to correspond with me, but given this opportunity, I could not help it. Our separation has been so long—so lonely! Will you take it to her, Lady Anne?"

Anne agreed, and he handed her a bulky packet. "Thank you for coming and telling me the news, ma'am," he said formally as she put the letter safely away in her reticule. "Tell Amelia she must not worry, that she must remain firm. Tell her I said that someday, somehow, we will be together."

"I shall," Anne whispered, awed by his determined

look. She watched his retreating back as he strode away from her, and then she put both hands to her mouth and choked back a sob. She could not deny her love for him any longer. It had taken every bit of self-control she possessed not to show it to him. But for his sake, and Amelia's, she must be strong so no one would ever suspect her feelings. Any confession of hers would do nothing but estrange her from her twin, perhaps forever, and she knew she could never bear that. Besides, James was in love with Amelia. He would never love her.

As she wiped her eyes and began to walk back to Berkeley Square, she became aware of a horseman cantering up behind her. She was reminded suddenly how improper it was for her to be here in the park alone, even at this unfashionable hour, and she tilted her chin. The gentleman would discover that she was not interested in dalliance, and in short order, she promised herself.

But when the horse was reined in, she found herself looking up into the furious eyes of her father. She knew he had seen James Galt leave her side when he held out his hand and said in a tighty, angry voice, "You will give me the letter Galt entrusted to you that you were about to take to Melia, Anne, and you will do so at once!"

VII

Those were the last words he spoke to her until they arrived home. He held his horse to a walk as he escorted her from the park, and when Anne saw he had no intention of leaving her to make her own way back, or conversing with her, she bit her lip. She had not heard that tone in her father's voice for many years, and she found she was sorry that her actions this morning, even if they were in a good cause, had forced him to employ it once again.

As she walked along in silence, she pondered the problem. Her father was so proud, so ducal, she knew he would never relent and agree to Melia's marriage, and in spite of what James Galt had told her, she herself did not see any way out of the impasse for the lovers but elopement. If only Melia were braver, she thought. Now I would not hesitate for a minute, if my happiness were at stake. James Galt could carry me off tonight! She forced her mind from the entrancing picture of a desperate flight through the darkness with him, and tried to concentrate on what was going to happen to her now. Surely the duke would punish her for her interference, if only by confining her to the townhouse, and treating her coldly for some time to come. He might even send her back to Severn with Melia. She was not looking forward to it at all.

When the groom had taken his horse, the duke escorted her up the steps. With his firm hand under her elbow, Anne felt very much a prisoner. Before he knocked, he said, "You will go to your room without attempting to communicate with Melia, and you will remain there until I send for you. Is that quite clear, Anne?"

"Yes, sir," she said, keeping her head as high as his. The duke itched to slap her for her willful meddling and unrepentance, and he went quickly to his library before he succumbed to the temptation.

He ordered coffee, and then he sat down at his desk and took the bulky packet Anne had given him from the pocket of his riding coat. He turned it over and over in his hands for several moments, somehow reluctant to open it and read it.

He had never insisted on inspecting the twins' post, as some parents did, for he felt such behavior a betrayal of the trust he had in them. Now, he knew he had no choice. Slowly, he broke the seal and spread the sheets out.

When Devett brought in the coffee tray, he was still reading, and his face was so black and harsh, his butler only put the tray down beside him, and bowed and went away.

The duke's eyes were bleak as he read the last words, and put the page down to join the others. He was surprised, no, astounded, at what he had read. He had expected promises of undying love, rosy pictures of the glorious life they would share, even detailed plans for an elopement. What he had not expected were calm, reassuring words, remembrances of all the times they had met, and the man's promise that no matter how long it took, he would wait for his Amelia forever. He made it very clear that until they had won the duke's consent, their marriage could not take place, and he pledged himself to be patient for as many years as it took to gain it.

The final sentences seemed to echo in the duke's mind, and he picked up the page and read them again. "You are too fine, too dear to me, to have it any other way, my Amelia. I would not separate you from those you love best, for even though we will love each other till death, I know it would only cause you pain. No, my dear, we will be steadfast, and we will not despair. I love you always. James."

As the duke drank his coffee, he thought long and hard. His face was still harsh with his displeasure when he rose at last to go and throw Melia's letter on the fire. Something stayed his hand, and, smoothing out the sheets, he unlocked the bottom drawer of his desk and put Galt's letter in his strongbox. He had had the strangest feeling that even he, her father, did not have the right to burn that letter, and that even if he had no intention of giving it to her, it must not be destroyed.

William Fairhaven was seen no more that day. He sent a note to the duchess, explaining the situation and asking her to release Anne from her room. And then he excused himself from dinner, saying he would speak to her the next morning. He also wrote another note, terser this time, and he gave it to one of the footmen to deliver before he went up to change his clothes to go to his club.

When Juliet came down the stairs late the following morning, she was stunned to see Mr. Galt in the hall, handing his hat and gloves to Devett. For a moment, she stood quite still, one hand going to her throat.

Mr. Galt bowed to her, but he did not speak for Devett was holding the door to the library open. Inside, she could see the duke, seated at his desk. When the door closed behind the Scotsman William had said he would never receive, she made her way to the morning room, completely in the dark as to the reason for his unexpected visit.

In the library, William Fairhaven was eyeing Mr. Galt with barely concealed dislike. As he studied the fellow close up for the first time, he wondered what there was about him that made Melia love him. Leaving his birth and fortune out of it, he was hardly a handsome man, for he looked stern and unyielding. The harsh planes of his face were severe, and his mouth was set firm. Altogether, he was not a pretty beau, nor from his appearance even a congenial, pleasant person. And this was the man Melia said she loved?

He shook off his abstraction as Mr. Galt bowed and said, "Thank you for seeing me, your Grace."

The duke nodded and indicated a chair. The Scotsman sat down, putting a leather case he had with him on the floor beside him.

"I have reversed my decision never to see you because I intercepted a letter you wrote to Melia yesterday, Galt," the duke began. He noticed how the man leaned forward a little, his deep-set eyes somehow accusatory, and he found himself saying, "As Melia's father, I had every right to read your letter, especially since I had forbidden her to have any correspondence with you. But perhaps you do not agree?"

At the sarcasm in his voice, James Galt shook his head. "No, it was your *right*, but whether it *was* right I must leave up to you and your conscience, sir."

The duke started to get up, and then he made an effort to control himself. "Be that as it may, I must tell you I was surprised by it. It was not at all the impassioned pleading for an early elopement that I expected from a fortune hunter."

The Scotsman's eyes flashed dangerously, and the duke raised his black brows. "You dislike the appellation? But that is why I have called you here. I want to make it very clear to you that if Melia persists in this mad love she claims to have for you, she will come to you penniless. Since I cannot approve the match, I intend to disinherit her. I imagine that news gives you pause, does it not, Mr. Galt?"

He leaned back in his chair and stared at the man sitting across from him. He was surprised to see him smile, albeit a little grimly.

"It does not give me pause at all, your Grace, it makes everything so much easier," Galt said. "I do not want Amelia's money, or her title, or her noble relatives. I never did. I want her, and she can come to me in her shift if you insist on it."

The duke tried to hide his astonishment. "Indeed?" he murmured. "Very fine talking, Galt, but I have been about the world a bit and I do not believe you."

The Scotsman reached down and picked up the case he had brought with him. Opening it, he withdrew some papers. "Here is a current accounting of my worth, your Grace," he said as he laid the papers on the desk. "As you will see, although I am not as wealthy a man as you are, I am well able to support a wife and family. Amelia would never be in want. I have a fine home in Edinburgh, carriages, and servants."

As the duke picked up the sheets, he added, "Perhaps you will understand me better if I tell you that the last thing in the world I ever intended was to marry an Englishwoman."

His voice as he spoke the last word was so bitter, the duke looked up at him again, his interest piqued. "No," James Galt was saying. "I am a Scots, a son of the Laird of Inverlochy, and until I met your daughter, I hated all Englishmen, not only for conquering my country, but for the way they have ravaged and exploited it ever since for profit. But even though I left Amelia and tried to forget her, I could not."

The duke tapped the papers on his desk and asked, almost gently, "But if you marry her and carry her to Scotland, won't you be condemning her to a life of unhappiness, sir? I am sure most of your countrymen feel as you do. How could they receive an English lady with anything but hatred and disdain?"

"They will receive her as Lady Amelia *Galt*, your Grace," his opponent said firmly. "As my wife, she will be accepted without question."

The duke nodded, and bent his head to study the

papers again. Until he finished, there was silence in the library.

"My apologies, Galt," he murmured at last as he gathered the papers together and handed them back. "I see you are not the penniless rogue I thought you."

As the Scotsman restored them to his case, he added, "I will be honest with you, as honest as you have been with me. I do not like this match. To my mind, Melia deserves someone better, someone with a title and wealth and position."

"I agree with you, your Grace," James Galt said. "But there is no man on earth worthy of Amelia. Since she has chosen me, let me assure you I love her very much, certainly as much as any noble English lord could."

The duke rang for his butler, and then he rose. James Galt was quick to follow suit. "I will send you my decision in a few days, sir," the duke said coldly.

He saw the disappointment in those keen hazel eyes, but the Scotsman only bowed his acceptance, and turned to take his leave. As Devett held the door of the library wide, the duke saw Melia coming down the stairs. Much like the duchess before her, she started, her hand going to her heart, and then she ran down the remaining flight directly to her love.

"James?" she asked, putting her arms around him as if she could not believe it was really he. "I am so glad to see you, my dear!"

The duke could see her face clearly, and the happiness and hope written there made him tighten his mouth. All he could see of Galt was his taut back and the stiff way he held his head.

"Aye, lass, I am glad to see you, too," he said, and then he reached up and took her hands from around his neck and put her away from him. "But your father has not given me permission to approach you as yet. We must be patient."

His words, although spoken in a constrained, quiet voice, were authoritative, and Amelia stepped back at

once, although her eyes never stopped searching his
face. "Of course, James. I understand," she said, and
then she smiled and curtsied deeply to him.

Galt hesitated only a moment, and then he bowed
in return and went quickly to the front door. Amelia
stood very still until that door closed behind him.

The duke watched her turn then, and run to the
library, her arms stretched wide. She wore a glowing,
delighted smile. William Fairhaven realized it was a
very long time since he had seen his Melia smile like
that, as she came and put her arms around him and
snuggled close to his chest.

"You did see him, you relented," she said, and then
she put her head back so she could search his face. "I
knew you would, father, I knew it! You could not let
me be so unhappy, for I know how much you love
me!"

The duke put his hands on either side of her face,
and as he stared down into her eyes, now filled with
tears of joy, he reached his decision.

It seemed to the Duke of Severn that things moved
very quickly in the days thereafter. Mr. Galt was summoned once again to Berkeley Square, and after only a
few minutes conversation, the duke sent for Lady
Amelia and left them alone together.

He was shaking his head a little and looking grim as
he joined his duchess in the drawing room, but she
would have none of it. She rose and came to kiss him,
and then she said, "You have done the right thing—the
only thing—my dear. I know Melia will never regret
her marriage. She will be happy with her James, no
matter how you still deplore the match. By relenting
at last, you have ensured her happiness."

A few days later, after the announcement appeared
in the journals, there was general mourning among the
young male population of the *ton*. They only managed
to console themselves finally by remembering the still
uncaptured Lady Anne.

William Fairhaven planned a gala ball to celebrate the betrothal, at which he intended to exhibit the portrait of his daughters that Claire Tyson had painted. The ball, and his calm acceptance of Amelia's future husband, would put paid to any unseemly gossip that might be developing about the Scotsman's unsuitability.

The townhouse in Berkeley Square fairly hummed with all the plans and preparations. Melia said she wished to be married in the gardens of Severn, and messages were sent to the staff there to get ready for the hundred guests who were expected. Some would only spend the night, but many of them would be there for a week or more. Both Amelia and James wanted a simple wedding, but this was not allowed. The duke, having capitulated at last, was determined to marry his daughter with all the pomp and circumstance he could bring to such a disappointing alliance. He agreed to the garden wedding, with only Anne as attendant, but in other matters, he was adamant. There would be a plethora of guests, the finest food and wine, and musicians, and he told the duchess to make sure Melia's gown was the most beautiful one ever made.

Juliet agreed, and when she went to discuss fabric and veiling with her stepdaughter, found she had some ideas of her own. Amelia brought out her sketchbook, and showed the duchess a design she had made that she wished embroidered on her wedding gown.

Juliet studied the drawing carefully. "How lovely it is, Melia, so delicate and yet so rich," she said. "Where did you get the idea?"

Amelia's eyes grew soft as she traced the entwined rose and thistle she had drawn. The duchess smiled when she was told its origin.

Carrying the drawing, the three Fairhaven ladies went to the modiste who had made the twins' ball gowns. Amelia explained exactly what she wanted. The gown would be made of yards and yards of the

finest white silk. It would have huge puffed sleeves
and a simply cut, tight-fitting bodice, embroidered all
over with her rose and thistle design in seed pearls and
silver thread. The design would be repeated on the
hem and sweeping train. Since the gown would be so
stunning, it was decided that the veil would be
nothing more than clouds of tulle, attached to the
Fairhaven diamond tiara, to be loaned by Juliet for
the occasion.

Anne's gown was to be a simpler version of the
bride's, in a blue silk that matched her eyes.

There was so much excitement, so many parties,
and so much gay chatter, that Juliet was sure she was
the only one to see that Anne was not happy. True, she
put on a brave front in public, but every once in a
while, there was a lost look in her eyes, as if she were
feeling already the separation from her twin that was
inevitable. The duchess promised herself that when
the wedding was over, she would be very attentive to
Anne, until the girl grew more cheerful. She did not
think that would take very long, for upon hearing that
the duke intended his family to spend the rest of the
summer in Brighton, many a young man had begun to
scurry around trying to find rooms in the seaside resort
the Prince Regent had brought to such popularity.

Anne was very gay the evening of the engagement
ball. Surrounded by her admirers, she did not sit out a
single dance, and she accepted all the compliments on
the portrait with as much delight as Lady Tyson did.

As she was standing before it with one of her
partners, the Earl of Burnham came and joined them.
He raised his quizzing glass to inspect it carefully, and
Anne found she was holding her breath.

"It is beautiful, no, exquisite, don't you agree,
m'lord?" Sir Whitney asked.

"An excellent likeness," the earl drawled, and then
he smiled a little and said, "Claire Tyson is an outstanding artist."

Anne was quick to agree, although inside she felt a

return of her customary annoyance at his nonchalance. Couldn't he have made some comment about the beauty of the sitters? she asked herself, trying to keep her expression from showing her thoughts.

"But any artist would be fortunate to have such loveliness to portray," Sir Whitney persisted.

"Didn't I just say so?" the earl murmured, and then he bowed and excused himself. Anne saw him waltzing a little while later with Lady Preston, but, as usual, he had not asked her to dance.

As she danced and flirted, Anne tried very hard not to let her eyes linger on the glowing Amelia and the man who stood so close beside her, his arm around her as he bent to whisper in her ear. They were so much in love, everyone remarked it, and one old lady said it brought tears to her eyes just to look at them. James Galt looked almost handsome in his dark evening clothes, for his stern face was relaxed in a broad smile, and his deep-set eyes softened whenever he turned to his lovely fiancée. As the set ended, Anne wished with all her heart that he was looking at her that way, and for a moment, her eyes grew sad and distant.

"Now why do you look so pensive, Lady Anne?" the earl asked as he took her arm and beckoned to a footman to bring them champagne. Anne made herself smile again. "I was thinking how much I will miss my sister when she is far away in Scotland, m'lord," she said. "I shall be lonely without her."

"Surely not for long, Lady Anne," he replied, seating her on one of the little gilt chairs that were placed at intervals along the sides of the ballroom. "It would not take much of a fortune teller to see your future, why, any one of a dozen men would be delighted to—er—assuage your loneliness. I expect to read of your engagement in a very short time."

Anne looked up at him quickly. There had been some tone in his voice that reminded her of the earlier challenge he had made at her presentation ball. But although she inspected his face carefully, she could read nothing there but a little amusement. Aware that the silence between them had gone on for much too long, she said in a haughty voice, "You are wrong. I am not interested in marriage, m'lord." Then her fair skin flushed a little under his intense scrutiny, and she turned her head so all he could see was her patrician profile.

"Indeed?" he asked in disbelief. "But what a terrible waste! It is most upsetting to think that such as you intends to continue to embrace the single state. But perhaps you might change your mind?"

As she shook her head, he leaned closer and added softly, "Or be induced to do so?"

Anne shook her head again, her mouth set firmly, but she spun around when she heard his chuckle. Her blue eyes sparkled with anger, and he took her hand and patted it. "How you do hate being teased, Lady Anne! But even though it might well incur your wrath, I must tell you that I would wager any amount you like that you will be following in your sister's footsteps within the year."

As she opened her mouth to hotly refute this statement, he added, "No, no, it is useless to protest! You must allow me to know your future."

Anne almost snatched her hand from his. "I shall decide my future, sir," she told him. "What I do is none of your concern."

To her surprise, he nodded, not at all perturbed. "Perhaps not at the moment. But in this instance I am sure I am right."

He rose then and bowed. "I am so sorry we must end our charming discussion, but the next set is forming and I am engaged for this dance. Excuse me, m'lady."

Anne could see Lord Anders hurrying toward them to claim her, and before she thought, she asked, "Why don't you ever ask me to dance, m'lord?"

She flushed again as his brows rose in astonishment, and his gray eyes began to twinkle. "I shall ask you to dance—someday, Lady Anne," he said. As she shrugged, pretending disinterest, he added, so only she could hear, "And I shall ask other things of you as well. And that you *may* wager on, my dear."

Anne was not sorry to rise and take a bowing Lord Anders's arm, for she could think of nothing to say in rebuttal to this bold threat. The earl watched her as she walked away, and when he went to claim his own partner, his face was alight with inner amusement.

Shortly after the ball, the Fairhaven ladies left London. Although many things had been done in town to ensure a perfect wedding, Juliet knew there was still a great deal to do at Severn. James Galt accompanied the ladies' carriage on horseback, for the duke had remained in London to oversee the final preparations there, and to bring Amelia's wedding dress himself when it was completed.

The Scotsman stayed only one night at Severn, which Juliet told herself was just as well when she saw the look on Melia's face after she came in from a moonlit stroll in the garden with him. He had business in Edinburgh, and he did not intend to return until just before the July day when he would finally claim Lady Amelia for his bride. Juliet and Anne were glad to wave good-bye to him, for very different reasons, but Amelia was depressed for some time. It was only when she was caught up in all the things that still remained to be done that she grew more cheerful.

At last the relatives and the wedding guests began arriving, and she woke one morning to hear the estate carpenters erecting the bower that was to be covered with flowers, where she would say her vows. For several minutes, she lay in bed dreaming of that happy moment, and then she smiled to herself. Even now, James was on his way back to her, she knew, accompanied by his brother and his family, and in only a little while she would become Amelia Galt. They had planned a short honeymoon in the English Lake

District that was so much admired by the poet Words-
worth, before going on to Edinburgh. Although
Amelia had some misgivings about leaving her family,
and especially her twin, she knew in her heart that she
would only find real happiness with her James.

He arrived the morning of the wedding, but she was
not allowed to see him. She had spent a long time
talking about marriage with Juliet the afternoon
before, and then her father had come to her room that
evening, to search her eyes one more time, to be sure
she was happy. At the look on his dear, somber face,
she felt tears clogging her throat, and wordlessly, she
put her arms around him and sobbed. The duke's own
arms tightened, but wisely he did not ask her what the
matter was. He seemed to know that this was her way
of saying good-bye—to her childhood, to Severn, and
to him. His own eyes were moist when he left her with
a kiss.

The hardest person to leave was Anne, and although
they cried together in each other's arms for a long
time, she could only be grateful when Anne made her
dry her eyes, in quite her old, brisk manner. "You
must stop, Melia," she ordered, handing her a handkerchief. "How awful if you appear tomorrow with
red-rimmed eyes! Poor James, to say nothing of father.
He would no doubt stop the ceremony on the spot, and
then what would our dear vicar do, all dressed up in
his best robes with his Bible open? Besides, there are
the guests. How sad, after coming all this way, if they
had to leave without even a glass of champagne!"

Amelia laughed at the picture she painted, and in a
little while, Anne tucked her in bed and kissed her
lightly before she went to her own room.

When Amelia was dressed the next afternoon, Juliet
clapped her hands in delight at the picture she made.
Anne smiled at her enthusiasm, although she agreed
Melia had never looked so beautiful, so regal. From
the sparkling tiara holding those clouds of veiling on
her black curls, to the tips of her satin sandals peeping

out beneath the embroidered hem of her gown, she was the vision all brides hoped they would be.

As Anne arranged her train, with the help of the excited maids, she heard a strange music outside, and she paused, her eyes puzzled.

Amelia laughed down at her. "It is the bag pipers, Anne. Father was a little sticky about them, but he came around. They are piping the guests to the wedding. It is a custom in Scotland."

As she spoke, she reached out and touched the sprays of white heather in her bridal bouquet. James had told her white heather meant good luck, and she smiled at the amount he had brought for her to carry, all the way from Scotland.

At last, everything was ready. Juliet had taken her place near the bower, and the guests were all assembled. The duke held out his arm to his younger daughter, his throat tight with his pride. He still did not like this match, but he knew Melia was happy, and with that, he told himself, he must be content.

As Anne walked slowly through the rose garden ahead of the bride on her father's arm, she kept her eyes on her bouquet. The music of the pipers who were lined up along the edge of the lake seemed a sad wail, almost a dirge to her. And then, unable to help herself, she looked up just before she reached the improvised altar, and she caught her breath. James Galt stood there waiting, his brother, the laird, beside him. They were both dressed in formal Highland garb, but she saw only James. His kilt of dress tartan was worn over silk stockings with scarlet garters and rosettes, and his shoe buckles, sword belt, and the shoulder brooch holding his plaid were all of highly polished silver. He wore the dress sporran at his waist. It was hung with an otter's head mounted in silver. His black velvet doublet showed a lace jabot and cuffs, and Anne thought him even more magnificent than Amelia. For once she felt safe gazing at him as she drew nearer, for he was looking beyond her, his hazel eyes eager. She knew Amelia was close when he reached up and almost reverently removed his bonnet. The sun struck chestnut hightlights in his dark hair.

As she took her sister's bouquet, and turned to face Vicar Manchester, Anne drew a deep breath to steady herself. She had never felt so sad, so left out, so forlorn. And she did not think she would forget until her dying day the look on James Galt's face as he took her twin's hand in his own.

From that moment on, the rest of the wedding day seemed to rush past Anne. She could only remember little vignettes of it later, her mind was in such turmoil. First, there was the agony of watching James kiss Melia at the end of the ceremony. She had been glad to busy herself with the long train as they went out among the guests, arm in arm, to the music of the pipers.

Anne followed on the laird's arm. She made herself smile at him. He was older than his brother, and stouter, and his face was not set in such severe planes.

She remembered little of the festive meal, the many toasts, the dancing, or all the guests who exclaimed over the bride and teased her about her own wedding someday.

One thing she knew she would never forget. She had just come from the dance floor with the laird after a spritely reel. He took her up to where the bride and groom were standing, for this moment at least, alone. The laird congratulated Melia on her gown, and then he began to chuckle. When he was asked why, he pointed to the design.

"Can it be you have not noticed it, Jamie, lad?" he teased his brother.

James inspected the gown, and a smile curled his lips as he lifted Melia's hand to kiss. "The English rose and the Scottish thistle. But how appropriate, my love," he said. And then he leaned closer and whispered, "In each other's arms at last."

Anne was standing so close, she could not help but overhear.

After that, she danced until she was breathless. She even danced a schottische with the bridegroom, who, in his happiness, seemed to have forgiven her her deception at last. Anne laughed and flirted with all the gentlemen, and generally had a wonderful time. She did not even lower her chin when Amelia and her new husband were driven away in their carriage, although she saw Juliet wipe a tear from her eyes, and her father's sad, set face.

But a little later, when all the guests had returned to the ballroom and the supper rooms, she made her way to the terrace that overlooked the lake and leaned on the balustrade there. It was almost full dark, with only a sliver of new moon and the evening star to light the scene.

Anne tried to put the sounds of merriment that she could hear behind her, from her mind. It is over, she thought sadly, but at least Melia never suspected my secret, no, nor anyone else. I may have to live with these sad feelings for the rest of my life, but I still have my pride.

And then she smelled the smoke of a cigar, and she stiffened, hoping the tears she wanted to shed so badly, did not show in her eyes.

As Hugh Moreley, Earl of Burnham, strolled up to join her, she suddenly recalled his angry expression when she had first turned from the altar following the ceremony. At the time, it had not registered consciously, but now she wondered what there was about a wedding to make the man look so black.

"Am I intruding, Lady Anne?" he asked, leaning on the balustrade beside her. His gray eyes searched her face, and Anne drew back a little, glad there was not much light.

"Not at all, m'lord," she said, and then she made herself laugh. "I was only getting a breath of fresh air.

Even here at Severn, it is warm, almost sultry. I am so glad Melia did not want to be married in London after all."

He did not reply for a moment, and she stole a glance at him, a little surprised. "You are very *gallant*, m'lady. My congratulations," he said, in quite the kindest voice she had ever heard from him.

"*Gallant?*" she asked. "I am afraid I do not understand you, sir." And then she added, "You must be thinking of what I told you in town, about how I would miss my sister."

She closed her lips firmly, determined not to say any more, and he reached out and took her chin in his hand. Gray eyes burned into dark blue ones as he said, "Of course, there is that, too."

Anne heard her brother Will calling her then from one of the terrace doors, and she excused herself, not at all reluctant to leave the disturbing, enigmatic earl. As she walked away, she heard him say behind her, almost as if he spoke to himself, "How glad I am that you are not to dance to that particular piper, Lady Anne. I, myself, have always considered bagpipes to be—er—vastly overrated."

VIII

The Duke and Duchess of Severn, in company with the Lady Anne Fairhaven, arrived in Brighton some three weeks later and took up residence in the charming villa the duke had hired on the Marine Parade. They had intended to be there at least a week earlier, but the duchess had not been feeling well since the wedding. When the duke would have taken her to London and the attentions of the best physicians, she had laughed at him before she told him that she was sure it was only the strain of preparing for the wedding that caused her to feel so poorly. Certainly the sea air and fresh breezes, to say nothing of the excitement of a new scene, would have her restored to good health in a thrice, and at last he had concurred.

Their delay had created great consternation among Anne's admirers, all of whom had made that part of the Front near the duke's villa, a favorite meeting place. Not a morning passed without four or five of them arriving to see if the knocker was on the front door and the shutters opened, and another group invariably appeared around tea time to check whether the carriages had come that day. There was great rejoicing when the duke's servants appeared in a huge fourgon loaded with boxes and baggage, but it was another two long days before the Fairhavens' dusty carriage, attended by the duke's grooms trailing the riding horses, appeared on the Parade.

When Anne came down from her charming bedroom facing the Channel late the next morning, it was to find that several gentlemen had called and left their cards, and she had received four nosegays as well. The duke, entering the hall after a gentle walk along the Front with Juliet, eyed these offerings with misgiving.

"One hates to even think of it, but I am very much afraid that the saying "Here we go again," is entirely appropriate at this time, my dear," he told his wife.

She squeezed his arm before she went to Anne's side and smiled at her. "Father!" Anne exclaimed. "Surely my indifference to them can hardly be considered encouraging!"

"Indeed?" the duke asked, giving his hat to his new butler. It had been decided to leave Devett at Severn, for he was growing old and disliked moving household. "But I believe I have mentioned before that you scarcely need to encourage them." He smiled at his daughter then, and added, "Pray you will not be as precipitate as Melia, Anne. Juliet is in no case to deal with another wedding at this time, and as for myself, a year—perhaps even two or three—in the interim would suit me nicely."

Anne picked up one of her nosegays and lowered her head to sniff its fragrance. "You need have no fear, father," she told him, her voice stiff, and then she changed the subject by asking the duchess how she did.

The duke left them together, and went out to stroll to the Royal Pavilion to pay his *devoirs* to his Prince, and apprise him of his arrival. William Fairhaven was not an intimate of the Prince Regent's, for he found some aspects of his character hard to admire, even though some day he would be King. But in matters of protocol, he was punctilious. Besides, he knew both Juliet and Anne would enjoy the receptions and musicales at the Royal Pavilion, and he was looking forward to seeing their reactions the first time they stepped into the Prince Regent's ornate, seaside retreat.

The Prince was not at the Pavilion that morning, and after he had left his card with the Prince's secretary, Colonel McMahon, and chatted for a few minutes with the other gentlemen gathered in the enormous Chinese Gallery, the duke excused himself.

As he stood outside, smoothing his gloves, he was joined by the Earl of Burnham. "You did not remain very long, your Grace," the younger peer remarked. "Can it be that you, like I, are not an admirer of stained glass skylights and Chinese canopies complete with dangling bells, to say nothing of what is certainly an excessive display of bamboo and lacquer?"

The duke smiled. "Prinny does have quite extraordinary tastes, does he not, m'lord? I am most anxious to hear Anne's comments, especially when she sees the Pavilion. I can only hope she remembers to whisper them."

"How is the Lady Anne?" the earl asked courteously, as the two men began to walk back to the Marine Parade.

"Very well, thank you," the duke replied. The earl wondered at the little frown between those distinctive black brows, not dreaming William Fairhaven was thinking of his duchess rather than his daughter.

As the two continued their walk, they chatted of the Season just past, and exchanged *on-dits*. The duke had just remarked on how crowded Brighton was in August when they reached the front door of his villa.

"Especially here, your Grace," the earl murmured, his gray eyes lighting up with amusement as two young gentlemen glared as they passed each other on the steps.

The duke nodded to Lord Anders and Mr. Collingswood as each of them gave him their most reverent bow. "Young puppies," he muttered, his voice disdainful.

The earl laughed. "It must grow tiresome, having them so constantly underfoot," he remarked.

"I have ceased to notice them unless I trip over them," the duke told him, and then he excused himself to enter the house.

He found Juliet alone in the drawing room with the morning's post, for Anne had gone upstairs to read a letter from Amelia, the first she had had since the wedding. As he closed the door of the drawing room, the duke was delighted to hear his new butler denying the gentlemen callers, for, as he told them firmly, the Lady Anne was not receiving that morning.

As William Fairhaven dropped a kiss on Juliet's soft hair, she looked up to smile at him. "We have a letter from Melia, William," she told him. "How happy she is!"

The duke took the sheets from her hand, and sat down beside her to peruse them. He was smiling broadly by the time he reached the last page, and then he shook his head. "You were right, and I was wrong, my dear, but to this day I cannot understand why she fell in love with the man. I doubt I ever shall."

His duchess laughed at his wondering tones. "Love is mysterious, is it not?" she teased him. "For example, who would have thought I could fall in love with you, my arrogant duke?"

The duke leaned closer to whisper in her ear, and she tapped his hand sharply in reproof, her eyes dancing.

Upstairs, in a chair near the window of her room, Anne sat staring out at the brilliant scene before her. The Channel was sparkling with whitecaps this morning, and the strand was crowded with holiday-makers, some of whom were entering the water in the square bathing carts with their large wheels that were provided for this purpose. It was a gay, colorful scene, but Anne's eyes were on the far horizon. It was obvious that Melia was happy, why, her joy fairly leaped from the pages. Anne's brows drew together in a little frown as she read the section of the letter again that begged her to lose no time finding her own bridegroom. "Marriage is of all things the most delightful in the world, dearest Anne," Melia had written. "I cannot tell you how glorious it is. I pray you will find the man who will make you as happy as James has made me, quickly."

Anne did not appear downstairs until lunchtime, but she was composed then, joining in the discussion of Amelia's letters with ease. At the end of the meal when Juliet went to rest, the duke asked his daughter if she would care to go for a drive.

"I shall show you all the sights, Anne," he said before she ran up to fetch her bonnet and sunshade. "Brighton is very festive, and I know you did not see much of it yesterday when we arrived."

As he tooled his phaeton along the Front a few minutes later, he pointed out The Old Ship and the Castle Inn where balls and assemblies were held during the week. Anne was more fascinated by the bathing carts drawn up on the strand.

"How delightful that looks!" she exclaimed. "I certainly must try it for myself, as soon as I purchase a bathing costume."

"I think not, Anne," the duke said sternly. "You will notice there are no awnings, unlike the carts at Ramsgate and other watering places. I am sure you will not be surprised when I tell you that it is a favorite pastime of the young bloods to sit in their windows with telescopes, so they might inspect any ladies so bold."

Anne laughed. "Perhaps you can arrange for awnings then, sir? Think how it would benefit Juliet to have a dip. I have been told salt water is an excellent restorative."

William Fairhaven appeared much struck, as she

had known he would be. Where his duchess was concerned, no effort of his was too great, too tedious.

As the Fairhavens continued their drive, they passed the Royal Pavilion. Its magnificence effectively silenced the Lady Anne. At last she said in a wondering voice, "How very bizarre, all those turrets and fretting and domes. Why, it looks positively pagan!"

The duke agreed, although he begged her to keep that opinion to herself. Anne pointed to a large rotunda. "What is that building, sir, set somewhat apart from the rest?"

On being told it was the Royal Stable, she dissolved in helpless laughter. "All that grandeur just for horses?" she asked when she could speak again.

"Of course. They are *Prinny's* horses," the duke told her, his lips twitching in response.

They spent the afternoon in perfect accord. As he handed her down at the villa later, the duke wondered how long it would last. Anne had been very subdued since Melia's wedding, and even as he agreed with Juliet that she was probably missing her twin, he was sure it would be no time at all before she recovered and was up to some deviltry. He resolved to watch her carefully.

But in the days that followed, his mind was more often on his wife. The duchess did not seem to be benefiting from the salt air and the gentle routine that had been established. Very often, she did not feel well enough even to chaperone her stepdaughter to the various parties, and it was left to the duke to take Anne about. Since he would have preferred to remain with his wife, he was preoccupied, and Anne often found herself left to her own devices.

She had made up her mind to forget James Galt, and in order to do so, she threw herself into a frenzy of gaiety and almost ceaseless activities. The duke had no interest in the amusements of the younger set, so he had no objection to Anne's walking or driving with all the young men who clamored for the privilege. He

even began to allow her to attend picnics and parties
without him. He felt it was more than safe to do so, for
she had had her Season and seemed in no danger of
succumbing to some callow youth's impassioned pleas
to let him make her his. Besides, the duke insisted she
always have at least two escorts, feeling there was
safety in numbers. He knew the beaux would watch
each other jealously; Anne would be as safe as if she
were under his all-seeing eyes.

True to his word, William Fairhaven had hired a
bathing cart for the family's exclusive use, and made
arrangements for it to be discreetly awninged. Anne
used it every fine day, although Juliet did not seem to
be interested. She was still very tired, and sometimes
she did not come downstairs until early afternoon.

Anne's most persistent admirers remained Sir
Whitney Blake and Stephen Young, who, denied
Amelia's hand, had transferred his devotion back to
her twin again. The two were nowhere near the
friends they had been a year ago, for they both felt
that if the other were out of the way, they would have
no trouble getting the Lady Anne to agree to marriage.
Anne could have told them what a misconception this
was, but since having them dance attendance on her,
write her fervent notes, and glare at each other over
her head, eased her wounded feelings and fed her
pride, she did not. Besides, it amused her that Mr.
Young, who only a short time ago had been mad with
love for Amelia, was so fickle he could forget her in the
twinkling of an eye. Anne had to bite her tongue
several times when she was tempted to remind him of
his impassioned words that evening at Ranelagh when
she had pretended to be Melia.

One evening in the Assembly Rooms of the Castle
Inn, the two young men almost came to blows. Sir
Whitney insisted that Lady Anne had promised him
the first waltz, and Mr. Young was hot as he claimed
the privilege. The Earl of Burnham put a stop to the
situation they were attracting. Coming over to where

Lady Anne stood between them, her expression demure, he held out his arm and said, "You must excuse the lady, sirs. I have a message from the duke."

He took Anne's hand in his arm and led her to the anteroom. Behind them, her two admirers glowered at each other for a moment, before they sought opposite ends of the room.

"Is it—is it about Juliet, sir?" Anne asked, forgetting them both in her concern. The earl noticed the strain in her voice, and he patted the slim white hand that was gripping his arm.

"Forgive me, I did not mean to alarm you, m'lady," he said in a soothing voice. "There is no message. I merely thought to remove you before murder was committed. Bloodshed at a Brighton Assembly is not good *ton*, you know."

He indicated a sofa, and as Anne took her seat, she chuckled. She was quick to frown, however, as he continued. "I wonder you did not stop them yourself, Lady Anne. Surely it was remiss of you to encourage them in their outrageous behavior."

Anne shrugged and waved her fan. "You would have me discourage my beaux, m'lord?" she asked in a disbelieving voice.

"In this case, certainly," he said. "I know you would never miss them, not when there are so many others begging for your attention. Besides, these two think themselves in love with you, or at least Sir Whitney does. I suspect the inconstant Mr. Young cannot bear to have his friend steal a march on him, so he must form one of your court as well. The longer you allow them to imagine their suits will prosper, the harder it will be for them when they finally get up their courage and propose to you. Of course, I know you have no intention of accepting either one of them."

Anne shrugged again in disdain, and, stung by her careless attitude, he added softly, "Surely you can understand and sympathize with the pain of unrequited love, can't you, Lady Anne?"

Anne swung around to stare at him, her dark blue eyes widening, and he nodded, his own gray eyes holding her gaze. "Of course you can. The feminine heart is always so tender, so merciful, is it not?" he added, his voice bland.

Anne could not lower her eyes or look away from his handsome, aristocratic face, those keen, knowing eyes. There was a long moment of silence, and then he said, "Allow me to warn you. Sir Whitney and Mr. Young are very close to calling each other out. I know how it would displease your father when it became known, as I am sure it will be probably even before the smoke from their dueling pistols has cleared, that the Lady Anne Fairhaven was responsible for the debacle. You cannot have considered the consequences. Such a duel would not only cause death or serious injury for one young man, and either exile or imprisonment for the other, it would also create a scandal that would be gossiped about from one end of England to the other."

Anne made herself relax the fingers that were gripping her fan so tightly, she wondered she had not snapped the sticks. "Why do *you* tell me this, m'lord?" she asked.

"You are asking what concern it is of mine, are you not, Lady Anne?" he asked in turn. "I shall be delighted to tell you. You see, I would prefer not to align myself with a lady who has made herself notorious, and I have every intention of marrying you myself, one of these days."

"You are very arrogant, m'lord!" Anne exclaimed, considerably startled. "As I told you once before, I have no intention of marrying you—or anyone!"

The earl continued to regard her, his eyes hooded. There was not a trace of a smile on his handsome mouth. At last Anne lowered her own defiant eyes to her lap.

"Yes, I am arrogant," he agreed. "As arrogant as you are, Lady Anne Fairhaven of Severn. We should make quite a pair, don't you agree?"

Anne's breathing had quickened, and without thinking, she said, "You said you would marry me 'some day,' sir. I assume then that I am to sit and wait until you decide that day has come? I shall not! I beg you will propose to me now, so I might give you my answer at once."

Her voice dared him to do just that, and he smiled, and picked up her hand and kissed it. As his lips touched her skin, it was all Anne could do to tear her hand away, and she shivered. "But I have no intention of being refused, my dear," he told her with another little smile. "I shall propose when it is appropriate to do so, and not before."

Now Anne raised her chin and looked mutinous. "Perhaps I shall accept another gentleman before that time, sir," she told him.

"I do not think you will, Anne," he replied calmly. "In fact, I know there is no danger at all of your doing so."

Seeing Lord Anders hurrying toward them as the musicians struck up the next dance, he rose and bowed to her. As he walked away, he smiled to himself. He had not meant to reveal his plans quite this early, but he had not been able to resist the opportunity. He was sure Lady Anne would think long and hard about what he had told her, and like all women, could not help but be intrigued by it. He knew she would always be on the lookout for him from now on, that she would watch him, and wonder, and wait. He told himself the waiting would do her a great deal of good.

Anne did think long and hard as soon a she was driven back to the villa after the Assembly was over. After she had been undressed, and her maid had left her, she lay in bed staring up at the ceiling. What had the earl meant when he said there was no danger of her accepting another man? Was it possible he knew of her love for James Galt? But that could not be! She had been so careful, why, not even her father or Juliet suspected.

But she knew the truth of his final words. She would never agree to marriage to anyone, not when she still thought so often of the Scotsman who was now her brother-in-law, not when she still cried herself to sleep wondering if he were taking Melia in his arms even then, and making love to her. She could still see those deep-set, frowning eyes, that rugged face, as clearly as if he were standing before her. He was as real to her as her twin, and she only had to look into the mirror to see Melia.

And then she began to wonder about the earl's calm assumption that someday they would be wed. How presumptuous he was, how sure of himself! Why, her father's pride paled in comparison. Even so, she could not help a little thrill of conquest that such a handsome, debonair, older man wanted her. He was so unlike her usual beaux. Beside Hugh Moreley they all seemed callous and noisy and crude. And she had to admit, there was something about the man that attracted her. She was never so conscious of her femininity as when she was with him. Tonight, when he had kissed her hand, she had shivered, but she knew it was not from revulsion, oh, no! It was all so confusing, so disturbing. She did not like the way he made her feel. Since she could not have James Galt, she wanted to remain intact, body and soul, an impregnable fortress that no one could ever get near, never mind storm. The only man who had been able to breech her defenses had been James; she must not allow the earl the privilege too.

The following evening the Fairhavens had been invited to the Royal Pavilion. The Prince Regent was holding a reception, and his own Wind Band was to entertain the guests in the huge, Oriental Music Room. Juliet was feeling better, and looking forward to the evening, so all three Fairhavens entered the duke's carriage for the short drive to the Pavilion.

William Fairhaven spent the time warning Anne to restrain herself when she stepped inside at last and, most especially, to keep her opinions to herself unless she spoke to her family, and then only in whispers.

Anne shook her head at him. "How worried you are, father," she said. "By now I know how to behave, don't I, Juliet?"

Her stepmother smiled at her. "Most of the time," she agreed cordially. Anne wrinkled her nose.

"I am sure you will captivate the Prince," the duke said. "He always has an eye for a lovely woman, and I doubt he has seen one like you, Anne, for many a day. Do not be offended if he gives you some ponderous compliments, or even flirts with you. He has never accepted the fact that he is not still the handsome young Prince Florizel the ladies swooned over so many years ago. In his own eyes, he is still that hero." The duke snorted. "It is unfortunate in a corpulent, middle-aged man, but he is the Prince."

"And do not go into another room with him alone, no matter how he opportunes you," Juliet said, adding a warning of her own. "You must be polite and take care not to offend him, but if he insists, say you are feeling ill. He is terrified of germs, and the night air."

Anne laughed as she smoothed her new gown of royal blue silk. It had tiny puffed sleeves and a pleated bodice that was very becoming. She was wearing the tiara and necklace of sapphires and diamonds that her father had given her for her debut, and she knew she looked well. Her maid had dressed her hair in a mass of ebony curls, and her excitement at meeting the Prince Regent at last had brought a flush to her pale cheeks.

But even with all the warnings, she could not restrain a gasp when she saw the inside of the Pavilion. Her father let her look about with wondering eyes for a moment, and then he led his ladies to where the Prince was receiving his guests, in the middle of the Chinese Gallery. Anne thought him as fantastic as his house. He had such a florid complexion, and he was so stout, that the red satin waistcoat embroidered all over with dragons in gold thread, and the tight-waisted coat he wore over it, did nothing to enhance his appearance.

The Prince was a genial man, well pleased with his Pavilion and his guests, and he beamed kindly at Juliet and the duke, and positively twinkled when Anne sank into a deep curtsy, her eyes lowered in girlish modesty.

"Now, why haven't I seen this young gel before, eh, Severn?" he asked the duke, poking him in the ribs. Not a muscle moved in William Fairhaven's face. "Such a dark beauty, why, she is outstanding, sir!"

As the duke nodded his thanks, the Prince took Anne's hand and patted it. "And I have heard there is another Fairhaven young lady, an identical twin. I am disappointed you did not bring her along, too. Together, they must be stunning."

"Unfortunately, I cannot produce her for you, Highness," the duke drawled. "My daughter Amelia is married now, and living in Scotland."

For a moment, the Prince pouted, and then he said, "Well, well, we must make do with the one, then. I shall hope to see you often, my dear young lady. You do my little seaside cottage justice. By the way, what do you think of it, Lady Anne?"

He dropped her hand to tuck both of his hands under the tails of his coat while he rocked back and forth on his heels, waiting for the compliments to come.

"I have never seen anything like it in my life, Your Highness," Anne told him honestly. Seeing he was waiting for something a little more effusive, she added, "It is so rich and grand it fairly takes your breath away."

The Prince beamed at her, and the Fairhavens were allowed to move away as he turned to greet his next guests. Seeing Juliet was looking a little uncomfortable in the hot room, the duke took her to a sofa near the door and beckoned a footman to bring them refreshments.

"You did that very well, Anne," he complimented his daughter. Looking around the room, he saw the Prince whispering to his sly little secretary, and pointing toward the sofa the ladies occupied, and he frowned a little. "I am afraid you will be asked to converse with him again, however, for here comes Colonel McMahon now, to do his master's bidding." The duke's voice was full of disgust, for he disliked the Prince's secretary immensely.

"Your Grace, ladies," the colonel said with a smirk as he bowed before them. "A little bird has told His Highness that the Lady Anne has an outstanding voice. He wishes her to sing for his guests after the Wind Band concert."

"Oh, no," Anne said, putting her hands to her flushed cheeks. "I could not—why, I am not prepared."

The colonel shook a playful finger at her. "But you must, dear lady! It is to be a Royal Command performance, you see."

The duke straightened as if he were about to protest, but Anne had seen the Earl of Burnham entering the gallery, and she stiffened and said, "Very well. I shall do my best, but you must allow me to speak to the musicians beforehand."

The colonel rubbed his hands together and agreed, and in a moment he was escorting Anne and a watchful Juliet from the room.

"Now what could possibly call for such a ferocious frown, your Grace?" the duke heard a voice ask as he watched his ladies disappear. He turned to see Hugh Moreley smiling and bowing. "Surely on such a *delightful* evening as this, in such *sumptious* surroundings, and in the company of your *Prince*, you should be wreathed in smiles."

"Prinny has insisted Anne sing this evening," William Fairhaven explained. "She has no music with her; she is not prepared."

"Ah, I see," the earl said. "But I think you worry

with no cause, sir. From my own observations of your daughter, I expect Lady Anne will carry all before her. She is, besides being such a beautiful young woman, a consummate performer."

The duke's eyes narrowed, even as he nodded his agreement. The two men exchanged glances, and then, without another word, the earl bowed and went to speak to some of his particular friends. The duke watched him as he walked away, an arrested look in his eyes.

To the other guests, and Juliet in particular, the evening seemed long, but to Anne it appeared no time at all before the Prince bounced up from his little gilt chair at the end of the concert and announced that they were all to have a special treat. Obediently, the guests settled back in their chairs in the ornate crimson and gold room, the ladies patiently wielding their fans, and the gentlemen trying to loosen their confining cravats.

Wisely, Anne had decided to do without the services of the Wind Band. It would be too difficult without rehearsals, and she was not sure her voice was strong enough to compete with all those flutes and oboes. Instead, she seated herself at the piano that had been brought forward by six liveried footmen, to accompany herself. She began with a simple, familiar ballad to gain confidence, and then, encouraged by the enthusiastic applause, finished with a lilting aria that showed off her range and expertise.

The Prince was loud in his praises when the Fairhavens took their leave of him a little later. "Such lovely purity, like a bird, my dear," he told Anne, pressing her hands between both of his. Anne tried to look suitably grateful for the compliment, but she wished he were not perspiring quite so much and she prayed that the overpowering scent he wore would not make her sneeze.

"You are to be congratulated, Severn," he said next, releasing her at last to turn to the duke. "Alas, it is a

sad thing to be middle-aged and have to observe such
talent and beauty, knowing it is not for the likes of us,
eh?" he asked. The duke was treated to another playful poke before they were allowed to leave. Juliet drew
some deep breaths of the cool, salty air as they waited
for their carriage.

"You were excellent, Anne," she told her stepdaughter. "I was so proud of you!"

Anne grinned, a mischievous light in her eyes. She
opened her mouth and was surprised to find her father
putting his hand over it. As her eyes questioned him,
he bent closer and whispered, "I know you are
bursting to imitate Prinny, you minx, but I must insist
that you wait until we reach home, and are behind
closed doors."

Anne gurgled with laughter, but she nodded
acquiescence to this plan. As they drove back to the
Marine Parade, she chattered about the evening, for
she was still flushed with excitement. She loved performing, and this evening had been a triumph for her.
Not only had a hundred of the *ton*'s more august
members been her audience, but she had held the
Prince Regent spellbound as well. She could hardly
wait to write to Melia and tell her of her success.

As she went up the steps behind Juliet and her
father, she admitted there had only been one disappointment. The Earl of Burnham had not come near
her all evening, and he had done nothing more than
nod carelessly when she looked his way as she was
being applauded at the end of her concert. What an
enigma he was, she thought crossly, but then she
forgot him in an instant when Juliet suddenly moaned
before she slipped to the floor in a dead faint.

IX

Before Anne could move, the duke was on his knees beside his wife, his dark face harsh with worry and concern. Picking up her limp wrist, he took her pulse, and then he said over his shoulder to his hovering butler, "Send someone for the doctor at once. Tell him to run!"

Anne pressed back against the wall, one fist covering her mouth in fear as the duke gathered Juliet into his arms and rose. He looked around and seemed to see his daughter for the first time, and he said, "Go and warn Juliet's maid that her mistress is ill, Anne."

Anne nodded, and hurried up the stairs, calling as she went. She held the door of the bedroom open so the duke could carry his precious burden to bed, and then she just stood there, terrified. What could be wrong with Juliet? she wondered. Oh, please God it was not serious, she thought, wishing there was something she could do to help. She watched her father removing Juliet's slippers, and holding her up so her dress could be unfastened and her laces loosened, but Anne had nothing to do but watch and pray. The maid was an older woman, and she did not seem nervous or incompetent. After she had the duchess comfortable, she covered her with a light throw, and then she went to get some water to bathe her temples. The duke sat beside his wife on the bed, his daughter forgotten as he chafed her hands gently. It seemed to Anne as if he were trying to give her some of his own strength, but it was a long time before the duchess groaned and opened her eyes. Her face was so white, the little mole beside her mouth was thrown into prominence. Anne clenched her hands together to keep them from trembling.

"William?" Juliet asked, in a thin, thready voice that was full of fear.

"Hush, love, do not try to talk," the duke said, his calm voice reassuring. "You fainted, but the doctor is coming and you will soon feel better."

Juliet closed her eyes, and then she moaned and shuddered again, and the maid leaned over to whisper to the duke. Anne could not hear what she said, but she saw her father's startled look, and the way he took the hand he was holding and pressed it to his heart.

It was only a few minutes later that the doctor came puffing up the stairs, but to the duke and Anne it seemed an eternity.

After brief introductions, and a whispered conference with the maid, the doctor insisted the duke leave the room. "I have to examine the duchess now, your Grace," he said firmly. "You must leave us, for you would be in the way. Your daughter, too—it would not be seemly."

At any other time, Anne would have laughed out loud at the very idea of a round, bald little man in a shabby black suit ordering her tall, elegant father around, but the duke nodded and left the room without a word of protest.

Anne followed him down the stairs to the drawing room. She knew she could not bear to worry alone in her room, and that even if her father wished for solitude in his vigil, she needed to be with him.

She found him leaning against the mantel of the empty fireplace, his back to her and his shoulders bowed.

"Father?" she said, pausing by the door. As he

looked up and turned, she saw the agony in his eyes, and she ran to him and put her arms around him.

"Don't look like that, don't!" she begged him. "Juliet will be all right, she *must*. How could we live without her?"

William Fairhaven put his own arms around his daughter and cuddled her close. "How indeed?" he asked in a strangled voice. When Anne started to cry, he patted her and handed her his handkerchief. "You must be brave now, Anne, for Juliet's sake," he told her, and then he added, "And for mine."

"Of course, father, I will do everything I can," she assured him, sniffing and wiping her eyes.

The two Fairhavens sat together for a long time. Faintly, they could hear sounds in the bedroom above where the duchess was lying, and every now and then, the patter of running feet on the stairs. They did not speak, and Anne knew her father was praying as fervently as she was herself.

Just as the clock struck two, the duchess's maid appeared in the doorway. She looked tired and the duke rose quickly. "Yes, Rose? How is she?"

"Doctor Canfield thinks she will be all right, your Grace, and the baby as well, but she must take the greatest care," the woman told him as she bobbed a curtsy.

The duke bowed his head, and Anne gasped and covered her mouth. Juliet was going to have a baby? Why, she had never even suspected it! Was this why she had not been feeling well since the wedding? Why she was always so tired, and only picked at her food?

It was very quiet in the house as she made her way up to bed. She paused for a moment outside her stepmother's room, but she did not try to see her. The doctor had said he would remain with his patient until he was sure she was in no danger, and Anne knew he had given Juliet a sleeping draught. There was nothing she could do until morning, and her father had sent her to bed as if he had to be alone now.

She did not sleep very well, although for once, her dreams were not troubled with James Galt's face, and it was late before she finally woke and summoned her maid. As she was dressed, she questioned the girl about Juliet, and was relieved to hear that she had slept through the night, and seemed a little better.

Anne would not allow her maid to fuss over her hair. She insisted she only brush it quickly and tie it back with a ribbon, she was so anxious to be belowstairs.

She met her father in the upper hall. He did not look as if he had slept at all, and for the first time, Anne saw his age plainly. His face was lined with strain, and although he had been shaved and was his usual impeccable self, his pallor told the story of his night's vigil.

They ate a late breakfast together, discussing Juliet's condition in hushed tones. The doctor had left earlier, and had sent a nurse in his place.

"If only we were in town!" William Fairhaven exclaimed at last. "I know nothing about this Doctor Canfield. He might be a bumbling hack, untrained and careless! In London, I could call in the finest doctors in England."

"He seemed to be competent, father," Anne told him, putting down the muffin she found she had no appetite for. "And he did save Juliet and—and the baby last night."

Her father nodded absently, and then the butler came in with a silver salver full of cards for Anne. She waved them away, and he coughed. "Beg pardon, m'lady, there is a Sir Whitney come to call. I have told him the duchess is ill, but he insists on seeing you. He is waiting in the hall."

The duke looked blacker than ever, and Anne felt a surge of anger as well. She rose and threw down her napkin, determined to get rid of Sir Whitney once and for all.

Unfortunately for him, just that morning the tall, blond peer had decided to ask the Lady Anne to marry him, and having come to this momentous decision, he could not wait another minute. He was sorry to learn the duchess was ill, but then, he knew she had been feeling poorly for some time. When he saw Anne, his face lit up and he held out the bouquet of roses he had brought. He was admiring the sparkle in her eyes so much, he completely missed the fury on her face.

"M'lady," he said, bowing deeply.

"What are you doing here, you stupid thing?" Anne demanded. She spoke in a harsh whisper for she did not want to wake Juliet.

"What? What did you say?" a bewildered Sir Whitney asked in a loud voice, sure he must have misunderstood.

"Do be quiet! Juliet is very ill," she told him. "I cannot see you now, the house is all upset."

"Just a few minutes of your time, dear Anne," he begged, holding out the roses once again.

Anne pushed them aside so violently, some red petals drifted to the carpet. Just then, the knocker sounded, and the butler, who had been lurking at the back of the hall, came forward to open the door. Stephen Young stood there, clutching his own bouquet. When he saw Sir Whitney, he put the butler aside and exclaimed, "So! You thought to serve me a bad turn, did you, sir?"

Anne put both hands to her head as the two suitors glared at each other, and then she said coldly, "Get out of this house, both of you! I cannot attend to you right now."

"But I have come to propose to you, Anne," Sir Whitney said.

"So have I!" Mr. Young echoed, determined not to be outdone by his rival.

"If you are not outside in one minute, I shall order the footmen to put you out," Anne told them. "There is no need for you to propose. I wouldn't marry either one of you if you were the last men on earth. Insensitive clods! *Out!*"

She turned on her heel and marched away, and for a moment, her two suitors stared at her stiff back before they looked sheepishly at each other. As the butler coughed, Sir Whitney looked down at the roses he held, and then he blushed bright red, and dropped them to the hall table. Mr. Young followed suit, and in only a little over the minute Anne had given them, the butler was able to shut the door behind them.

It was not long before all Brighton knew that the Duchess of Severn was very ill. The door knocker had been muffled so the noise would not disturb her, but still it seemed to be in constant motion. Flowers and baskets of fruit and cards poured in, and even the Prince Regent sent his sympathies, and offered to call his own physician down from London if the duke felt it necessary.

To Anne fell the task of replying to all these good will offerings. She was glad to do so; she only wished there was something more she could do to help. She had seen Juliet for a few moments the first day, and although she was horrified at her pallor and the fright that lingered in her hazel eyes, she took her clue from her father. Whenever he was near his duchess, he was a tower of quiet strength, reassuring her by his calmness.

One afternoon, a few days later, as Anne was passing her room, she heard Juliet begin to cry. She paused by the door, wondering if she should go in and try and comfort her.

"I almost lost the baby, William," she sobbed. "And now I must be an invalid for so many months!"

Anne held her breath until she heard her father's voice. "My dearest wife, you must not despair. I will be with you, and all will be well, you'll see."

Anne heard the bed creak and knew he had sat down beside his weeping wife to gather her in his arms. "You must be calm and try to regain your strength and good health, Juliet," he said. "You are the most precious thing in the entire world to me."

Anne closed her eyes for a moment, and then she tiptoed away. It was wrong for her to listen to such naked emotion between two people so much in love. As she went down to the library and the letter she was writing to Melia, she wondered she had not noticed it before. But then, her father was always so formal, so contained. She had not thought a man his age could feel love, or passion, the way a younger man did. She realized she was nowhere near the grownup young lady she had imagined herself to be, and she shook her head at her naivete.

As soon as Juliet could travel, the duke made arrangements to take her to Severn House in London. Dr. Canfield told him he thought the quiet of the seaside would be better for her than the noise of town, and the fresh salt air more conducive to good health than the odors and filth of London, but the duke was adamant. He did not feel Juliet was regaining her strength as quickly as she should, and she continued to feel weak and nauseous and tired.

Anne helped him make all the arrangements to close the villa and transfer the servants and baggage and horses. She was so busy, she was not seen at any more parties and assemblies, to the chagrin of her beaux. She refused each and every invitation for a walk, a picnic, or a ride, and she was rarely at home to callers.

She did see the Earl of Burnham once. She had been hurrying up to Juliet's room herself with an eggnog the chef had prepared one afternoon, and they met in the hall.

"My dear Lady Anne," the earl said, waving the butler away. "I shall not detain you for I know how busy you are. Please convey my best wishes for a speedy recovery to the duchess. Her charming smile is much missed."

Anne stiffened, sure he had been looking at her scowl when he said that. She was cross because she was wearing her old sprigged muslin today, and had not had her maid put her hair up. With it streaming down her back under her hair band, she knew she must look about twelve years old.

As the earl turned to go, he said, "By the way, I am glad you took my advice."

"Your advice, sir?" she asked, one foot already on the bottom step.

"Discouraging those two duelists we were speaking of, I mean," he said. "Everyone has remarked the rebirth of their friendship, and since they have not been at all reticent, it is well known that you not only had the gall to refuse their offers, you did not even allow them to make them. My congratulations, ma'am!"

He grinned at her and left her, and Anne tossed her head. It had not been like that at all, but she had no time to tell him. She had more important things to do.

A week later, the Fairhavens were back in Berkeley Square. They had traveled at such a slow pace, they had had to break their journey overnight on the road, the duke was so anxious Juliet suffer no discomfort.

For a few days, Anne was still very busy. There was the house to see to, and the staff—all the things Juliet normally took care of—but eventually a routine was established, and she found she had time on her hands. It was hot and sultry in town, and most of the houses around the square were shuttered, the knockers off their doors. The duke had summoned London's finest physician to attend his wife, and Juliet was on the mend at last. She even rose every afternoon now, and took tea with them in her sitting room.

Anne busied herself riding in the park with her father and going on shopping expeditions with her maid. She went to the various museums, and she opened a subscription at a fashionable library in Bond Street. She found she was taking out as many books for herself as for Juliet, for the evenings were long and lonely. The duke had no interest now in any plays and concerts, and there was no one in town that she could go with in his place. She began to grow impatient with the quiet life she was forced to live, and her boredom increased.

She was in Hecton's Library one morning, exchanging her books, when she met a new friend. She had rounded one of the stacks and run right into a lovely little blond. As the two ladies struggled to keep their balance, Anne moved her foot and heard the ominous sound of ripping.

"I do beg your pardon, ma'am," she said, putting out a steadying hand. To her surprise, the lady laughed, seemingly not at all put out by the damage that had been done to the flounce of her smart pink walking dress.

She looked down to see it dragging on the floor, and then she said in a breathless contralto, "It was as much my fault as yours. I was hurrying and not looking where I was going. My maid can fix it in no time. Besides, I have never cared for this gown above half."

"You are very good," Anne told her, smiling back at her. "But you cannot walk about the streets dragging your flounce behind you. Please, won't you come home with me so I might have my maid repair it for you?"

Anne heard the woman behind her give a warning cough, and she knew it was not because she resented the sewing chore. The other lady seemed aware of her hidden meaning as well, for she laughed and held out her hand.

"Your maid means to warn you that you do not
know me, ma'am," she said. "Why, I might be a
number of unsuitable things . . ." She paused and
looked beyond Anne's shoulder at the disapproving
maid, and then she chuckled. "None of which I dare
mention right now! But that is soon remedied. My
name is Kitty Whittaker. My husband is an officer in
the Light Bobs."

She put her hand to one side in consideration. "Let
me see. Ah, yes! He is a younger son of Viscount Booth
of Northumberland, and he is distantly related to
Lady Jersey. There! That takes care of the proprieties,
does it not?"

She looked so smug and pleased with herself that
Anne had to laugh before she could introduce herself
in turn. It seemed only a moment before the ladies,
and a somewhat mollified maid, were seated in the
duke's town carriage being driven to Mrs. Whittaker's
house in Hanstown.

"Do say you will come home with me," Kitty Whittaker had begged. "We can have a cup of tea and a
good coze while we get to know each other. I was
feeling so blue-deviled this morning, for Gerry is on
duty this week, you know, but now my spirits have
quite revived."

Anne was delighted to do so, for she had been
feeling "blue-deviled" herself, with all the whole long
empty day stretching before her. As they neared the
Whittaker house on Eagle Street, the little blond said,
"You can see we are not in a fashionable part of town,
but you must not regard it. We decided we would
rather spend our money on more important things—
clothes, and amusements, and parties. And it is not a
bad little place after all."

Anne had never seen anything like it. A tall, narrow
building with only two rooms on each floor, it was like
a doll's house. When she was shown into the drawing
room, she stopped in surprise. There was a monkey

there, dressed in a gold coat, and over by the window, a pair of love birds in a gilded cage.

When her hostess came back, attired now in green muslin, she introduced her pets. "The love birds are Kitty and Gerry, of course," she said. "One of my husband's madcap friends gave them to us as a wedding present. And that is Lord Horatio."

At the sound of his name, the monkey leaped into her arms and wound his own skinny ones around her neck, chittering to her.

"Lord Horatio?" Anne asked, a little bewildered.

Her hostess gave her silvery laugh. "For Gerry's father, my dear. Horrid old thing! He did not like our marriage the least bit, you see. I am sorry now I burdened my dear little friend with his name, for *he* has such a nice disposition, and he loves me, don't you, Lord H?"

By the time Anne took her leave almost two hours later, she was feeling happier than she had for a long time. She had joked and laughed and talked to her new friend almost the way she used to with her twin. Kitty had begged her to come on Sunday evening when she always had open house, to meet her husband and some of their friends, and to join their party for a riding expedition and picnic early next week.

Life was very different after that. The duke, apprised of her new acquaintance, only nodded. He was glad Anne had someone to go about with, for he knew neither he nor Juliet was very good company for her at the present time. He did make some inquiries, of course, but on hearing of Captain Whittaker's respectable background and noble family, made no objections.

If he had not been so preoccupied with his duchess, he would have been more careful, but there was no way he could know that his daughter had been taken up by a set that included every rattle in a scarlet coat, more than a few rakes, and some ladies of very du-

bious reputation. And if he had inquired further, he
would have discovered that Kitty Whittaker had been
no more than an innkeeper's daughter. There was no
harm in her, but neither was there much merit. She
lived only for amusement, and the people she found
amusing were very often not those welcomed in the
forefront of society.

Anne was delighted to join her in every one of her
madcap pranks. Without Amelia to temper her behavior and prevent her wilder starts, she was soon a
popular member of the set. She had a whole new
group of admirers now, and she enjoyed them so much
more than the stuffy society beaux she had known
before.

Many evenings, she was driven to Hanstown, supposedly to a quiet family party, and then bustled out
the back way to attend a masked ball at Ranelagh,
a discreet gaming house, or a play of questionable
taste.

It was the middle of September now, and society
was trickling back to town for what was called "The
Little Season." Juliet was feeling stronger every day,
but, concerned for the child she carried, could not be
persuaded to attend any parties. The duke began to
wonder if travel to some warmer clime might not be
the answer. He knew he could send Anne to her sister
in Scotland while he took Juliet abroad. Perhaps a
change of scene, just the two of them, would help, he
thought.

If Anne had heard of his plans, she would have been
vocal in her dismay. She had no desire to go and live
with the Galts, of course, to have to see her lost love
every day, to pretend to Melia. Besides, she had met a
man at the Whittakers who was quite the most
unusual, intriguing gentleman she had ever encoun-
tered.

He was the Viscount Yates, a tall, rangy man in his
late twenties, who would have been handsome if the

pox had not marked his face. Somehow, though, even the scars could not detract from his virile appeal, for he had brilliant red hair, and blue eyes that seemed very knowing and devil-may-care. To Anne, he was the epitome of sophistication, and she was proud of her ability to attract him. There was something dangerous about him that she found impossible to ignore. Kitty Whittaker had made a half-hearted effort to warn her, but when Anne only laughed at her tales of the heartbroken ladies he had loved and left, the duels and gambling debts, and the exile imposed by his family, she had shrugged her round, white shoulders and continued on her merry way.

Cary Holden had no intention of marrying Anne, but he did his best, which was very good indeed, to interest her in an affair. Anne would have none of it, and seriously angered him by telling him that for a Fairhaven of Severn, such behavior was completely unacceptable, leaving him with the impression that although the lady enjoyed their light flirtation, she was, after all, only slumming. He called her his Cruel Fair, and continued to implore her to be kind to him. Anne took great care to remain with the group, and she never allowed him more than a stolen kiss when she could not find a way to avoid it.

She had been to the theater with him and the Whittakers one evening, and as they waited outside for their carriage, she remarked, "The soprano was truly dreadful tonight, wasn't she? I am surprised she was engaged, when she has so little voice."

"But she has—er—other charms, that more than make up for her lack of musical ability," Lord Yates pointed out.

The Whittakers laughed uproariously, for the lady had been very voluptuous, but Anne ignored the jest. "I could perform better than she did," she told them.

"Then why don't you, my Cruel Fair?" Yates suggested idly.

The rake, although he had a very real physical attraction for Anne Fairhaven, cared for her no more than he had for any of the other ladies he had known. He knew it would ruin her socially if she even appeared on the stage, but he did not care. Perhaps if the arrogant lady were to become an outcast, he would have more luck enticing her into his bed, he thought. More than most men, Viscount Yates disliked playing a losing hand. He began to discuss the possibility of Anne's triumphant assault on the London stage.

"What a lark it would be!" Kitty Whittaker said in her breathless way.

"It will be no trouble at all to fill the house with scarlet coats, m'lady," her husband promised. "You know how they would cheer you!"

"But I don't quite see how it can be managed," Anne said, with a little frown. "I would have to be incognito, of course."

"Naturally you would wear a mask, perhaps a wig," m'lord pointed out.

Anne thought hard, but at last she shook her head. "No, I see it would be impossible, and just the sort of thing to set up everyone's backs. And my father— well! He would probably send me back to the country, and I would never be able to leave Severn again."

"But no one would know for sure, my dear," the viscount whispered, taking up her hand and pressing it. "Can it be that you are afraid of the gossiping of a few stuffy dowagers? Why, I thought you were ripe for every rig in town!"

The carriage had arrived in Berkeley Square then, and she was not required to try and answer him. Calling out her good nights, Anne ran up the steps of Severn House.

It was a long time before she got to sleep that night. Every time she closed her eyes, she seemed to see a picture of herself on center stage, smiling as she accepted the applause and cheers of a packed house as they threw flowers and clamored for another encore from the talented, mysterious performer all London was flocking to see.

X

The Earl of Burnham arrived back in town a few days later. The Little Season was in full swing, and he was surprised when he did not see Lady Anne Fairhaven at any of the festivities. He made a few discreet inquiries, and discovered that although the Fairhavens were in residence, the duchess was still living secluded and the duke was seldom seen.

He thought perhaps the young lady he was so anxious to see might be traveling, until he chanced to meet Percival Collingwood one morning at Brooks's.

"It is the strangest thing, m'lord," the freckle-faced young peer complained. "I went to call several times, but she was never at home. And when I found out her stepmama was still unwell, I had m'mother write and beg the honor of chaperoning Lady Anne herself to some of the more festive occasions."

He fell silent, his good-natured face set in discontented lines, and the earl prodded gently, "Yes, and she replied . . . ?"

"She thanked my mother for her kindness, but she said she was not interested in any parties. Lady Anne! Not interested in parties? Did you ever hear of such a thing?"

"It does sound most unlike her," the earl murmured, his gray eyes intent.

After he left Brooks's, he went to Berkeley Square. He decided he would call on the duchess to ask how

154

she did, and he would try to get further news of Lady Anne. But as he entered the Square, he saw a dashing perch phaeton pull up before the Fairhaven town-house, and a young soldier run around to lift the Lady Anne down. The earl leaned against the palings of a house four doors away, and watched the young man say something, still holding the Lady Anne high above the cobbles. He heard her gay laugh, and saw the way she shook her head until her escort was forced to set her on her feet.

The earl decided to call another day.

That afternoon, he was stunned when he saw Lady Anne in Hyde Park. She was walking with a couple he did not know, a captain in the Light Bobs who had a luscious little blond clinging to his arm. His eyes went to her own escort, and he drew in a startled breath. Where in the name of heaven had Anne Fairhaven ever met Viscount Yates?

The earl's face grew grim as he watched them stroll along. It was a merry party, and it was obvious to anyone that Lady Anne was very much the life of it. She appeared to be on excellent terms with Yates, not objecting to the tight way he was holding her close to his side, nor the intimacy with which he leaned over to whisper in her ear.

Viscount Yates was not unknown to the earl. He was one of the wildest, most dissolute men in London, and there were no hostesses who cared anything at all for their reputations who would include him in their parties. He was a gambler, a rake, and, some said, no better than a murderer. The earl recalled several unsavory episodes from the man's past, and his lips tightened.

It was obvious that in his distress over his wife's health, the Duke of Severn had loosened the leading reins where his daughter was concerned. Hugh Moreley would be willing to wager anything you liked that he had no idea of the company Anne was keeping.

He walked along behind the foursome, and

somehow was not surprised when he saw them hailed by the notorious courtesan Harriet Wilson and her latest protector.

The earl took another path than that led to the Stanhope Gate. He needed some time alone to think how best he was to handle this situation before it became too late. Knowing Yates as he did, he was sure there was scandal brewing.

In the days that followed, he made arrangements with a private agent to have the Lady Anne Fairhaven followed, and it was not very long before he discovered the little house in Hanstown, and all her current friends and activities. As he flipped through the agent's report, his lips tightened. She had attended a public ball, masked to be sure, as if that were any protection against the opportunings of drunken commoners and wild young lords out on a spree, she had visited a gambling house in Euston Street where he knew the stakes were high and the play suspect, and she had also gone three times to the theater. What was so unusual about this last item, was that it was to the same theater, and the same performance, every time. The earl made a note to attend that evening, to see what could possibly be so fascinating about a musical farce entitled "What the Young Lord Did."

The farce was not very good, although it was attracting sizable crowds, mostly of the male sex. The earl understood why when he saw the voluptuous soprano, billed as The Golden Nightingale, in her flimsy, extremely low-cut gowns. As he left the theater, and pushed his way through the crowds, he decided that if any nightingale in his vicinity sang as badly as Miss Clorinda Carstairs did, he would have shot it on the spot, to put it out of its misery.

And then he stopped dead. No! Anne could not be contemplating *that*, not seriously, could she? A man jostled his arm, and he began to walk again. Knowing Anne Fairhaven as he did, he had to admit it was entirely possible. And why else would she have subjected herself to three evenings so tedious, so full of sly sexual inuendoes and bad singing? It was not at all her style, unless she really were planning to take over the lead role.

It seemed such a mad idea, he was still not entirely persuaded that this was what she had in mind, and so he went the next morning to call in Berkeley Square.

The duchess received him in the morning room, explaining that Anne was using the drawing room for vocal practice. Faintly, the earl could hear her playing and singing, but he could not be sure that the piece she was working on was from the farce he had heard the evening before. He put her from his mind as he inquired after the duchess's health, and said how delighted he was to see her looking so well. Secretly, he was appalled at the violet shadows under her eyes, and her thinness, even though she smiled and chatted with her usual pleasant manners.

"Yes, I am quite recovered now, thank you, m'lord," she said. "And a good thing, too, for Melia and her husband are coming from Scotland to spend Christmas at Severn with us, and all the boys will be home."

"Lady Anne must be delighted that she will have her twin with her once again, your Grace," he remarked.

He thought the duchess looked a little troubled, but she only nodded as she agreed. "It has been hard on her, for they were so very close," she explained. "I do not think I will ever forget her face when she discovered Melia was in love with Mr. Galt. I thought she would faint, she was so shocked. But she seems to have grown accustomed, and she is very busy these days."

Indeed she is, your Grace, the earl thought grimly to himself. For a moment, he toyed with the idea of telling Juliet Fairhaven what he had learned about her stepdaughter, and enlisting her aid in separating Anne from her undesirable acquaintances, but she seemed so fragile in her early pregnancy that he did not like to add to her troubles.

As he took his leave of her, he wondered if there were any sense in going to the duke instead. It was what he should do, of course, but he knew it would put paid to any chance of his marrying Anne some day. She would have nothing to do with a tattle-monger who had gone behind her back and interfered in her life. No, he must watch her from afar, ready to step in if things got out of hand, hoping all the while that she would see the light and realize her mistake herself.

Two evenings later, Anne came face to face with the earl. She was standing by the E.O. table in Mrs. Lowry's gambling establishment, a little pile of *rouleaus* beside her, and she was accompanied by the same threesome he had seen her with in the park.

Her face flushed a little as he bowed, for he looked so surprised and disdainful to see her in this place. Anne tilted her chin and introduced him to her companions. For some reason, she wished Kitty had not worn that fussy puce silk and those large ostrich feathers in her coiffure, and that Captain Whittaker did not look so rakish. When Viscount Yates put his arm around her, she gave him a darkling look and moved away.

"I am acquainted with the viscount," the earl told her as she presented him. Anne was sure she heard disapproval in his quiet voice.

"Not that we ever seem to come in each other's way, eh, Burnham?" the viscount asked rudely as he put down another bet. His sneer was very pronounced. Then he turned to Anne and said, "Do you bet the red again, Cruel Fair? It cannot lose all night, you know."

"Of course," Anne said brightly, putting down her bet. Mrs. Lowry beamed at them, and spun the wheel. The ball landed in the black.

"Lady Anne should not lose, terrible thing to see one o'her beauty on the outs," another gambler, somewhat the worse for claret declared. He raised his glass to her and smiled, his eyes bleary. "Here's to you, fair lady, and to better luck next time!"

He lurched toward her then and, tripping, spilled his wine down the front of her primrose gown. Anne jumped back, frowning.

"Now look what you've done, Reggie, you clumsy thing!" she exclaimed. The captain handed her his handkerchief and she began to try and repair the damage as Reggie offered profuse, muddled apologies. Kitty Whittaker was rummaging through her reticule, and at last she came up with a tiny square. "Here, my dear, take mine, too," she said, and then she joined in the general hilarity, for of what possible use two square inches of cambric and lace would be, it was hard to see. The viscount took out his own handkerchief and began to assist her, his hand very close to her bosom, and the earl had had enough.

"If you would allow me to see you home, Lady Anne," he said, coming to take her arm. "You cannot remain here with your gown ruined, and I was thinking of leaving myself. Somehow the tables are not very enticing tonight."

Anne flushed and pushed the viscount's hand away. She wanted to refuse, but there was something in the earl's eye, some little cold flash of steel, that told her it would be most unwise.

Before she could say anything, the viscount spoke up. "Very good of you, Burnham, but I will take the lady home."

"Oh, I would not think of troubling you, dear fellow," the earl replied. "Berkeley Square is very near my house on Charles Street, but for you, it would be quite out of the way. If I remember, your rooms are not in Mayfair, are they?"

The viscount shook his head, looking grim.

"Shall we, m'lady?" the earl asked, and then he nodded to the others and led her from the room.

"Don't forget our appointment tomorrow, Cruel Fair!" the viscount called after her.

When they were seated in his carriage, the earl still had not said a word to her. Stung, Anne said, "I suppose you are going to lecture me, are you not, m'lord? Well, I don't know what business it is of yours!"

"I would not dream of it, Anne," he said, to her surprise. "As you so *nicely* put it, it is none of my business. Not yet, at any rate."

"And it never will be," she told him, turning to look out at the streets they were passing through.

The earl smiled, but he had no further comment. They rode in silence until the duke's townhouse was reached, and then as he helped her down from the carriage, he held her arm for a moment. Anne looked up into his handsome face, now cold and stern once again.

"I suppose it would be no use to suggest to you that your current companions are not worthy of you, Lady Anne? That it would be more appropriate for you to return to your correct *milieu* in the *ton*? That you are treading on very dangerous ground here that could well lead you into disaster, and cause those who love you to suffer a great deal of pain and disappointment?"

He saw the determined look in her eye, and shook his head. "I was afraid you would not agree. However, whether it is my concern or not, you may be sure I shall be swift to act, m'lady, if I discover you have decided to do something definitely *outré*. Remember I told you so, and be warned."

Anne tossed her head, and then she took a deep breath. In the soft light of the oil lamps, she looked very lovely, even in her stained gown. To his surprise, she curtsied without a word of argument, and bade him a civil, if chilly, good night.

The earl was not the only one to notice Lady Anne Fairhaven's new set of companions, and a few whispers began to circulate. Unfortunately, Juliet did not hear them, and the young men who were whispering were not likely to be honored by a conversation with the duke. The earl waited, secure in the knowledge that with his agents watching her, he would be quick to learn when she finally stepped over the line that marked the difference between good taste and bad.

He had a moment of hope when he learned she had lost her voucher to Almack's. It seemed the Lady Anne had not been able to resist mimicing Mrs. Drummond Burrell one afternoon as she walked in the park, and although her audience had found her hilarious, the lady herself was not amused. The earl managed to ask the duke about it the next day, and William Fairhaven frowned and shook his head.

"It is typical of Anne, m'lord," he said. "You may be sure I scolded her for it. It does no good to get people's backs up that way, and although I, myself, consider Mrs. Drummond Burrell a haughty bore, puffed up with her own conceit, and care nothing for her opinion, it is not for a young girl barely out to be so bold. Anne has apologized to me and to Juliet; I have every expectation that we will see no more public theatricals."

The earl sincerely hoped he was right, but he would not have wagered a ha-penny on it. He would not even have wagered that when he learned from his agent that Lady Anne Fairhaven, in company with the Viscount Yates, had made a call on the management of the Abbot Theatre in Piccadilly. The earl ordered his carriage then, and made his own call at the same establishment.

It was unlikely that the manager, Mr. Theodore Bodkins, had ever been honored by so many of the nobility in one day before. But where he had been smiling and rubbing his hands together at the thought of future profit as he bowed Lady Anne Fairhaven and her escort from his office, he was nowhere near as pleased when the Earl of Burnham left him.

"I believe you had a young lady here this morning,

sir," the earl said, as soon as he had introduced himself.

Mr. Bodkins begged him to take a seat, but eyeing the faded velvet that looked none too clean, the earl refused.

"In the theatrical world, I see many young ladies, m'lord," Mr. Bodkins said, trying to keep the upper hand.

"This lady's name is not important. Suffice it to say, she is the daughter of a duke. A very proud duke, moreover, who would take it very seriously if his daughter were ever to—er—grace your boards," the earl told him, his face grim.

"Indeed?" Mr. Bodkins asked, brushing a suddenly perspiring hand over the few greasy strands of hair that still adorned his gleaming head. "But why was she here then, auditioning for the part? And what concern is it of yours, m'lord?"

"It is nothing but a madcap prank, which I, as the duke's emissary, intend to stop. As for the rest of your inquiry, I intend to marry the young lady; what she does is very much my concern."

Mr. Bodkins began to extend his best wishes, but the stern, implacable expression of his visitor's handsome, haughty face made him sputter into silence.

"Come, come, my good man! When was the lady to perform? Under what name, and for what renumeration?"

Mr. Bodkins stopped dissimulating, and gave him the answers he sought. The earl curled his lips when he heard the sum he had promised to pay The Bird of Paradise.

"She insisted on wearing a red wig and a mask, m'lord, and she said she did not want me bruiting it about that she was a member of the nobility," the manager whined, hoping the earl might still relent. "And as she was leaving, I heard her tell that there viscount she was with that he would owe her their wager now."

"I shall be glad to reimburse you the sum you were to pay her, sir," the earl told him. Mr. Bodkins brightened a little. Of course, it would in no way repay him for the money that would have poured in, night after night. He had heard the lady sing, and her voice was as outstanding as her beauty. He had had no intention of keeping her family background a secret. He knew Londoners would pay, and pay well, for the privilege of applauding a duke's daughter. It really isn't fair, he thought, barely hearing the earl's suggestion that he engage another red-headed performer to take the lady's place.

"Were there to be rehearsals?" the earl asked next.

"Yes, starting tomorrow. The lady told me she was a quick study, so she was only to rehearse four days. The performance was set for Friday evening."

The earl thought for a moment, caressing his chin. "Let her have her rehearsals," he said. "In fact, I do not want her to know she is not to be the star until the night of the performance. Can this be done without her knowing it?"

Mr. Bodkins waved his fat little hands. "Of course, m'lord, but you are asking me to pay the musicians, the stage hands, the dressers, for nothing. I cannot do it, it will ruin me."

"Send the reckoning to me this afternoon, and I shall see you are none the worse for it," the generous earl announced. Mr. Bodkins knew the man must be besotted with the lady to take on such an expense. "I suggest you engage someone who can step in at the last moment," the earl continued. "Otherwise you will have a howling mob on your hands when you cannot produce your Bird of Paradise, sir."

"Aye," Mr. Bodkins agreed, wiping his brow. "I'll keep Clorinda on, as understudy, like. If she wears the red wig, perhaps it won't be known who she is."

The earl bowed slightly, sternly repressing his comment that the lady in question would only have to sing two notes before the oranges and tomatoes began to fly.

When Anne had finally agreed to go on the stage, her friends had applauded her daring, and made so much of her that she began to feel very adventuresome. After all, as the viscount had promised over and over again, no one would know it was she. He went with her to select the bright red wig she would wear, the headdress made up of multicolored feathers, and the golden half mask.

But when she finally appeared at the theater, she began to have serious doubts about the wisdom of what she had agreed to do. It was all so different from this side of the footlights, common and tawdry and dirty. The other performers were unlike any people she had ever met in her life, and they were unkind to her. Clorinda Carstairs was rude. Anne ignored her, as she did the members of the chorus who looked her up and down with so much animosity. She was shocked when she saw the dressing room all the women used, for it was separated from the men's side by only a ragged curtain. Before and after rehearsals, there were a great many ribald comments called back and forth, some of which were so explicit, they made her blush.

She was also horrified when she saw the gown—if you could call it that—that Mr. Bodkins said she must wear. It barely covered her breasts, and it was so flimsy, she was sure you could see right through it under the stage lights. Anne refused in a cold voice, to the hilarity of the others.

"Coo-er!" Miss Maisie Fetherington, the second lead, exclaimed, striking a pose with her nose in the air. "Wot a thing it is to be one of the *haut ton*, woi, it makes one downright above the rest o' us poor mortals, now don't it?"

Mr. Bodkins took the rejected gown away, shaking

his head. It was replaced by one only a little more modest.

Once Anne was on stage, things were a little better, although she could not care for the leers she received from the bass, or the tenor's bad breath washing over her when he held her clutched in his arms. It was certainly a world removed from the Prince Regent's Music Room in the Pavilion.

By the day of the performance, Anne was praying she would get laryngitis, or perhaps come down with a severe case of influenza. But she had no such good fortune, and having set this all in motion of her own free will, she knew she must see it through to the end.

She had no idea that Viscount Yates had been very busy in the interim, getting the word about that the Lady Anne Fairhaven of Severn was to take the leading role Friday evening in "What the Young Lord Did." Mr. Bodkins had been sold out for two days, and he could have sold a hundred more tickets, if he had them. He groaned at the money he was going to lose.

Anne drove to the theater early that evening, accompanied by Kitty Whittaker, who was to act as her dresser. She hoped to be in costume and made up before the rest of the cast came in to tease and taunt her.

Kitty was bouncing on the seat of the carriage in her excitement, and talking nonstop about what a wonderful lark the whole thing was. Anne wondered she had never notice what a chatterbox Kitty was, and some of her suggestions for Anne's future made her frown.

"Why, that Harriet Wilson won't have a thing on you, my dear," she said, her blue eyes sparkling. "You can pick and choose any man in the *ton* you want, after tonight."

Glumly, Anne remembered that she had always been able to do that, and without making such a spectacle of herself, as the carriage halted in the alley near the stage door.

Kitty climbed down first, still chattering, and as Anne followed her, she was startled to find herself swung up into a man's arms and carried briskly away. She looked up into Hugh Moreley's blazing gray eyes and realized she had never been so glad to see anyone in her entire life.

"Here now!" Kitty called, running after them. "What on earth do you think you're doing?"

The Earl of Burnham whirled and glared at her, and she skidded to a halt. "I am removing Lady Anne from this very inappropriate location, Mrs. Whittaker," he said. "I suggest you remove yourself as well. Go home and try to learn some common sense!"

Anne found herself deposited in the earl's carriage, and before she could think of escape, he had climbed in beside her and grasped her arm, and the carriage drove away.

"But I must perform, m'lord," she said when she had caught her breath. "I promised! I must keep my promise!"

The earl folded his arms across his chest. Staring straight ahead, he said, "That has all been taken care of, m'lady. Mr. Bodkins does not expect you this evening. Miss Carstairs will become The Bird of Paradise tonight, or at least she will be until she is booed from the stage."

"You did this!" Anne said, her voice shaking a little. "How dare you interfere in my life?"

"Be quiet!" the earl ordered. "We will discuss this later!"

Anne heard the anger in his rough voice and noticed the white lines around his mouth and the way a small muscle twitched there for a moment, and she made herself very small and quiet on her side of the carriage. They rode in silence until the earl's townhouse in Charles Street had been reached.

As the groom opened the door, he grasped her arm again, and made her follow him down the steps and up to the front door. As his butler opened it, he thrust her inside.

"See that we are not disturbed, Cawley," he ordered, still grasping her arm, and then he marched her to the library and shut the door firmly behind them.

Anne had never realized what a strong man Hugh Moreley was, and when she saw his angry face, she moved away from him, rubbing her arm.

"Why have you brought me here, m'lord?" she began with a hint of her old arrogance. "You know it would ruin my reputation if—"

He barked a harsh laugh. "Your reputation, m'lady? *You* prate to me about your reputation?" He started toward her, and then he checked, making a visible effort to control himself. "For your information, I have brought you here until it is too late for you to return to the theater and your—er—your performance," he told her.

"How . . . how did you find out?" she whispered, cringing at the scorn she had heard in his voice. She wondered why knowing she had lost his good opinion could upset her so much.

The earl went and poured them both a glass of wine. As he handed it to her, he said, "I can assure you it is common knowledge all over town. Your friends— the Viscount Yates in particular—have been very busy."

Anne put her wine down untasted. "No, no, that cannot be! They knew I was to perform incognito, wearing a mask and a wig. It must have been that greasy Mr. Bodkins, or that horrible Clorinda Carstairs who bruited it about."

Hugh Moreley gave another bitter laugh. "How naive you are, m'lady, how grass green! Did you really think your 'friends' could keep this to themselves?

Why, it is the jest of the century, an *on-dit* to be chewed over for years! I told you before they are not very nice people, but you did not believe me."

"You are wrong, you must be! They *are* my friends, bright and amusing, and full of fun," she said.

"Even though they encouraged you to do something they knew would ruin you? Something you would never live down until your dying day? You have an odd conception of friendship, m'lady."

"But no one was to know, they promised! You must be wrong!" she exclaimed.

"Am I? Then why is there a sizable wager down in the betting book at White's laying five to one odds that the Lady A.F. will perform this evening? The wager was made by Viscount Yates, m'lady," he told her.

Anne gasped and covered her face with her hands. The earl waited for the flood of tears he was sure would come, but Anne surprised him. In only a moment or so, she lowered her hands and faced him proudly, her shoulders squared. He knew the effort it cost her, for her blue eyes were huge in her white face, and he wanted to go to her and take her in his arms, to comfort her.

"So, you were right, and I was wrong, m'lord," she said in a voice that barely quivered. "I must beg your pardon."

"Drink your wine, Anne," he said, his voice kind now. As she picked up her glass again, he suddenly remembered something. "I believe *you* have a wager with the viscount too, do you not?"

"Do you know everything?" she asked, with some of her old snap.

He smiled, and then he leaned against the large center table. "Where you are concerned, my dear Anne, I could wish I were infallible indeed. Suffice it to say, I know enough. I have made it my business to know—and you know why."

Her chin came up at that, and he added, "May I suggest you write to the viscount when you pay your wager, and tell him you never had any intention of performing, that it was all a hoax on him? And when the story gets out, as it will, of course, you can laugh at the very idea of the Duke of Severn's daughter ever doing such a thing. I shall do all I can to help you."

"But why should you . . ." she began, and then she flushed and lowered her eyes to her glass.

"Exactly," he said wryly. For a moment they stared at each other, and it was Anne Fairhaven who looked away first.

As soon as she had finished her wine, he suggested that he take her home.

She saw him looking at the Cartel clock on the mantel, and she rose and said quietly, "There is no need for your concern, m'lord. I have no intention of returning to the theater. Not now, not after what I have learned."

"Do you wish me to call for the carriage, or will you walk, m'lady?" he asked as they went to the door.

Anne said she would be glad to walk the short distance to the square, and he nodded, taking her arm.

He looked down at her as they headed in that direction, and he saw the little frown she wore. She was biting her lip, and he said, "Yes, I must tell your father. He will hear about it soon enough, you know. I shall try to temper it."

She nodded. "I realize there is no way of keeping it from him, or from Juliet either, but I wish it did not have to be. Not for my sake," she added quickly, as if she thought he might think her afraid, "but for theirs."

The earl let his eyes linger on her profile for a moment, thinking what a valiant woman she was. And then he reminded himself she was also impulsive, maddening, hot to hand, and arrogant to boot, lest he become maudlin.

The duke was not at home when they arrived, so the earl asked for the duchess. When he learned she was in the drawing room, he told Anne to go to her room.

"There is no need for you to be present, m'lady," he

assured her when he saw the doubt in her eyes. "I am sure her Grace will come up to you shortly, and you can make your own explanations, but I must insist on a few minutes alone with her first."

Anne wanted to object, but the stern look was back on his face, and she nodded. "Thank you, m'lord," she said, holding out her hand. "You have been a good friend to all the Fairhavens this evening."

The earl kissed her hand, and then he followed the butler to the drawing room. Anne went up the stairs, her head high.

He tried to make the story he told Juliet less horrifying than it really was, but by the time he had finished, her face was white with shock. To his surprise and chagrin, she burst into tears.

"M'lady!" he said, considerably startled, "I did not mean . . . I would never have told you . . ."

"My fault, all my fault," she moaned from behind her handkerchief.

The earl let her cry for a moment, and then he came and sat down beside her. "Why is it your fault, m'lady?" he asked. "It was, after all, Anne's doing, her impulsiveness that caused the debacle."

The duchess shook her head, and then she wiped her eyes. "No, it must be laid to my door, m'lord. You see, if I had not been so preoccupied, if I had not indulged myself because I—I was with child, I would have seen what Anne was up to. I would have noticed her new friends and activities, and I could have stopped her. I have been self-centered, and it is especially bad because I know Anne so well, know the kind of trouble she can get into. I have let her down—and William, too—most lamentably."

The earl took one of her hands and patted it. "My dear lady, do not refine on it too much," he said. "But now I must beg a favor of you, if I may."

"Of course," she said. "There is no way we can ever thank you for putting an end to all this before it became a disaster. You have only to ask."

"Then I would like to ask that you do not mention anything about what I have told you to the duke this evening. Not until I have had a chance to see him tomorrow."

He saw she was looking puzzled, and not too pleased, and he pressed her hand. "Please, m'lady. I have a very good reason for this request."

At last she nodded, and he rose and bowed to her. "Anne is waiting to see you, m'lady. She is very contrite. For the Lady Anne, that is," he added sharply, and he was glad to see a little smile on her lips.

He paused at the door. "Perhaps you would be so good as to tell the duke I will be here at ten in the morning. And if my visit could be kept from Lady Anne, I would appreciate it."

Although she did not understand him, she agreed, and he took his leave.

XI

When the earl arrived the following morning, Severn House was very quiet. As he handed his hat and gloves to the melancholy butler, Hugh Moreley wondered at it. It was almost as if no one was at home.

The butler interrupted his musings, saying in mournful accents that the duke was waiting for him in the library. As the earl followed him there, his brows rose a little. Was it possible the man knew? And then he reminded himself how difficult it was to keep anything from the servants.

The butler announced him, and withdrew, closing the doors behind him. The earl moved toward the desk where the Duke of Severn was sitting. One glance at his harsh face, the anger that burned in his dark eyes, and he knew the butler was not the only one who had learned the truth. He was disappointed, but he made himself bow.

"Thank you for receiving me, duke," he said. "I can see you have been apprised of the situation."

The duke nodded as he got up and came around the desk to offer his hand. "I cannot thank you enough for what you did, m'lord," he said, his voice stiff as the two shook hands.

The earl made a careless gesture. "It was my pleasure, sir, you may be sure," he said easily.

When he had been seated and was sipping a glass of sherry, he said, "I had hoped to tell you about it myself, but of course I see now, that as distraught as she was, the duchess could not restrain herself."

"Juliet did not tell me, m'lord. Anne did," the duke said.

The earl paused, his glass halfway to his lips. "Anne?" he asked.

"She waited up for me last night to make her confession," William Fairhaven told him. Seeing his guest's surprise, he explained, "Whatever else can be said about Anne—and I can think if a number of uncomplimentary things this morning—she is not a coward. She felt it was her place to tell me herself."

He paused for a moment, and then he said, his voice harsh again, "I have never been so close to whipping her, and believe me, there have been many occasions in the past when I longed to do so. She has always been willful, careless, and improvident."

"She is a very young woman," the earl reminded him.

The duke ignored him. "When I think of what she was planning to do, the shame it would have brought to our name, I cannot understand why she ever agreed to it in the first place," he said. "Of all my children, I would have said Anne understood best what I expected of the Fairhavens. She is so proud."

"Yes, but if I may . . . ?" the earl asked. He waited until the duke nodded his permission, and then he said, "I believe it was her arrogance that led her into this trouble. She thought herself infallible, you see, for if Lady Anne Fairhaven decided something was all right, naturally the world must agree with her. She really believed that because she is who she is, she could do anything. That is arrogance indeed." As the duke looked bleak, the added, "She will outgrow it eventually, sir."

"One hopes we will all be able to avoid social ostracism until that happy day," the duke snapped.

"What are your plans for her, your grace?" the earl asked next.

"To be truthful, I am somewhat confused about the course I should take," the duke admitted. "Even before this happened, I intended to take the duchess abroad, and I had thought to send Anne on a visit to her sister. Of course I could confine her at Severn. I have a cousin I know I can persuade to go with her as watchdog. I am only sure of one thing. Anne will not appear in London again for a very long time."

The earl crossed one well breeched leg over the other. "I hope I can change your mind about that, duke, and solve all your problems as well. You see, I am here to ask your permission to address Anne."

William Fairhaven's black brows soared. "You want to marry her? Now, after what has happened?" he asked, as if he thought the earl had gone mad.

"Yes, I do," Hugh Moreley said, holding his eyes. "I have wanted to marry her for a very long time, but I did not speak of it because the time was not right."

"And you think it is right now?" the duke asked. "Now, when all London is talking about her, reviling her?"

"I am no more concerned about 'all London' than you are, sir," the earl said firmly. "And I cannot conceive a better time. No matter how much talk there is, she did not appear on that stage, after all. And when our engagement is announced, that news will still any malicious tongues most effectively."

The duke stared at him. "Of course, I see the truth of what you say. But I must ask you, does Anne know your intentions? Does she care for you?"

"She knows that I want to marry her someday," the earl replied. "She does not care for me that way— yet. But there is something between us even so."

The duke was frowning again. "But I cannot like a match for my daughter, no matter how advantageous it is, where there is no love, m'lord."

For the first time, a slight flush stained the earl's cheekbones. "You may be assured there is a great deal of love, your Grace. It may be one-sided at the moment, but I have great hopes of changing that."

The duke rose to stride the room, and the earl rose as well, his gray eyes intent. He held his breath.

At last the duke turned to stare at him, his black eyes boring into his face as if to see into his heart and soul. The earl did not look away. "Very well," William Fairhaven said finally. "I know you for a good man, and certainly it would be a fine match I would have to approve. I will give you permission to speak to Anne. But if she refuses you, I will not pressure her, nor must you. Do you agree, sir?"

The earl nodded, his throat tight. "Certainly, your Grace."

"I shall send her to you now," the duke said, walking to the door. And then he paused and turned, one black brow quirked. "Now why do I have the lingering feeling that in doing so, I am serving you a very bad turn, m'lord? And after all you have done for us, too. It is too bad."

The earl smiled at him, and he shook his head and left the room.

Lady Anne came into the library only a few minutes later. She was wearing a gay blue muslin gown, and her hair had been arranged in charming curls, but still she was subdued, and she did not look as if she had slept very well.

"M'lord," she said as she curtsied. "You wished to see me?"

He took her hand and drew her to her feet, his gray eyes searching her face. Anne wondered why he looked so serious, so stern, and what he and her father had just been discussing. And then he raised her hand and kissed it. Once again, Anne felt those little tremors inside, and she made herself stand very still.

"Your father has given me permission to speak to you, Lady Anne," Hugh Moreley began, and her heart jumped.

"To speak to me?" she asked in a wondering tone.

"Come, come, m'lady, this can come as no great surprise," he said, in much his old manner. "After all, I did tell you I intended to ask you to marry me someday. That day has arrived."

"After last night, I am surprised you still want to do so, sir," she said, turning away from him a little.

"No doubt it is very foolish of me," he agreed, his voice cordial.

She looked at him suspiciously, to see a little smile curling his lips. He put his hands on her arms, and then he said, his deep voice warm, "I do care for you, Anne. You need not fear that I ask you because of some noble desire to save you from social disaster. I am not so chivalrous as that!"

His hands tightened for a moment on her bare skin, and then they moved in a soft caress. Anne looked at him, and when she saw the light burning in his eyes, she lowered her own, totally confused.

"Perhaps you would like some time to consider my proposal, m'lady?" he asked politely. "I shall be glad to wait outside."

"No!" she exclaimed, for she had just had a sudden vision of James Galt's face, and she was remembering how he had pulled her into his arms and kissed her with such intense hunger, the passionate words of his proposal when he thought she was Amelia. "No, I will not marry you, m'lord," she said in a firm little voice.

The earl stepped away from her. "Then what will you do?" he asked in a normal tone.

She looked perplexed, for she had not expected such a calm reaction to her refusal. He sounded as if she had just denied him a dance, or his escort on a drive, instead of the marriage he claimed he wanted. "I do not understand what you mean, sir," she said.

"I had a long talk with your father this morning, Anne," he said. "He is very displeased with you."

Anne twisted her hands together. "I know," she

said. "So is Juliet. I knew they would be. I . . . I am sorry for it."

"Sorry for it you may be, my girl, but that will not appease your father. He intends to take his duchess abroad for her health, so he is planning to incarcerate you at Severn with some guardian cousin as watchdog. You will not be permitted to set foot in London again for months, perhaps years." The earl paused, and then he added, "Or he may send you to your twin and her husband in Scotland. I doubt you would care to reside there in the company of a bridegroom who was wishing you at the devil most of the time."

Anne turned away to hide the pain in her eyes. Yes, she knew all too well why James Galt would not want her in his house, she could never go there. And when she thought of being buried at Severn, with only Cousin Martha to keep her company, she did not see how she was to stand it. She had always disliked the lady, with her cold formality and disapproving sniffs. Anything would be better than that!

"But if you accept my proposal, m'lady, neither of those horrid fates would await you," the earl continued calmly.

"I do not love you, m'lord," Anne said, determined to be honest.

Hugh Moreley moved closer and watched her where she stood with her hands clasped before her, her eyes troubled.

"Not at the moment," he agreed.

Anne took a deep breath. "If you are thinking that some day I will come to do so, I must tell you I never shall. There is a reason why I—I cannot love you."

The earl waited, but he was to be disappointed, for she compressed her lips, as if in saying more she would reveal a desperate secret.

"I shall take my chances on that, my foolish lady," he teased her, and then he tilted her chin so she was forced to look at him. "I love you quite enough for both of us," he told her, putting his arms around her to draw her close. Anne stared up at him, her blue eyes wide, as he bent his head to kiss her.

The reluctance, almost aversion, he saw in her eyes, stopped him. For a moment, he remained only a few inches away, and then he straightened and let her go. Anne moved away from him, her breath coming fast and her heart pounding. He took her hand, clasping it in his own warm one as he said, "It will be all right, my dear. My word on it." His deep voice was even, and so kind, she felt herself relaxing. "Know that I shall love and cherish you always. And instead of months of unhappiness, you will soon come to see how happy I intend to make you."

Anne felt as if she were in the midst of a bad dream. How could he still want her after she had told him she did not love him? That she never could? And even if he did still want her, for some reason she could not understand, she knew she must not accept him. It was not fair to him, for he was such a good, true, honorable man. He deserved better.

"I cannot," she whispered. "I like you too much to disappoint you."

He tilted her face again, but he did not try to hold her, and she was grateful. "I will not be disappointed, my dear, and I cannot tell you how much it buoys my spirits to hear you say you like me."

They stood quietly together for a long moment, his gray eyes burning into hers as if to convince her by his very intensity. "Say yes, Anne," he ordered. "Say yes."

Anne moved away from him and lifted her chin. "All right," she said in the voice of one hard pressed. "Since you want it so badly, m'lord, I guess I might as well."

An unholy amusement gleamed in his eyes for a second, and then he threw back his head and laughed. "I am sure no man has ever been more graciously accepted," he told her when he could speak again. "Do not change, Anne. I don't think I could bear it if suddenly you became all meek and mild and conventional."

He reached out then and took her hand again. "There is one thing, however, that we must have straight between us," he said in a serious voice. "Understand I am not offering you a marriage of convenience, Anne. I will have my heir—in fact, I would like several children. If you do not feel you can accept that part of our marriage, tell me now, and I will not hold you to your agreement."

"Of course. I understand, m'lord," she agreed, wondering why she felt a shiver run over her skin, and that little tremor deep inside again.

"What do we do now?" she asked, trying to put all thoughts of his future lovemaking from her mind.

He led her to a sofa, and then he went and poured her a glass of sherry. Anne watched him in spite of herself. He was so handsome, so strong. She still felt his masculine presence, even now that he was across the room. And then she told herself she was being ridiculous. She loved James Galt, not Hugh Moreley. It was only that since she had to marry someone, it might just as well be the Earl of Burnham. At least *he* wanted her. Her father and Juliet could not wait to be rid of her, that was plain to see, and Melia and James were wrapped up in their own happiness. She would only be an intruder there. A most unwelcome intruder.

She knew she could do a great deal worse than the earl, for he loved her, and he was a handsome, appealing man. And he will never have any reason to regret our marriage, she vowed to herself as he handed her the sherry.

"First we drink to our future happiness, my dear," he said, recalling her to the present. "Then you will tell your father and the duchess while I go and write an announcement for the papers. This afternoon, or tomorrow at the latest, we must begin to plan our wedding. What say you to the end of October, my dear? That should give us enough time to plan the finest, most elaborate ceremony the *ton* has ever seen. I expect it to surpass royalty. Do you agree with me that only Westminster Abbey would be a fitting setting for us?"

Anne nodded, speechless.

"We must have an army of attendants, some pages, even a little flower girl or two," he went on. "Choirs, of course, and perhaps a string trio as well as the organ? Your gown must be breathtaking, for I intend all the world to envy me my beautiful bride. And I want you to wear pearls, for they will not detract from your sparkling eyes. I shall select them at Rundell and Bridges this very afternoon."

He smiled then, at her amazement. "And for our honeymoon, we will go abroad ourselves. To Greece, do you think? Perhaps the Caribbean would enchant you? Or should you like the gaiety of Paris better? I could buy you so many lovely things there, as a show-case for your beauty."

Anne put her hands to her hot cheeks. "Enough, m'lord! It is too much to think of, all at once."

He took up her hand and turned it so he could kiss her palm, and she shivered. "I intend to wrap you up in luxury, and spoil you with a lavish hand, dear Anne. But I will not speak of it again until you become more accustomed."

He put his arm around her lightly then, and kissed her cheek. Then he murmured against her hair, "Do you think you could do one little thing for me, Anne?"

"Of course," she assured him, a sinking feeling in her stomach for the kiss she was positive he meant to ask. She only hoped she could comply without showing him her reluctance.

To her surprise, he rose and bowed to her. As he strolled to the door, he said over his shoulder, "Then do try and force yourself to call me Hugh. It is only a small step, to be sure, but it is a beginning." He sent her a mocking smile, and added, "Until later, my dear."

Anne stared at the door he closed softly behind him, and then she put her hands to her cheeks again. What had she done? Oh, why was she so impulsive, so unrestrained? She hated to think she was the kind of woman who married to the best advantage, but wasn't that, in truth, exactly what she had just agreed to do? Because she had been denied James Galt, she had said she would marry a man she did not love, because he was rich and had an exalted title, and he wanted her. And she had to admit she had been influenced as well by the life she would have had to live if she did not accept him. He was her escape from imprisonment at Severn, or deception in Scotland. It was a terrible thing she had promised to do, but it was too late to change her mind now.

She was still sitting there when her father came back.

"The earl has left, Anne?" he asked, and she nodded. "What answer did you give?" he persisted.

"I said I would marry him, sir," she told him.

William Fairhaven came and took the seat beside her, his dark eyes searching hers. He remembered Melia's glowing face, the joy that had shone in her eyes when he had given his consent at last, and he could not like Anne's quiet, contained manner. It was so unlike her usual exuberance, her sparkle when she was happy.

"Do you love him, Anne?" the duke asked. "I would not have you marry a man you did not love."

Anne returned his glance, and then she made herself smile as she lied. "Yes, I do. Perhaps not as much as he loves me, but I do."

Her father did not look entirely convinced. "You did not accept him as a penance for your bad behavior these past few weeks, I hope, or as a way to make up for Melia's disastrous match?"

"Certainly not," Anne said, her eyes flashing.

The duke sighed, and then he took her hands in his. "Hugh Moreley is a fine man, Anne. He deserves a good wife, someone true and honest and loving. I hope you intend to be that kind of wife."

Anne could not speak past the lump in her throat, but she nodded.

"Run along then, my dear, and tell Juliet. I know she will be pleased, for she has often remarked how much she likes the earl."

As Anne rose to do his bidding, he added, "And since Hugh has shown us he can control you and your wild starts so well, both Juliet and I can look forward to a serene existence from now on. How restful it will be, knowing you are the earl's responsibility."

"Why, father," Anne chided him, "you sound as if you will be glad to be rid of me." She smiled again, to hide the ache in her heart, for she knew the truth of her jesting words.

The duke did not deny it as he went to his desk, waving a dismissive hand.

Juliet was much more difficult to deceive, and Anne needed every bit of the acting ability she possessed to convince her stepmother that she was happy and content, and that Hugh Moreley had swept her off her feet this morning, making her realize that she had fallen in love with him, all unbeknownst to herself.

At last the duchess clapped her hands, and looked happier. "I am delighted for you, dear Anne," she said. "The earl is a wonderful man, so kind and good! You will remember that I told you once there is nothing in the world to equal marriage to a man you love. I am so glad you are to know its joy, as well as Melia."

She stopped, and then she said, "We must write to her at once with the good news. Of course she must be your honor attendant. When does the earl want the ceremony to take place?"

When Anne told her the end of October, Juliet looked a little surprised. "So soon?" she asked. "We shall have to bustle about, my dear, won't we?"

And then she laughed. "All bridegrooms are impatient, but perhaps besides his eagerness to claim you, he wants to travel before the winter storms set in. Fetch me that pad and pencil, Anne. We will begin making plans at once."

Anne brought her the articles from her desk, delighted that the more prosaic planning for the wedding itself had ended a most uncomfortable discussion of married love.

By the time the two went down for luncheon, Juliet had sent a note to Charles Street, asking the earl to join them that evening for dinner. Without even waiting for his reply, she ordered a festive meal, and her warm smile and spirited conversation throughout luncheon, made the meal much less an ordeal for Anne.

That evening, when the earl was announced, Anne was waiting with the duke and duchess in the drawing room. As he stepped in, she made herself go to him quickly, holding out her arms. As he took her in his own and looked down at her, his eyes asked a question. She only smiled, and reached up to draw his head down to hers to kiss him lightly on the lips. "My dear Hugh," she said.

The blush that suffused her cheeks removed completely any doubts of her happiness from her father's mind.

There was a wicked gleam in the earl's eyes as he whispered into her black curls, "Splendid, Anne, perfectly splendid! My congratulations."

Anne only had to spend a few minutes alone with the earl at the end of the long, gay evening. At the table, she had been amazed at everyone's happiness, why, even the butler and footmen were beaming. And the toast her father proposed, the earl's gallant reply, were everything an enraptured bride-to-be could desire. She twisted her hands together under the cover of the table for a moment, as she gave them both a glittering smile of thanks.

But when the duke and duchess left the drawing room, she was nervous again. Hugh Moreley seemed to sense it, for he sat down across from her to tell her what he had done that afternoon, making no move to kiss or embrace her.

"I rather think a drive in the park tomorrow might advertise our intent, my dear," he concluded. "And then there is the Cowper ball the following evening. We must attend that together, for that is the day the papers will carry the announcement. Do wear something stunning."

"Of course, Hugh," Anne agreed. "I have a scarlet ball gown I have been saving for a special occasion."

He rose then, and came toward her, and Anne concentrated on keeping the little smile she was wearing pinned to her face. He took out a long velvet box from his pocket, and held it out to her. "I am sure you will look even more lovely wearing these," he said.

Anne opened the case with trembling hands. Inside were ropes of creamy, perfectly matched pearls, ear bobs, and a matching bracelet. They seemed to glow with life as she stared at them.

"They are beautiful, thank you," she said in a tight little voice.

"They will become even more so, once they have rested next to your skin." His eyes caressed her neck and shoulders, displayed this evening in a soft blue silk gown. "Did you know that pearls grow more luminous the more they are worn, Anne? Their beauty is enhanced by the warmth of the body."

His voice was soft and intimate, and Anne swallowed. She knew the earl was wooing her, and she wished he would not.

"Then perhaps I should wear them to bed tonight," she said before she thought. "They are so lovely, they deserve to be at their best for the ball," she added hurriedly, as his eyes gleamed with amusement for her predicament.

"I shall take the picture of you doing so to my own bed with me, Anne," he murmured. "Somehow I doubt I will get much sleep."

To Anne's relief, he changed the subject then, and it was only a few moments more, before he rose and came to draw her to her feet. She waited, her heart jumping, but he did not attempt an embrace. Instead, he bowed over her hand, and only kissed it softly before he said good night.

From that moment on, time seemed to accelerate for Anne. She was caught up in plans for the wedding, and the festivities that were to preceed it, and the end of October seemed to be racing toward her with all the speed of a runaway team.

She managed to keep up her pretense of happiness, whenever she was in company, and her composure slipped only a few times. Melia had replied at once to the letter announcing the engagement, and her effusive words of joy for her twin's happiness sorely tried Anne's acting ability. But after she said she would be delighted to be the honor attendant, she offered her own wedding gown, saying how pleased she would be if her twin wore it, for she was sure it would be good luck. Anne threw up her hands in horror.

"No!" she exclaimed, causing Juliet to look at her, surprised at her vehemence. "I will never wear that gown, never!"

Seeing the little frown between her stepmother's brows, she took a deep breath and said more calmly, "It would not be at all appropriate, dear ma'am. What have Hugh and I to do with English roses and Scottish thistles? I want my own gown, for the earl insists on it."

Juliet agreed, and Anne was quick to change the subject. The design she finally chose was a slim white satin slip with an overdress made of the finest hand-made Chantilly lace, which had long tight sleeves and a close-fitting bodice fastened with tiny buttons. The overdress stopped at the waist in front, extending into a sweeping ten-foot train behind. On her hand, Anne was to wear a matching lace veil, and around her neck, Hugh Moreley's ropes of pearls. She would be magnificent, the modiste assured her at one of the innumerable fittings. Anne tried to smile.

She found the despondency of her former beaux amusing. She had never encouraged a one of them to think they had any chance with her, yet still they went around looking for all the world as if they had suffered a jilting from which there was little possibility of recovery. The earl finally had to speak to Mr. Collingwood, telling him he was making a perfect cake of himself, dressed constantly in unrelieved black.

Anne had refused all of Kitty Whittaker's invitations, and in a short time, she and her entire set dropped from sight as if they had never even existed. The only one of them Anne saw was the Viscount Yates, in the park one afternoon. She was seated beside the earl in his phaeton then, and when the viscount gave her a mocking bow, she looked right through him, disdain in her eyes.

Hugh Moreley was sitting with Anne and the duchess in the drawing room, the afternoon the Galts arrived from Scotland. He was telling them his plans for the wedding trip, but all Anne's interest in weeks in Paris, and a villa by the sea in the south of France, disappeared the minute Amelia ran into the room, straight into her twin's arms.

Anne laughed and cried with her, and hugged her tight, bracing herself for the moment she must look into James Galt's unobtainable face. When Melia went to kiss the duchess, Anne tried to smile naturally at the man standing before her. He was just as she remembered him, handsome and rugged, but he looked much happier, she thought, admiring the smile that lit his hazel eyes. Galt drew her into his arms to kiss her cheek, and Anne closed her eyes, her breathing shallow as she forced herself to remain very still. Then, as he moved away to greet the earl and Juliet, she took a deep, steadying breath before she turned to join them.

"So, you have captured the other lovely Fairhaven twin, have you, m'lord?" Galt asked as he bowed. "I can assure you from my own experience, that you are to be congratulated. You will be the happiest of men."

"I am sure I shall be," the earl said, his deep voice calm. Anne looked at him and was surprised at how keenly he was studying her face. She made herself smile at him, her head held high. "Very sure," he added, still staring at his fiancée. Anne shivered a little, and she was glad when Melia asked a question and she could look away finally from those intent gray eyes.

She was much more accustomed to the idea of their marriage now, and she had grown easier in the earl's company. He had finally kissed her one evening, and to her surprise, she found his embrace enjoyable. His mouth had been as warm and eager as his caressing hands, and she discovered that she was able to return his kiss with some fervor.

When he raised his head at last, his voice had been husky as he murmured, "My darling Anne! How much I love you . . . want you!"

Anne would have replied, but he put his hand over her mouth, shaking his head as she did so. "No, don't say anything, my dear," he had told her in his normal tone of voice. "I know it would be a lie right now. Someday, I hope to hear you say you love me, but you must not tell me you do until you mean it. Do you understand?"

Anne had looked troubled, but she had nodded. As he drew her into his arms again, he gave her a little squeeze, and then he said, his breath stirring the dark tendrils over her ear, "There is no need for any such pretense between us. Besides, you will remember that I told you I love you quite enough for two."

XII

The Earl and Countess of Burham returned to England in late February, after a wedding trip of almost four months. They went immediately into Devon to visit the duke and duchess before going on to the earl's own estates in Oxfordshire.

As their carriage passed through Severn's familiar wrought-iron gates, Lady Anne smiled and gave a contented sigh. The earl looked at her from where he sat on the far side of the carriage.

"There are some bridegrooms who might take offense at that heartfelt sigh, my dear," he remarked.

"How fortunate that you are not so sensitive, Hugh," Anne told him absentmindedly as she leaned forward for her first glimpse of her old home.

The earl stared at her patrician profile, noting the rapt expression in her eyes, and then he shrugged before he turned to inspect the view from his own window. The park and frozen lake glistened under a light mantle of snow.

When the carriage entered the courtyard and rattled over the cobbles, he admired anew the grandeur of the duke's principal seat. He helped his wife down himself, and then he shrugged again when she shook off his arm impatiently to run up the long flight of stairs. As he followed her at a more leisurely pace, he studied the towering columns and the statuary.

The massive front doors had barely been thrown open before Anne swept inside, beaming at the old butler she had known all her life.

"Devett, how glad I am to see you, to be home again!" she exclaimed.

"And we are very glad to have you here, m'lady," the butler told her, signaling to the footmen to assist the earl's servants in unloading the coaches before he came to bow and take m'lord's hat and greatcoat. Anne put back the hood of her sable cloak just as Juliet came from a nearby drawing room, her arms wide.

With the birth only a month away, the duchess was heavier, although she carried herself with dignity. She looked much better, for the sparkle was back in her hazel eyes and her face glowed with happiness.

For a moment, there was nothing but excited conversation and kisses exchanged all around, but then Juliet drew back to hold her stepdaughter at arm's length so she might inspect her. "What lovely furs, Anne," she said, her eyes admiring.

Anne handed the huge muff to Devett, and allowed the earl to remove her cloak. "Hugh bought them for me in Paris, ma'am," she said carelessly. "But where is father? I cannot wait to see him."

As the three walked to the drawing room, the duchess explained that the duke was expected momentarily. Not knowing the exact day of their arrival, he had driven into Barnstaple on business.

The duchess ordered tea, and then, as the earl and his hostess took their seats beside the comfortable fire that was blazing on the hearth, Anne walked with quick, impatient steps about the room. She paused to admire the view from one of the long windows, and to touch a grouping of porcelain figurines that had always been favorites of hers. The earl watched her without saying a word. Juliet looked from one to the other, a little confused.

Anne looked so different to her somehow, and she wondered why. It was not her smart Paris gown, nor the more sophisticated way she was doing her hair, it was something in her face, her posture, her expression. Was it ill-concealed petulance? Indifference? A coldness that had not been there before? Juliet did not know. She only knew that Anne did not seem anywhere near as beautiful as she had before her wedding. There was a brittleness about her, and she looked much older, even in such a short time.

The duchess told herself she was being fanciful, as she smiled at the earl and began to question him about their journey. She watched his face carefully as they talked. Hugh Moreley was as pleasant as he had always been, and when Anne came to join them as the tea tray was brought in, he rose and smiled at her. But Juliet sensed that he had changed too, in some subtle way she did not understand. She found her heart sinking a little. She had had such hopes for Anne and Hugh, but unless her intuition was misleading her, all was not well with their marriage.

The hour they spent together was full of quick conversation, as they all caught up on family affairs.

"Perhaps I am telling tales out of school, but I cannot wait for her to tell you herself," Juliet said as she passed Anne a plate of cakes. "Melia is in an interesting condition, too. Isn't that wonderful?"

She saw the way the earl looked quickly at his wife, and heard Anne's startled exclamation, before she said, "Wonderful, indeed, ma'am. And when is the happy event to be?"

"In late September," the duchess told her. "We had hoped that she and James could come and visit this summer, but that is out of the question now. Besides Melia's condition, James is very busy these days. He has finished his book at last, but he is hard at work on a new invention. Something to do with a reaping machine, I believe."

"A reaping machine?" the earl drawled. "I was not aware Mr. Galt was agricultural."

"According to Melia, machinery fascinates him. He is constantly searching for better ways to mine and farm," the duchess said.

"But if Melia cannot travel, I will not be able to see her," Anne complained, frowning in her disappointment. "And it has been so long, months and months!"

"Perhaps we should travel to her then, my dear," the earl suggested. Anne smiled until he added, "You have never been to Edinburgh, have you? It might be quite an—er—interesting experience for you."

His eyes held his wife's for a moment, and then she turned away, her color a little heightened. Again, the duchess looked from one to the other, and she was not at all displeased when the duke entered the room and the Galts and Scotland were forgotten.

That evening at dinner, Anne returned to the subject. "I see we shall have to treat you with even more respect now, father," she said, her eyes twinkling as they used to do when she was bent on mischief. "After all, you are not only the illustrious Duke of Severn, and a soon-to-be father again, but a soon-to-be grandfather as well. Why, you have become a patriarch!"

The duke's black brows creased in a sudden frown. "I had not considered it in that light," he said, nodding to Devett to refill his wine glass. "And I will confess that at my age, I do not feel at all prepared for the role of grandfather. Now I know why I should have insisted you and Melia marry later, instead of sooner. You are making me old before my time."

The duchess chuckled a little. She could see William was not at all pleased by this new picture of himself. She, too, found it hard to imagine him in the part. He was still so lean and virile, and there was very little silver in his black hair.

"At least you must acquit *us* of contributing to your

venerable image, sir," the earl said smoothly. "Isn't that so, my dear?"

His gray eyes sought his wife's where she sat across from him, and Anne tossed her head, looking displeased. This evening she was wearing a low-cut, narrow gown of Pomona green. It seemed to have been chosen to set off the magnificent waterfall of emeralds and diamonds she wore at her throat. In the candlelight, the jewels glittered with a fire that was matched by her blue eyes.

Now she nodded to her husband coldly, before she turned her shoulder to ask Juliet a question about Severn. The duchess noticed her husband's slightly raised brow at his daughter's rudeness.

The newlyweds had not been with them for many more days before Juliet was seriously concerned. She made it a point to ask Anne about her marriage one afternoon when the men were out riding, but the conversation could not be said to have been a success. To all her questions, Anne returned a light, evasive answer. It was obvious that she had no intention of confiding in her stepmother. Late that same afternoon, Juliet told the duke of her worries.

William Fairhaven frowned as she spoke. "I agree with you, my dear," he said when she had finished. "I am concerned myself. They are so cool to each other, they almost act as if they were barely acquainted. Hardly the behavior of a couple just returned from their wedding trip, is it? I wonder what could be wrong?"

Juliet sat down beside him. They were in her rooms, as was their custom, so they might enjoy some privacy. "I don't know, William," she said slowly. "I have tried to speak to Anne about it, but she will not discuss it. And since I am only five years his senior, I do not feel I can approach the earl, even though I am his step-mama-in-law. But stay!"

Her hazel eyes brightened, and she took the duke's

hand in hers. "Why can't you speak to him, my dear? A good man-to-man talk. I cannot bear to see Anne becoming so cold, so secretive! There must be something we can do!"

The duke caressed his chin, deep in thought. "I cannot speak to Hugh about his marriage unless he himself initiates the conversation, Juliet," he said finally. "And I can assure you, he has no intention of doing so." As the duchess looked disappointed, he added, "I will, however, speak to Anne."

The next morning, he sent a footman to ask the countess to join him in the library. While he waited for her, he read the morning's post. It was a good thing he had something to occupy himself with, for Anne did not make an appearance for nearly an hour.

As she entered the library, the duke rose to his considerable height and leaned his knuckles on the desk. "How glad I am you have been able to come, finally," he said with a little frown. "I do hope my summons did not put you to any extraordinary trouble?"

Anne flounced into the seat across from him without waiting for him to give her permission, and his frown deepened. "Am I late?" she asked carelessly, smoothing her elegant morning gown. "I did not know. My maid was so slow and stupid this morning, I gave her a thundering scold."

When the duke did not reply, she looked up in surprise. "There was something important you wanted to see me about then, sir?" she asked. William Fairhaven thought he detected a defiant note in her voice and a militant look in her eyes.

"There is indeed, daughter," he said as he took his seat again. "Both Juliet and I have noticed that things do not appear to be going very well for you and the earl. I thought perhaps you and I might talk about it. We are concerned. We had hoped you would find contentment in your marriage, but it appears that has not been the case."

Anne rose to pace the room, and the duke watched her carefully. That beautiful face was frowning now, and she looked annoyed. "I don't see why everyone is making such a fuss!" she exclaimed at last. "There is nothing wrong with my marriage!"

"No?" her father asked. "But anyone can see that you are not as pleased with your husband as Melia is with hers."

"There can be no comparison, sir," Anne said quickly. "Let me tell you it is a very different thing to be the Countess of Burnham, rather than plain Mrs. Galt."

"I was not speaking of your differences in rank, Anne," her father said. "Melia is happy with her James, but I am afraid you are not happy with Burnham."

"Happy! Happy!" Anne cried as she came to lean on his desk and face him. "I am sick of everyone prating to me about happiness! I am content, and I am sure the earl is, too. Why, how could he not be? Besides, look at the things he has bought me—the furs and jewels and gowns. Everything I admire the least little bit is instantly mine."

The duke studied her pale face. "Is he perhaps trying to buy your love, Anne?" he asked in a quiet voice. Anne started, as he went on, "I know how much Hugh Moreley loves you. It seems to me you are not living up to your word in the way you treat him, nor in the way you act."

Anne's face had gone very white, and he saw how her breathing had quickened and the glitter of tears in her eyes. He waited for her to collect herself and answer him.

"The earl knew how I felt when I accepted him, father," she said at last. Her voice was quiet now, and she held herself erect, her shoulders squared and that defiant chin tilted. There was a dignity about her bearing that he could not help but applaud. "I told him how it would be, and he agreed to it," she went on. "I also told him I would never change, and he accepted that as well. I am living up to my wedding vows. I deny him nothing."

Her dark blue eyes dared her father to question her further, and then she drew a deep breath and curtsied. "Please excuse me, sir," she said. "I must be alone now."

The duke waved his hand, and she turned and left the room. Eyes narrowed, he watched her straight back and proud head, her regal carriage. And then she was gone, and he was left to stare with unseeing eyes at the papers before him.

Anne went to her room, but as soon as she heard the earl speaking to his valet in the adjoining room, she left without telling him she was there. She stood for a moment in the hall, wondering where in all this vast mansion she might go for some privacy. And then she nodded a little to herself, and climbed the stairs to the schoolroom. She knew no one would think of looking for her there, and she did not think she could bear seeing anyone—Hugh, Juliet, even a servant—until she had time to think.

There was no sound but the steady ticking of the wall clock after she closed the door. It was chilly in the big, cluttered room, but she did not notice as she went and sat down at her old desk. In a moment, she reached out and touched the one beside her, where Melia had bent over her lessons. It seemed so long ago that they had been there together, young and happy, and full of a thousand madcap schemes. And now, their lives were changed forever. Anne put her head down on her arms and cried softly for a moment, as she remembered those two children, all long black hair, enormous eyes, and thin, angular bodies. How little had they suspected what the future had in store for them.

In a while, she composed herself and went to sit on the window seat, to stare out past the huge columns of the portico at the gardens of Severn. It did no good to cry, she told herself. There was no going back now to those long-ago days. Melia was married to her James, and carrying his child, and her own future was settled as well. Permanently settled.

The reluctant Countess of Burnham drew her knees up so she might rest her arms on them as she forced herself to think of the problem at hand. She had not imagined that her father and Juliet would be so quick to see that she was not in love with the earl. Perhaps she had been too careless, but she did not feel she could playact anymore. Besides, it was different now that they were married. Hugh would mock her if she tried to pretend an affection he knew she did not feel. He would be polite, of course, but he could be just as sarcastic as the Duke of Severn, when he chose to be.

Anne sighed. She had not had the least idea of what marriage would be like when she had agreed to it. For the last four months, she had been constantly in his company, and the only other person she had ever been so close to before was her twin. But where she and Melia were one person, happy in their closeness, she and Hugh were not, in spite of their physical intimacy.

She remembered her wedding day when she had stood beside him in the Abbey and said her vows. It had been just the elaborate spectacle that Hugh had wanted, and she herself had reveled in all the pomp and ceremony. And then there had been the drive to the coast, and their first night in the inn at Dover. She had felt a little trepidation when the earl had risen after a late supper in their private parlor, but all he had done was to kiss her cheek before he took her to her room, saying he knew how tired she must be. It was the same as they traveled through France, and by the time they reached Paris and the *hôtel* he had hired on the Rue Dauphin, Anne wondered if he had changed his mind about a marriage of convenience after all. She tried to tell herself she was relieved, although she could not help but wonder at it.

But he came to her that first night in Paris. Anne could still remember how he had looked when he took her in his arms, and how eagerly, yet how slowly and carefully, he had made love to her. She had not liked the initiation. It had hurt, and none of his assurances that things would be better soon had convinced her. He had fallen asleep beside her, his arms holding her close, but when he heard her weeping quietly later that night, he had risen without a word and returned to his own room. He came to her often after that, but he never stayed beside her again.

Anne discovered that lovemaking was not only bearable, but pleasant as well. She never told him how she felt, because when she experienced the waves of pleasure he was able to stir her to, she was sure she was betraying herself and everything she believed in. Surely it was wrong to love one man with all her heart and soul, yet be able to find contentment in another man's arms. Confused, she grew colder and more haughty as a result.

She sighed again, remembering. It was true he had bought her everything she wanted, although he seemed to be mocking himself as he did so, with his curling little smile. Anne had adored Paris—the shops, the modistes, the theaters and music halls, the elegant palaces and parks and cathedrals. As she and the earl had explored the city, they had had many light-hearted moments, and many times had enjoyed a hearty laugh together. Anne discovered a great deal about Hugh Moreley during those weeks. He was not just arrogant, he was quick-witted and kind, and constantly concerned for her well-being. She enjoyed feeling loved and pampered, even though she fought any dependency on it.

She regretted it when the weather turned colder and they left the city for the south of France.

The villa he took her to was on a cliff, overlooking the sea near Cannes. It was warm there, almost summery, and a complete change from the sleety rain of the capitol. The earl had arranged for his yacht, *The Bluebird*, to anchor nearby so they might sail when they wished, and Anne soon relaxed to enjoy the lazy days that were full of the scent of roses and heliotrope, yet still had a refreshing, briny tang.

There was a little cove below the villa that was reached by a narrow, rocky path. It was almost enclosed between high cliffs that stretched like enfolding arms toward the sea, and it was very private. The earl often ordered an *al fresco* luncheon served there, and one afternoon, after the servants had toiled back up the cliff carrying the empty baskets, he had come to lie down beside her. Anne was stretched full-length on a blanket on the sand, her straw hat tipped over her face as she dozed, listening to the sound of the little waves that lapped the shore. She was almost asleep when she felt his hands on the buttons of her gown, and she stiffened.

"It is all right, my love," he told her, one warm hand slipping inside the gown and under the straps of her chemise, while the other moved up her leg in a soft caress. "There is no one near to see us. We can even have a swim later, without your smart bathing dress. Would you like that?"

Anne sighed as his hand closed over her breast. She felt so drowsy, so relaxed. In a few moments, she found herself responding to the earl as she never had before. There was something about the hot sun beating down on them, their isolation, that awakened an answering hunger deep inside her. She forgot her love for James Galt and her aloofness as she moved closer to Hugh, her arms as eager, and her lips as demanding as his.

But when she felt herself sliding into what seemed to be a pit of complete oblivion, she cried out. The earl raised his head, and she stared up at his handsome face, taut now with passion. She tried to twist away, but he would not let her go. Even as she tried to fight it, she was engulfed in a whirlpool that threatened to consume her with its urgency and power. And then, quite simply, the world as she had always known it, dissolved.

Afterward, she lay very still, feeling weak and shattered. Hugh bent over her to kiss the hollow in her throat. "Anne, darling," he said, in a husky, uneven voice, "my dear love."

His voice broke the spell, and Anne felt a sudden rush of tears. They ran out the corners of her eyes to mingle with the black hair fanned out beneath her on the sand. As Hugh reached up to caress her face, he felt their dampness, and he raised his head, his keen eyes dark with his concern.

"Do not cry, my love," he said. "Sssh. It is all right. What you feel, what you have just experienced, is what love between a man and a woman is all about."

Anne sat up, pushing him away. She stared at him. He was so big, so strong. His powerful chest that was covered with black hair was rising and falling, and when she looked into his face, she saw his blazing, triumphant gray eyes, and she felt very cold and very frightened.

"No," she cried, drawing away from him. "I won't! I *won't!*"

Without a word, he rose and ran into the water. She watched him swim out to the headland, his long stroke powerful, and for one terrifying moment, she thought he meant to swim until he disappeared. She sighed as he headed back to shore, and then she dressed.

He did not speak a word to her until they had climbed the cliff, but at the top, he took her hand and kissed it. "I shall never forget today, Anne," he said. "I must thank you for a beautiful memory."

His voice sounded mocking to her, and she saw he

was wearing his sardonic little smile again. Anne lowered her eyes as she turned away.

In the days that followed, she thought she detected a waiting look in those gray eyes, an expectant tilt to that dark head, even though she had reverted to her earlier cold, aloof manner. He had not questioned her, not even when he came to her room on those soft, scented nights. She never experienced the wild feelings she had had on the little beach again, and she remembered that she had not known whether to be glad or sorry that this was so.

After another week, there was no more anticipation in the earl's eyes, and he himself grew more formal, more distant. Anne had told herself she was glad everything was back to normal.

But still she had been very uneasy, and it was with some relief that she had boarded *The Bluebird* at last for the sail across the Channel, and home.

Now Anne turned from the window of the schoolroom, and swung her legs to the floor. She did not have the faintest idea what she was going to do now. She wondered if she should tell Hugh about the talk she had had with her father, and beg him to take her away from Severn. And then, as she shook out her crumpled skirts, she nodded. Yes, it would be better when they left here. The duke and Juliet were too all-seeing, and she could not relax, but surely when she was at her new home, busy with her household, she would be more content. She would not have to hear her father's lectures, or parry Juliet's loving concern; she would not have to pretend anymore. And she was sure the earl would prefer it too, for she knew he had a great deal to do on his estate after his long absence.

As she left the schoolroom, Lady Anne Fairhaven Moreley, Countess Burnham, put up her chin. She had been endulging herself this past hour in maudlin thoughts and weak depression, but she would do so no longer.

The past was gone forever; she could not will it to return. And even if she could not look forward to the future she saw stretching before her, she could still face it bravely, with her head held high.

XIII

It was almost the end of March before Anne found herself in Scotland at last. Juliet had had her baby, a little girl they named Amy Julia, and both mother and child were doing well. Anne had sent her new sister a sumptious present, but she was not at all sorry that she and Hugh had left Severn.

There had been just as much to do in Oxfordshire as she had anticipated. The earl's estate, called Burnham Hall, had been a surprise to her. Somehow, she had not imagined it would be so grand. Why, it was almost as impressive as Severn, she told the earl during their first dinner there together. Hugh Moreley's eyes had crinkled in amusement, and he had laughed at her, in quite his old way. Anne smiled back at him. She had determined to try harder to make him happy. On the journey there, she had had a lot of time to think about what her father had said to her, and she had come to see that she had been selfish. Since they were married, she must fill her role as wife with more than a cold petulance, for if any man deserved it, Hugh did.

With this new resolve of hers, life became almost pleasant for the earl and his countess. Anne threw herself into all the new activity with a will, and a guilty little feeling of relief. They were both busy, but of necessity, their different tasks kept them from too much intimacy, and it became easier when they were

forced to be together. Then too, there was so much to
talk about, so many plans to be made. Anne thought
Burnham, just like Severn, was like a bustling little
country, entire unto itself. There was the red-bricked
mansion and the numerous outbuildings, the grounds
and park, the tenant farms, woods, and village, and
the army of indoor and outdoor servants to oversee.
She was quick to confess to the earl that she knew very
little about household matters, and he laughed at her.
He assured her he did not want a homebody for a wife,
and that Mrs. Clark would be most indignant to be
supplanted as housekeeper. Anne liked the older
woman, who had known the earl since his childhood,
at once, and she was glad to learn from her, although
she discovered she herself was not at all domestic.

Before the thrill of being chatelaine at Burnham
could wear off and she grew bored, they took coach for
Scotland. Spring was late this year, and as they
traveled north it grew steadily colder. Anne was glad
she had thought to bring her furs.

She found Scotland very different than she had
imagined it would be. For one thing, it was wilder
than the English countryside, and sometimes they
drove for over an hour without seeing anything but
wandering flocks of sheep and an occasional lonely
croft. Secretly, Anne wondered how Melia would ever
become accustomed to this lonely land that was so
barren and windswept.

Edinburgh was a revelation and a relief when they
finally reached it. The New Town was impressive with
its fine buildings, wide streets, and squares. Towering
high above it was the massive castle. It seemed to
brood over the valley below, and Anne was glad when
the buildings of Charlotte Square shut it from sight.

The Galts' house, like all the others on the north side
of the square, had been designed in 1791 by James
Adams in the true Georgian style. Not that Anne was
allowed to see much of the exterior, for Amelia flew

down the steps and into her arms before she really had a chance to look around. Arms entwined, the two sisters went into the house, talking as if they had seen each other only yesterday. The earl followed, smiling a little at their happy reunion.

It was sometime later, after tea had been brought to the large, well-proportioned drawing room on the front of the house, that Anne thought to ask for her host.

Amelia chuckled. "I must apologize for him, must I not? James is down at the manufactory in Auld Reekie where his reaper is being built. He spends most of his time there lately, although he has promised, on his sacred honor, he will not fail us for dinner."

The earl, lounging against the mantel, saw the puzzled look in his wife's eyes. "But isn't he always here for dinner, Melia?" she asked.

Her twin laughed again. "Some weeks I do not see him one night in seven," she admitted cheerfully as she refilled their cups. "It depends on whether there is a problem with the plans, or some of the parts."

Anne was amazed that Melia did not seem to mind being left alone so much of the time. She knew she would hate it, herself. Why, Melia was with child, too, and James was neglecting her, all for a silly piece of machinery.

She studied her sister over the rim of her teacup. Melia did not look deprived. If anything, Anne realized, she had never looked better. Even dressed in an afternoon gown Anne remembered from two years ago, she was beautiful. Her cheeks glowed, her eyes sparkled, and a happy smile played over her mouth almost continually. And instead of being shy with her new brother-in-law and letting Anne control the conversation as she always had in the past, she conversed easily with Hugh. Anne realized she was very much mistress here, and as such, had gained a maturity and poise she had not possessed before.

When Amelia showed them to their rooms at last, she apologized for the lack of space. "Our servants do not live in, you see," she explained. "I do hope it will not inconvenience you not to have your maid and valet within constant call."

"They don't live here?" Anne asked, as if she had never heard of such a thing. From where she stood in the narrow upstairs hall, she could see her maid putting her gowns away in the wardrobe in her room.

"There is no room for them. What with James's study and workroom, and my studio, we have filled every nook and cranny," Amelia said, and then she added with a twinkle, "Actually, I think they prefer to have their own place. The Scots are so independent!"

The earl assured her there would be no problem, when he saw that his wife, resplendent in her furs and jewels, was speechless. Amelia told them she had already made arrangements for their servants to lodge at a boarding house a little distance away.

She excused herself then, saying she must speak to the cook about dinner, and Anne went into the small bedchamber that was to be hers. There was a tiny frown between her black brows, and Hugh Moreley smiled to himself as he left her.

He did not smile that evening when he saw how eagerly she looked at James Galt as she entered the drawing room. The Scotsman stood up and bowed as Amelia came to lead them both to chairs near the fire.

"It is so cold this spring," she said, hugging her sister a little. "I must admit the weather in Scotland was quite a surprise to me, after the more temperate climate of Devon."

Her husband smiled at her, and Anne saw a little message exchanged as their eyes met. She felt a pang of anger that Melia could behave with him as she had only been able to with her twin before, and she felt envious as well. What must it be like to be so happily married? she wondered. She looked over to where the earl was standing talking to James Galt, her eyes speculative. Hugh was taller, and there was no denying he was a handsomer man than his host, and certainly much better dressed. James was wearing old-fashioned evening clothes, and he wore them so carelessly, Anne knew he was not even aware of his appearance. Beside him, Hugh was all smooth-fitting perfection and modish elegance.

Dinner was delicious, even though Anne was surprised again when she saw her sister made do with only an elderly butler and a little maid to serve them. She noticed James was absentminded, and sometimes Melia had to call him to order when he did not appear to hear a direct question. As dessert was being served, she shook her head and sighed, a rueful little smile on her lips.

"What is the problem at the manufactory, James?" she asked, her head tilted to one side in inquiry.

James looked up from where he had been frowning over some patterns he was drawing on the linen cloth with his fruit knife. Once again, Anne saw his eyes soften as he studied his wife in the glow of the candles between them.

"I beg your pardon, dearest," he said, and then he turned to his guests. "I beg your pardon as well, for I have been most remiss. But there is a serious problem, and at the moment, I do not see how it is to be resolved."

His eyes dropped to the cloth again, and he frowned.

"Do finish your dinner, my dear," Amelia told him. "And then perhaps you had better excuse yourself. From past experience, Anne, Hugh, I can tell you he will not be very good company until he has solved whatever is bedeviling him."

James Galt made a half-hearted attempt to assure

them he would be delighted to return to the drawing room and some pleasant conversation, but his wife was firm in her dismissal. After a glass of port with the earl, he came to say his brief good nights. Amelia went with him to the front door, and Anne could hear them murmuring together very clearly. And then there was silence, and it seemed a very long time before she heard the door close behind him.

She looked up to see the earl studying her face, his expression cold, and she wondered why her cheeks grew warm. She hoped he had not thought she was eavesdropping!

Amelia had planned a few dinner parties, and there was an occasional assembly, but outside of those evenings, and the sightseeing they did, Anne thought Edinburgh a very quiet place. Certainly it was nowhere near as exciting as London, where sometimes she had attended four parties in one evening! Then, too, she thought the people she met narrow and provincial in their outlook. Their conversation seemed limited to Scotland and its affairs to the exclusion of all else, and the topic that seemed to be discussed most was the Highland Clearances, of which she knew nothing. And although it was obvious that Melia was regarded with warm affection, her sister was aware of the aloofness, almost disapproval, masked by politeness, to which she and the earl, as English, were treated. Used as she was to whole-hearted admiration, she was not prepared for indifference and barely concealed dislike.

Even Melia seemed strange to her. Her only concern was for her husband, the child she was carrying, and her household. She seemed to take it for granted that Anne was as happy as she was, for she never asked any questions about her twin's life, nor did she try to communicate with her mentally as she was used to do. Anne was saddened that their childhood closeness had been severed by their new roles as wives.

One cool, breezy afternoon, some two weeks after their arrival, Anne went out for a solitary walk in the square. As she strolled over the still dormant grass, she could not help feeling a little depressed. Melia was busy in her studio, James was at the manufactory, and Hugh had gone for a drive, leaving her to her own devices. She frowned a little. True, he had asked her if she would like to come along, but she had refused. Now she felt cross and neglected and very bored.

As she started back across the square, she saw James Galt striding toward her, and her face grew animated as she waved. For a moment, she saw him quicken his pace, and a smile light his hazel eyes, and she felt a little tremor inside. But as soon as he noticed the sables she wore, his smile became a mere politeness for he had realized she was not his Amelia.

He stopped and bowed to her, and then he offered his arm. As they walked to the gate, he explained he had returned home for some papers he needed that he had left in his study.

"You are very industrious, James," Anne told him. "You make the rest of us look like gadflies."

He looked down at her briefly. "We Scots tend to take ourselves too seriously, I know," he admitted. "Amelia tells me it is a very good thing she married me, for otherwise I would have turned into nothing but a sour old recluse."

He laughed, his eyes glowing with his memories, memories Anne could see he had no intention of sharing. Trying to regain his attention, she put her other hand on his arm.

The earl's carriage had just driven up to the door of Number 7, and as he stepped down, Hugh Moreley saw his wife walking close beside James Galt in the square. As he watched, he saw her lean toward him, and put her hand on his arm, and he felt a sudden sick rage. Anne never touched him unless she could not help it, and she had never looked up into *his* face with her heart in her eyes.

Ordering his coachman to stay where he was, he strode to the gate, arriving there just as Galt and Anne did. He did not notice the Scotsman's open-faced welcome, for he was staring at his wife. When he saw the little shadow of regret on her face for his appearance on the scene, he stiffened.

"There you are, Anne," he said keeping his voice even with a great effort. "I have come to take you for a short drive."

Anne began to refuse, but he was insistent, and in only a minute more, he was helping her into the carriage. Anne heard him give a terse order to the coachman before he climbed in beside her.

Anne turned to ask him what he thought he was about, but when she saw the rage he did not trouble to hide now in his gray eyes, she cowered back on the seat. He looked as if it would give him a great deal of pleasure to strike her, and she was confused. Hugh had never looked at her this way; whatever was the matter with him? She tried to question him, but he waved an impatient hand.

"Not now!" he ordered. "When we arrive at Arthur's Seat, we will take a walk. I have a great deal to say to you, madam, and I must insist on complete privacy."

Anne looked puzzled, but she did not try to question him further. She was alarmed, for she had never heard that tone in Hugh's voice before. He not only sounded cold and angry, but distraught as well.

They left the carriage near the base of the huge, flat-topped hill that was an extinct volcano, to make their way up a winding path. The earl helped her when the going was steep or rough, but he did not say a word. By the time they reached the wind-swept top, Anne was breathless, and warm under her furs.

The earl looked around. On this cool late afternoon, there was no one in sight, and he nodded grimly before he turned to his confused wife. He stared at her, even in his distress admiring her flushed cheeks, those beautiful eyes. As he watched, she reached up to brush back a tendril of black hair that had escaped her hood.

"Well, m'lord?" she asked pertly. "We are certainly private here!"

Hugh Moreley nodded. "I have brought you here, Anne, because I think it more than past time to tell you I know all about your infatuation with James Galt."

Anne started, one hand going to her throat as her eyes widened.

"Oh yes," the earl continued, staring down at her. "I have known it this age. Even before we were married, I knew of it."

"When did you find out?" Anne whispered.

He noted bleakly that she made no attempt to deny it, but he knew Anne was not capable of being devious. "I suspected it last Season, but I was not sure until I saw your face as you walked toward him at your sister's wedding," he said coldly.

"Yet you still asked me to marry you, knowing I was in love with another man?" she asked in some surprise.

The earl made an impatient gesture. "You mistake the matter, Anne. You were not in love with him then, and you are not in love with him now. I am sure you were just fascinated by the man, and more so, I daresay, by the situation."

She stared at him, aghast. "Oh, yes," he went on, his voice rich with sarcasm. "It was *so* romantic, wasn't it, my dear? The star-crossed lovers, the stern, implacable father; the painful separation, the joyous reunion and happy ending! Why, it had everything that girlish dreams are made of, did it not? I am sure you were disappointed that Galt did not storm the house, sword in hand, and carry Amelia away on a huge white steed. But how shattering for you, that *you* were not the heroine of the piece! And I know, from personal experience, how you love center stage, do I not?"

He paused, but Anne was incapable of speech, although her eyes never left his taut, angry face, those bitter, accusing eyes. She felt suddenly chilled.

"But Mr. Galt did not have the good sense to choose your wonderful, elegant self, did he? No, he chose Amelia. In your conceit, you could not bear that, so what must you do but imagine you loved him too? I thought once you were married to me, you would forget him, for even now I find it hard to believe that your infatuation for a dearly beloved sister's husband could continue all this time."

"It is not infatuation! I do love him!" Anne cried, stung into response.

The earl quirked a brow. "Do you, my dear? Even now, when you have seen the kind of life you would have led as his wife? Imagine it, if you please. He would have buried you up here in Scotland, never taking you anywhere. He would have neglected you for his work, and expected you to live in a small townhouse with few servants, and no pretty clothes or the numerous entertainments that you crave."

"It would have been different if James had married me—" Anne argued, but the earl interrupted her.

"No, it would not. He chose the better twin for his wife after all. You are too used to attention and admiration and luxury to change, and James Galt is too strong a man, too determined on his course, to change for you. You would have made each other miserable."

Anne tried to steady a quivering chin. She could feel the tears welling up and threatening to clog her throat, and she swallowed. "You do not understand, Hugh.

You think it mere fancy, but I tell you, it is not. James kissed me, I—I know I love him."

The earl moved forward to grasp her arms. "What foolishness is this? Kissed you? When?"

"It was when he first came to London," Anne whispered, her lips almost white. "He called on us, and since I was the only one home, I went to him, pretending to be Melia. I wanted to meet him, for I was sure he was the reason she had been so unhappy. And when he saw me, he thought I was Melia, and he—he proposed, and then he kissed me."

The earl's gray eyes were stormy. "When did he discover your playacting, Anne?" he asked.

Anne looked down at the dry brown heather at her feet. It looked as dead as she felt inside. "Almost at once," she admitted.

"He *must* have been pleased with you," the earl said, his voice sarcastic. "I wonder he did not beat you for it."

"He was very angry, that is true. It was not until after Melia married him that he forgave me," Anne told him.

"I see. And on that one brief encounter, you built this fantasy, this ill-fated love?" he asked. "How disappointing and tame our marriage must have seemed after such a *consuming* passion!"

Anne felt he was blaming her for accepting him, and she said hotly, "I told you how it was, Hugh, I did not mislead you! I told you I could never love you, so you cannot accuse me of deception!"

He nodded, his eyes as cold as gray metal. "What you say is very true, Anne. Yes, I knew, and I have only myself to blame for not having this out with you before we wed."

He turned away from her then and stared down at the city, and the dark palace of Holyrood House that crouched at the foot of the Seat. Anne stared at his stern profile, his taut posture, and when she saw the way he clenched his fists, she was a little afraid.

And then he turned back to her to study her for a moment. When he spoke, his voice was quieter and slower, and Anne clasped her trembling hands together. "Because I loved you so much, Anne, I was willing to marry you, even knowing what I did," he said. "You see, I really believed that behind that young, careless facade that was the Lady Anne Fairhaven, there was a great deal more. How disappointing to discover that you are nothing but a beautiful face and lovely voice, after all, and that what I see is all there is to you. Do not continue to imagine you love James Galt anymore, Anne. You are incapable of loving anyone but yourself. You are selfish and spoiled, and this love you claim has never been anything more than jealousy of your sister, and her happiness."

Anne listened to him in disbelief, feeling colder than she ever had in her entire life. Her sables could not warm her now. And then to her surprise, he put back his head and laughed. "And you are the Countess of Burnham, my wife! The woman I thought indispensible for my happiness and my future! What delicious irony! No doubt I shall spend the rest of my life in bitter regret. No matter. You are my countess, and so you shall remain. I am sure we will grow accustomed, and in time, learn to rub along fairly well with each other. At least it will be easier, now that there is honesty between us."

Anne put out her hand. "Hugh, please . . ." she said, her voice imploring.

He would not take her hand. "No, no more now, Anne. There is no need to tell me you will *try*, no need to pretend. I only regret that I did not know about that kiss." He shook his head at his folly, and then he added, "I must ask you to tell me one more thing, m'lady."

He waited until she nodded, and then he said, "I know your sister does not suspect your secret attraction for her husband just by the loving way she treats you. But does James Galt know?"

Anne drew herself up. "Of course not! You insult me, Hugh, if you think I would ever, ever do anything to cause Melia pain. He has no idea."

He nodded, and then he turned and studied the sky. Over the Firth of Forth, dark storm clouds were massing against the horizon, and it was getting colder. "Come," he said, holding out his hand. "It is time we went back. I shall discover an urgent reason why we must leave Edinburgh shortly, for although of course I am desolated to deny you the opportunity to remain close to your lost love, I cannot be expected to put up with being made to look the foolish husband. Know that I shall never permit you to be foolish either, Anne. You are the Countess of Burnham, and as my wife you will conduct yourself accordingly."

Anne did not try to speak as they started their descent. She felt frozen and battered by his cold, angry words, but she put up her chin.

I may be his countess, but I am still the Lady Anne Fairhaven, she reminded herself. I am not some little nobody to be chastised and insulted. I was honest with Hugh, I told him I would never love him. And he is wrong, wrong! I do love James, I always will. And no matter how futile my love for him, it will be a part of me until I die.

She stumbled a little on the steep path, and the earl was quick to steady her with a strong arm. She turned away from him then, hoping to hide the feelings she was sure were written plain on her face. Her legs felt weak and trembly. In spite of her brave thoughts, she wanted nothing more than to reach her room and cry, cry for hours, to rid herself of the pain she felt deep inside that he had discovered her secret.

And then she realized that it was not only for herself she wished to weep. No, it was also because she had hurt Hugh Moreley. She might not love him, but she had never intended him to discover the reason why.

XIV

Anne sent her excuses to the Galts that evening, saying she was suffering a severe headache, but she did not dare give in to her grief until Melia had come to see her to make sure she was all right, and she had dismissed her maid. She heard Hugh moving in the adjoining room, but he made no attempt to speak to her. She told herself that was just as well, for she did not know how she was ever going to face him. She sobbed herself to sleep, but when she woke early the next morning, she was herself once again.

Very well, she told herself as she dressed, it was unfortunate that he had learned her secret, but she had never misled him, and so she had nothing to apologize for. Neither had she betrayed herself to Melia or James. In fact, this whole quarrel was more Hugh's fault than hers, even if the initial reason for it could be laid to her door.

She squared her shoulders as she inspected herself in the pier glass. She looked just the same. No one would suspect that she had suffered such a shattering experience, or been so horribly insulted by her supposedly *adoring* husband. As she went down to breakfast, she was prepared to behave just as she always had. Hugh had told her what he expected of his countess, and she would be an exemplary one, dignified and cool.

She managed to playact very well, but she was not

at all sorry when they left Edinburgh two days later,
the result of a fictitious summons from one of Hugh's
relatives in Oxfordshire.

As she sat alone in the coach, for Hugh had said he
preferred to ride, she stifled her regret that James had
not been present to say good-bye. He had been called
to his manufactory very early, and had only left his
apologies and his farewells for his wife to deliver.
Anne had been annoyed, but Melia had laughed and
said it was typical of him, before she waved to her
sister and Hugh and went back into the house. Anne
had the feeling she forgot them before the coach
rounded the corner of the square, and she sighed. Was
everyone in the world busy and content and happy?
Everyone but herself?

The journey was long and tiring, and she was glad
to see the gates of Burnham Hall ahead at last. But she
discovered that evening at dinner that she was not to
be allowed any respite.

"I have it in mind to travel to London by week's
end, ma'am," Hugh told her during the fish course.
When she looked surprised, he added, "The Season has
begun. Surely you do not care to remain quietly in the
country when there is so much gaiety to be had there.
Besides, think how painful your absence is to all your
throngs of admirers!"

Anne ignored the sarcasm. "Certainly, Hugh," she
said, "I can be ready any time."

He busied himself cutting his Dover sole before he
said, "If you do feel pressured, you must not put yourself to any trouble, ma'am. You can easily come later,
at your convenience. There is no need to travel with
me, after all."

Anne had looked at him suspiciously, before she had
assured him again, in a light voice, that she preferred
his escort. As she ate her dinner, she wondered how
long Hugh would continue on his current course. He
had not come near her since that afternoon at Arthur's

Seat, and she had found in the last few days that she was lying awake at night, waiting for him to do so. He had never been able to stay away from her before, not even after her outburst on the beach at the villa, and she was sure he would not be able to do so now.

But the earl did not knock on the connecting doors, and by the time they arrived at Charles Street, Mayfair, late one lovely spring afternoon, Anne was becoming seriously alarmed.

She made more of an effort to look beautiful for him, and when he told her to buy whatever she wished, she purchased several stunning outfits and ball gowns to entice him. She had her hair arranged in a new style, *à la Grecque*, she began to wear a heady scent that she had heard whispered would drive a man wild, and she experimented with some discreet cosmetics. It was all to no avail. Hugh never failed to tell her she looked lovely, and he admired the low-cut gowns and form-fitting habits and walking dresses, but still she was left to her solitary nights. Sometimes he did not even accompany her home after the latest ball, and she would lie in bed, staring up at the ceiling, wondering where he was and what he was doing. Surely a male card party could not compare with her charms!

Hugh Moreley knew very well what she was about, and for the first time since their confrontation in Scotland, he began to feel a glimmer of hope that all was not lost after all. When he had first seen Anne on the morning after he had told her he knew her secret, he had wanted to shake her for her cold dignity and barely hidden air of injury. He himself had spent a restless night, not only reviewing her admissions, but also the cutting things he had said to her. At the time, he had wished there was some way he could recall those hateful words and bitter accusations, some way he could go back even to the sham marriage they had shared before. But the words had been said. He had called her selfish and conceited, and consumed by jealousy, and he knew a woman of Anne's caliber would not find it easy to forgive, or forget. He could not excuse himself by saying he had only lashed out at her because she had hurt him so badly, and because he loved her so much.

At first, ashamed of himself and smarting under her indifference, it had been no trouble staying away from her. But as the days passed, he realized with a rueful shake of his head that he loved her and wanted her still; he always would. He began to pray that she would come to see her infatuation for Galt for what it was, and perhaps even begin to love him at last.

Sometimes, as he had ridden beside her carriage on the journey to Burnham Hall, and subsequently to London, he would recall that one brief interlude on the beach in France. Remembering Anne's total surrender, and her joy in their lovemaking, he told himself he must not become discouraged. He knew she was not incapable of love, even if he had accused her of the failing. In truth, he was sure she would love more deeply than her twin when she finally surrendered. Anne was all passionate fire and conviction, but she had yet to learn that love's bonds were soft and silken. They were not the cold chains she imagined them to be as she clung to her pride and her independence.

When the earl noticed her puzzlement and her dismay at the way he was keeping his distance, he had an idea. And after their arrival in town, he began to make some definite plans when he saw her feverish shopping and the way her eyes seemed to beg for his approval and capitulation. Desiring her the way he did, leaving her to go on to his club after a party was the hardest thing he had ever done in his life, but he knew it was the only way he had to bring his difficult, proud Anne to her senses. Sometimes, it was all he could do not to pull her into his arms and kiss her until she was breathless, for besides looking so beautiful, the new scent she was wearing was just as successful as its makers had promised.

As a result of his strict control over himself, and his enforced celibacy, he became even more formal and distant as the days went on.

Anne found that all her pleasure in London and its multitude of activities and excitement, had disappeared. Even her old beaux, still fervent in their admiration, only annoyed her, and many times she had to count to ten before she told Lord Anders he was a fool, or Percy Collingwood, an idiot.

She wished Juliet were in town, for then, she decided, she would be quick to seek her advice. She knew it would hurt her pride to have to admit her failure as a wife to the duchess, but she did not know where else to turn. Unfortunately, the duke and duchess were not expected in Berkeley Square this Season. Because of the baby, they had decided to remain in the country.

Anne did not feel she could entrust her confession to the post. Sometimes, she thought she should go down to Severn for a visit, but she could not bring herself to leave the earl. Even if he had decided on a loveless marriage, she felt she had to be near him.

Anne made herself become very gay, because only in that way could she banish all her doubts and fears, if only for a little while. She accepted every invitation she received, and she kept herself busy during the day shopping and riding, walking in the park, and attending tea parties and luncheons that only last Season she would have stigmatized as dead bores.

She thought the earl seemed amused by her endless round of activity. Although he was not with her often, it could not be said that he neglected her in any way, for he served as her escort to all the more august parties and balls, and he was so polite and attentive to her in public that Anne knew no one in the *ton* suspected their estrangement. She was grateful for it. She knew she could never bear it if anyone learned that the beautiful lady Anne, the toast of the town, had been scorned by the man who only a few short months before could hardly wait to make her his bride.

Yet even with all her feverish activity, there were times when she was alone, times when she was forced to think, and think hard. Those rainy afternoons when riding parties had to be cut short, or picnics canceled, hung heavy on her hands. She did not seem to be able to read a book, do needlework, or think of a new arrangement for the drawing room furniture to distract her mind; instead, she would find herself sitting quietly, wondering why in the world this had happened to her, and what on earth she was to do about it.

She even began to think that perhaps she had been more at fault than she thought. She knew she should not have accepted Hugh, feeling as she did, even if he had told her he did not care at the time. And when she tried to concentrate on James, telling herself how much she loved him, she had difficulty regarding him with any real fervor anymore. Remembering the recent trip to Scotland, she came to see that he had been rude to her, rude and careless. He was a selfish man, wrapped up in his own concerns, when all was said and done. And always, as she pondered her change of feelings about him, she seemed to hear Hugh's cold accusation ringing in her ears. Was it possible that he had been right and that she did not love James Galt after all? She did not know anything about infatuation—perhaps less, she told herself with a little frown, than she knew about love.

Hugh had said she was selfish and spoiled, and she was forced to agree now that his assessment of her was probably true. And perhaps he was also right when he claimed that she was only jealous of Melia's happiness.

Anne shook her head, her frown deepening. It was painful to think she might be capable of such an ugly trait. But even if none of these things could be laid to her door, she had to admit Hugh had been right about one thing. She would have hated the life Melia was leading. Marriage was not all breathless passion— there were all those hours and hours in between to be filled. How awful to have a husband who put his own concerns first, who was absentminded when he wasn't ignoring you!

As the days and nights went by, instead of picturing James Galt's rugged face, she found herself, more often than not, remembering Hugh and that afternoon at the beach. Sometimes, if she closed her eyes, she could almost hear his husky voice calling her his dear love, and she could see clearly his long muscled legs, that powerful chest covered with curly black hair, those strong arms and caressing hands.

She wished they were back there now. She wished she had a chance to turn back the clock and change things somehow.

And then she would shake her head at her silly daydreams, reminding herself that he seemed content with a loveless marriage, that he considered her incapable of real love.

One afternoon, as she was leaving her modiste's, she saw Kitty Whittaker again. The little blond was about to trip up the steps of the shop as Anne came out, but she paused to give her former crony a deep curtsy.

"Why, countess, what a delightful surprise to see you again," she said, throwing a saucy smile to her companion, an improbable redhead Anne did not know.

"How are you, Kitty?" Anne asked quietly as she came to stand beside her.

"Just fine and dandy, m'dear," Kitty told her. "And you?" Before Anne could reply, she said in her breathless way, "I must say I am surprised to see you looking so well. We were all sure you would be devastated when we heard."

"Heard?" Anne asked, a little frown between her brows. "Heard what?"

"Why, can it be you don't know?" Kitty cried, with a fine display of false concern. "Oh, I shouldn't tell you, then, should I, although it is too bad! And you a bride, too! Whoever would have thought the lovely Lady Anne would not be able to hold a man? Not I!"

Anne reached out to grasp her former friend's arm as the redhead tittered behind her handkerchief. A dangerous light burned in her eyes, as she said, "Tell me what you mean, at once!"

Kitty did not bother to protest. She had been nursing a sense of injury ever since Anne had dropped her, and after she had been such a good friend, too. And, she told herself, it would do the proud bitch good to be put in her place. "Of course, m'dear," she said, leaning closer to whisper. "I am surprised you have not heard, for it is all about town that your new husband has set up a mistress."

"You lie, Kitty!" Anne declared, her face white.

"Indeed, I do not, do I, Clarissa?" she asked, seeking confirmation from her companion. Clarissa shook her head, her pale blue eyes avid. "No, indeed," Kitty went on. "He's Mary Crandall's new protector. How else could she afford to move into that smart little house at Number 12, Adams Street? Or sport such lovely gowns and jewels? She hasn't had a stage part this age!"

As Anne stared at her, speechless, Kitty shook off her hand and picked up her skirts. "I do feel so sorry for you, dear," she murmured sweetly as she started up the steps. "It will be so uncomfortable for you once the news reaches your set, now, won't it?"

When Anne did not answer, she smiled, and then she beckoned to her companion and went into the shop. As Anne stood there, she could hear them laughing behind the door, and she raised her chin and went quickly to her waiting carriage.

As she took her seat, Anne felt as if she might explode. To think that Kitty Whittaker was laughing at her! To think that all of the fringes of society were whispering about her, and pointing her out whenever they saw her! And how long would it be before this delicious *on-dit* was common knowledge of even the patronesses of Almack's? Oh, how could Hugh do this to her? How could he humiliate her this way? Anne took a deep breath and gritted her teeth, not noticing her maid's anxious look. He would *not* do it, for she would see to it before the gossip spread to even one more person. She banged on the roof of the carriage with her sunshade, and when the coachman pulled up and opened the trap, she told him to take her to Number 12, Adams Street. Her maid began to shake her head and make breathless little tuts of disapproval, but Anne ignored her.

Adams Street was in a discreet backwater of Chelsea, and Number 12 not very different from its neighbors. Anne ordered her maid to wait for her in the carriage, and then, with only a quick look around, she marched up the marble steps and banged the brass knocker. The very young maid who admitted her to the hall looked startled when she gave her name and asked to see Miss Mary Crandall at once.

She was taken to a neat drawing room which had a canary in a cage in the bow window, vividly reminding her of Kitty Whittaker's house in Hanstown. While she waited, Anne paced up and down the room. The bird sang gaily behind her, but she did not hear it. Somehow, some way, she must get this Miss Crandall to give Hugh up. She was sure she had enough money of her own, banked at Hoare's, to buy her off. After all, she told herself, it was not as if the woman was in love with Hugh. No, it was only a business arrangement. Her eyes darkened with anger and her cheeks flushed with delicate color as she considered what that business arrangement entailed, and she had never looked so handsome as she did when Miss Crandall came in at last.

Anne inspected the woman she had come to see carefully, and she was startled. Mary Crandall was at least Hugh's age, and perhaps even older. Although she had a voluptuous figure, fully revealed in a low-cut gown, and lovely blond hair, her face was nowhere near as beautiful as her guest's.

And then, as the two women stood regarding each other, Miss Crandall smiled, and Anne knew what Hugh saw in her after all. Her smile transformed her face, it was so full of charm and personality.

"Lady Burnham?" the woman asked. At Anne's nod, she indicated a chair. "Won't you be seated, m'lady? I must say this is a surprise."

She sounded a little amused, and Anne paled. She knew many men took mistresses, of course, but their wives, to the woman, ignored the fact. Certainly they did not call on these ladies of easy virtue!

"Thank you," Anne said, sitting down and keeping her back ramrod straight. Miss Crandall sat on the sofa across from her, and tilted her head in inquiry. "There was some special reason for your call, m'lady?" she prompted, when Anne hesitated.

"There is indeed," Anne said at last, raising her chin and looking straight at her adversary. "It has recently come to my attention that Hugh—the earl, I mean—has become your . . . is visiting . . ."

Her voice died away, and Miss Crandall laughed. "You will not offend me, m'lady, by honest speaking. We both know my place in your husband's life. There is no need to be at all reticent about it, I assure you."

As she had been speaking, she had admired the fire in Anne's eyes. She was all haughty pride, and every inch the countess.

"Of course you are right, Miss Crandall," Anne said. "And I have come to put a stop to it."

Miss Crandall smiled a little. "Indeed? But this is

most unusual, m'lady. And although I am sure there are other wives who would like to—er—'put a stop' to their husband's amatory adventures, I have never known one who was quite so direct."

Anne waved an impatient hand. "I do not care a snap of my fingers about other wives," she said. "I am only concerned with my husband. I am sure we will be able to come to some agreeable solution. I am a very wealthy woman, the daughter of the Duke of Severn."

Miss Crandall sat back and folded her hands in her lap. Anne was almost sure she could see a twinkle in her eyes. "But I must admit I am not very interested in your proposal, m'lady," she said. "Hugh is such a wonderful lover, is he not? I find I adore him, quite beyond any monetary considerations."

Anne stiffened. "I shall pay double what he gives you," she said. As the woman only looked politely interested, she added, "Or perhaps you would prefer a cash settlement of a thousand pounds?"

Miss Crandall's carefully plucked eyebrows rose. "That is generous indeed, m'lady," she said.

"I am sure you will be able to find another protector," Anne told her. "One whom you will 'adore' quite as much as you 'adore' Hugh." Her tone was sarcastic and scathing in her condemnation.

"No doubt you are right," her hostess said meekly.

There was silence in the little drawing room. Even the canary had stopped singing. And then Miss Crandall rose and Anne held her breath. "Very well, I shall accept your offer, m'lady," she said.

Anne felt a stab of triumph as she rose, too. "I shall direct my bank to pay you the money as soon as I hear that you have left this house, and told Hugh you will not see him again. Send me your new direction."

She swept to the door, her head held high. Behind her, Miss Crandall said softly, "It shall be as you say, ma'am, but if I may . . . ?"

As Anne turned, intrigued, she went on, "May I

suggest you ask yourself *why* the earl saw the need for a mistress? You are young and very beautiful. Now that I have seen you, I find it hard to believe that Hugh does not want you."

"It was all a misunderstanding," Anne said, surprised into response. There was such a look of kind concern on the older woman's face that it had caused her to lower her guard.

"I see," Miss Crandall said. "Then may I also suggest you do your best to repair that misunderstanding, ma'am? Besides being so wealthy and open-handed, Hugh Moreley is a wonderful man. And even though you have managed to send me away, I must point out how many women like me there are who would be delighted to take my place. I do not think you would care to make many more calls like this, or to have to pay such munificent sums in the future. Please believe I tell you this for your own good."

When Anne stood staring at her, speechless, she added gently, "It is necessary, when you are a woman, not only to be beautiful and clever, but to be kind as well. If you love Hugh, you will take great care of him, always. And you do love him, do you not, my dear?"

Anne swallowed, as the canary burst into trills of song. "Yes," she whispered, "I find that I do."

Miss Crandall smiled her lovely, winsome smile. "I must wish you both well then, ma'am," she said, and Anne nodded curtly before she left the house.

For a long moment, Mary Crandall stood very still in the center of the drawing room, and then she smiled a little and went to her writing desk.

On the drive home, Anne pondered what she had just admitted. The words had seemed to come from somewhere deep inside her, and although she had spoken without thinking, she was forced now to admit the truth and what she had said. She had not gone to Adams Street only to salvage her pride in any way she could, she had gone because she could not bear to think of Hugh in anyone else's arms but her own. He was *her* husband, *her* lover, and she would never share him with any other woman. It was more than jealousy, or wounded pride, it was her love for him that had caused her to act as she had this afternoon. She realized now that everything Hugh had accused her of, was true. She did not love James Galt; she never had. Oh, she had thought herself the victim of a great, secret passion that had doomed her to a sad, unfulfilled life, but she knew now that she had been dramatizing the situation as she had always been so apt to do. Whatever she had felt for the Scotsman, it could not compare to the fury and pain and loss she had felt this afternoon when she had learned that Hugh was involved with another woman.

And when she remembered that Hugh had always known that she thought she loved James Galt, and had married her in spite of it, her heart went out to him. Now she knew how he must have suffered, and for so many months, too, not just the hour she had today.

When she reached Charles Street, the earl was not at home. Anne was glad, for she wanted to think before she met him again, get over this absurd shyness she was feeling toward him. They were to attend the Throckmorton ball this evening, and Hugh was to escort her. She set her maid to preparing a bath and laying out her finest Paris gown, while she herself unlocked her jewel case to take out the pearls he had given her for a wedding gift.

She was smiling a little as she put them on her dressing table, and then she stopped, an arrested look coming over her face. What was she going to say to him? When? And more importantly, would he believe her? She sank down on a chair near the window. What would he do when he found out his mistress was no longer in residence in Adams Street? Why, oh, why hadn't she made the woman promise not to tell him anything about her visit? He was sure to be furious with her for her interference. And how could she suddenly claim she had acted that way because she loved him now. He would not believe this sudden about face, no, he would be sure she was only pretending to love him to save her pride. Somehow she would have to convince him she was not playacting, that she meant every word.

It seemed no time at all that Anne was forced to join Hugh for dinner before the ball. She thought he seemed strangely excited this evening, and somehow very pleased with himself, and the speech she had been rehearsing died on her lips. Perhaps he was remembering his last call in Adams Street, she thought as she toyed with her pheasant and new peas, and then she put down her fork.

"Not hungry, ma'am?" Hugh asked courteously. "Then perhaps we should be on our way."

As Anne rose obediently, he said, "You are looking very beautiful tonight, ma'am. My congratulations. The pearls are perfect with that ivory silk. It is one of the gowns you bought in Paris, is it not?"

Anne could only nod as she preceded him to the hall to accept her gloves and stole from the butler. She was glad Hugh seemed to have so much to chat about on the short drive to the Throckmorton townhouse, for she could think of nothing but the confession that, sooner or later, she would have to make.

The ball was a perfect crush, and this evening Hugh did not leave her side. She began to wish he would ask someone else to dance, join other gentlemen in the card room, or engage in a spirited conversation with his particular friends. Instead, he was most attentive, and the only time she could escape him was when he was forced to give her hand to someone else. They had danced the first waltz together, and Anne knew she would never forget how wonderful it had felt to be in his arms, held close while his gray eyes lingered on her face, especially now that she knew how much she loved him. She had sighed deeply, and then her eyes flew to his face. She was so surprised to see his little smile that she lowered her lashes at once, and began to chat about the other guests. The earl did not question either her sigh or her burst of vivacity, but Anne wished the evening was over and they could go home.

When that happy moment finally arrived, she found it nowhere near as comfortable as she had thought it would be. As the carriage carrying them back to Charles Street turned into Berkeley Square, the earl remarked, "I shall not come in with you, ma'am. The night is still young, and I have another—er—engagement."

Startled, Anne swung around to face him. "Oh, no, you must not go!" she cried. The earl's brows rose.

"Not go?" he said, sounding incredulous. "Why ever not?"

"I must speak to you, m'lord," Anne said in little above a whisper.

"Surely whatever you have to say can wait until tomorrow, ma'am," he said. "I cannot like a change of plans, and my—my friend will wonder if I do not come."

"No, it cannot wait!" Anne cried, wondering at her suddenly dry throat. "It must be now . . . tonight!"

"Very well," the earl said, to her considerable relief as the carriage stopped before their front door. "I can spare you a few minutes before going on to my—mm —rendezvous."

Anne bit her lip as the groom helped her down the steps, and then she tried to compose her features as she greeted the butler and let the earl escort her to the library.

He went to pour them both a glass of wine, and Anne stood where he had left her in the middle of the floor, her hands clasped before her. When he came to give her her glass, he was smiling, and her heart sank.

She knew he would not be smiling for very much longer.

"Now, ma'am, what is this matter you would speak to me about, that is of such earth-shaking significance that it cannot wait until morning?" he asked, looking at the Cartel clock and frowning a little.

"I have a confession to make to you, m'lord," Anne said, trying to keep her voice from trembling.

"A confession? How very singular," he said, putting his glass down on the desk top and then leaning against the desk, completely at his ease.

"Yes, for I have done something that I do not think will best please you," Anne told him, stealing a glance at his handsome face.

She paused, trying to collect her thoughts, but the earl did not prompt her. He only waited, a polite look of inquiry on his face.

"You see, I found out something this afternoon, and I . . ." Anne whispered, and then her voice died away.

"Yes? And you . . . ?" he was forced to ask.

Anne put up her chin, and said, all in a rush, "I found out about your mistress, and I went to Adams Street to see her."

She wished she could lower her eyes, but she did not seem to be able to look away from him. His face was very still and composed. When he made no comment, she hurried on, anxious now to be done. "I told her I would pay her a large sum of money to give you up, and she agreed. So you see, I had to tell you tonight, for if you were planning to go to Adams Street, she will not be there."

Hugh straightened up and came to take her forgotten wine glass from her hands. "Why did you do such a bizarre thing, Anne?" he asked, sounding to her confused ears no more than a little curious. He put her glass on a table nearby and then he came back to encircle her bare arms with his hands. She shivered at his touch. From only a few inches away, his gray eyes burned down into hers, and a little muscle quivered for a moment beside his mouth.

Anne willed herself to be brave and completely truthful. "I did it because I could not bear it . . ." she began.

"Could not bear to have your considerable pride wounded, ma'am?" he interrupted her, his voice a little rough.

Anne shook her head. "No, it was not only my pride, Hugh, although I do not wonder you think that the reason. Of course, my pride was hurt, and I do not deny it, but it was much, much more. I was so jealous I could not stand it, for you are *my* husband. I realized today that I loved you too much to share you with any other woman."

She thought she saw doubt in his eyes, and she said with as much passionate conviction as she could muster, "You must believe me, Hugh! I have never felt less like playacting; I am in deadly earnest! Ever since we left Scotland, I have had many lonely hours to think, and I have come to see I have been a fool, as spoiled and self-centered as you said I was. I only pray you can still forgive me, for I do not think I could bear it if you did not love me anymore. You see, I do love you with all my heart, and if you will let me be your wife again, I will show you that I have changed at last. I only regret that it took me so long to discover that you are my one true love. You always will be."

The earl looked down into her pleading blue eyes. He knew what such an admission had cost his proud Anne, and he waited no longer. With his heart singing, he put his arms around her to pull her close to him, and locked against his long, hard body, Anne raised her face for his kiss. She was breathless when he finally took his lips from hers, and exultant, her whole body pulsing with her joy that she had won him back.

"I should beat you, you know," Hugh remarked in a husky drawl.

She nodded, her face hidden in his coat until he
tilted her chin to stare down into her beautiful face.
"But this time I will not," he added, generous to a
fault.

"This time?" Anne asked, a bewildered frown creas-
ing her brows. "Are you implying there will be other
times, other mistresses, Hugh? Oh, no, no!"

"Perhaps not," he said, burying his hands in her
black curls. "Not if you continue to love me in the
future, that is."

"I will! I promise!" Anne said, her voice so fervent
with her determination that he chuckled.

"I sincerely hope so, Anne," he said, his eyes
twinkling. "I hate to think you might be forced, unlike
all those other wives that you do not care a snap of
your fingers about, to march into Chelsea many more
times, waving a thousand pounds." He chuckled again
as she gasped, and leaned back in his arms to stare at
him.

"You knew all along," she accused him, grasping his
lapels tightly.

"Of course I did," he said. "Mary wrote to me right
after you left to tell me that the scheme I had con-
cocted to bring you to your senses had succeeded
beyond my wildest dreams, for not only had you
bearded the lioness in her den to put a stop to our
liaison, but you had confessed your love for me as well.
I have been walking on air ever since, my darling."

"Do you mean to tell me, Hugh, that she was not
your mistress after all?" Anne asked grimly.

He ignored the dangerous undertones he heard in
her voice, as he kissed the tip of her nose. "Not, er,
recently, ma'am," he confessed. "I have had no
mistress since I met you, my lovely Anne. Shall we say
she is just an old—mm—acquaintance of mine who
happens to be a fine actress as well as a good friend?"

He waited for his arrogant Lady Anne to make up
her mind what she was going to do about his deceit.
Suddenly, to his surprise and delight, she burst out

laughing, and then she put her arms around his neck again.

"Hugh, you are very, very bad," she said when she could speak. "I know I should punish you for making me suffer, but somehow I find I have no desire to lash you with angry words and storm out of the room."

She stood on tiptoe and raised her lips, as her hands caressed the back of his neck. His arms tightened, and she murmured, "It would mean spending another lonely, sleepless night, my dear, and I have spent quite enough of them lately to last me a lifetime!"

A little breathless at her daring, she kissed his cheek. Before he turned his head to capture her lips again, he whispered in her ear, "Make that two lifetimes, love. Two, at the very least!"

About the Author

BARBARA HAZARD was born, raised, and educated in New England, and although she has lived in New York for the past twenty years, she still considers herself a Yankee. She has studied music for many years, in addition to her formal training in art. She added the writing of Regencies to her many talents in 1978, but her other hobbies include listening to classical music, reading, quilting, cross-country skiing, and paddle tennis. THE TURNABOUT TWINS is the third book in a series; it was preceded by THE SINGULAR MISS CARRINGTON and THE DREADFUL DUKE.

*Introducing a new
historical romance by Joan Wolf*

DESIRE'S INSISTENT SONG CARRIED THEIR PASSION THROUGH THE FLAMES OF LOVE AND WAR ...

The handsome Virginian made Lady Barbara Carr shiver with fear and desire. He was her new husband, a stranger, wed to her so his wealth could pay her father's debts, an American patriot, sworn to fight Britain's king. But Alan Maxwell had never wanted any woman the way he wanted this delicate English lady. And a hot need ignited within him as he carried Barbara to the canopied bed, defying the danger of making her his bride tonight . . . when war could make her his enemy tomorrow. . . .

Coming in July from Signet!

27 million Americans can't read a bedtime story to a child.

It's because 27 million adults in this country simply can't read.

Functional illiteracy has reached one out of five Americans. It robs them of even the simplest of human pleasures, like reading a fairy tale to a child.

You can change all this by joining the fight against illiteracy.

Call the Coalition for Literacy at toll-free **1-800-228-8813** and volunteer.

Volunteer Against Illiteracy.
The only degree you need is a degree of caring.